SECRET SOLDIERS

BY THE SAME AUTHOR

Soldier Boy

KEELY HUTTON

SECRET SOLDIERS

FARRAR STRAUS GIROUX
New York

Farrar Straus Giroux Books for Young Readers
An imprint of Macmillan Publishing Group, LLC
175 Fifth Avenue, New York, NY 10010

Printed in the United States of America by
LSC Communications, Harrisonburg, Virginia
Designed by Aimee Fleck
First edition, 2019
1 3 5 7 9 10 8 6 4 2

mackids.com

Library of Congress Cataloging-in-Publication Data

Names: Hutton, Keely, author.
Title: Secret soldiers / Keely Hutton.
Description: First edition. | New York : Farrar Straus Giroux, 2019. |
Summary: In 1917, Thomas, a thirteen-year-old coal miner seeking his missing brother, James, joins the clay kickers, who tunnel beneath the battlefields of the Western Front as they learn to be men.
Identifiers: LCCN 2018039223 | ISBN 9780374309039 (hardcover)
Subjects: | CYAC: Coming of age—Fiction. | Friendship—Fiction. |
Soldiers—Fiction. | Miners—Fiction. | World War, 1914–1918—Campaigns—Western Front—Fiction.
Classification: LCC PZ7.1.H913 Sec 2019 | DDC [Fic]—dc23
LC record available at https://lccn.loc.gov/2018039223

To my secret soldiers,
Greg, Aidan, Colin, and Maximus.
Without your love and support,
I'd have lost many a battle.
Thank you for standing by me
during the setbacks and
celebrating with me
each small victory.
You ignite my imagination,
inspire my words,
and fulfill my dreams.

DULCE ET DECORUM EST

WILFRED OWEN

Bent double, like old beggars under sacks,
Knock-kneed, coughing like hags, we cursed
through sludge,
Till on the haunting flares we turned our backs,
And towards our distant rest began to trudge.
Men marched asleep. Many had lost their boots,
But limped on, blood-shod. All went lame; all blind;
Drunk with fatigue; deaf even to the hoots
Of gas-shells dropping softly behind.

Gas! GAS! Quick, boys!—An ecstasy of fumbling
Fitting the clumsy helmets just in time,
But someone still was yelling out and stumbling
And flound'ring like a man in fire or lime.—
Dim through the misty panes and thick green light,
As under a green sea, I saw him drowning.

In all my dreams before my helpless sight,
He plunges at me, guttering, choking, drowning.

If in some smothering dreams, you too could pace
Behind the wagon that we flung him in,
And watch the white eyes writhing in his face,

His hanging face, like a devil's sick of sin;
If you could hear, at every jolt, the blood
Come gargling from the froth-corrupted lungs,
Obscene as cancer, bitter as the cud
Of vile, incurable sores on innocent tongues,—
My friend, you would not tell with such high zest
To children ardent for some desperate glory,
The old Lie: Dulce et decorum est
Pro patria mori.

SECRET SOLDIERS

ONE

MACHINE-GUN FIRE TORE across the narrow, lifeless stretch of muddied earth separating the armies of the Allies and the Central Powers. The soldiers called it no-man's-land, but the battlefield was not barren of men. British and German. Belgian and French. It claimed them all. Without prejudice and without mercy.

A young soldier crouched behind a trench wall. He clutched his rifle to his chest and strained to hear through the din of gunfire, but only the thundering booms of the German howitzer cannons interrupted the rapid pulse of the machine guns. The enemy launched artillery shells high into the sky above no-man's-land. They screeched like banshees as they plummeted back to earth, exploding on impact—before, behind, and inside the Allies' trenches—with deafening blasts.

The soldier covered his head as clods of dirt and splintered wood rained down on his helmet. Shrapnel sliced through the trench, embedding in sandbags, timber, flesh. Seconds later, medics carrying stretchers squeezed past the soldier in their rush to aid the injured and remove the dead.

The Allies returned fire. Bursts from their machine guns rattled through the soldier's bones. Each explosion and answering volley of gunfire twisted his muscles, tighter and tighter, until he feared that when the command finally came, he wouldn't be able to move. Securing his rifle in the crook of his arm, he rubbed his hands together to regain some warmth and feeling. When they tingled again with circulation, he raked his fingernails across his arms and neck to relieve the constant itch of body lice. He scratched until he drew blood, welcoming the momentary distraction the pain produced, but the itching and fear returned the second he stopped.

Hardened candle wax filled every seam of his shirt and trousers, and scorch marks marred the heavy wool of his uniform, evidence of his desperate attempts to burn the rice-sized lice from his clothes, but it was a losing battle. In the trenches, there were always more lice to kill. Just as there were always more enemies to fight.

A spray of bullets slashed across the sandbags at the top of the parapet. The young soldier looked to his brothers-in-arms, pressed shoulder to shoulder along the trench wall. The officer to his left stood closest to the ladder. His right hand held his rifle. His left gripped the fourth rung. He would be the first to go over the top. The young soldier would follow.

Cold tension seized his muscles again at the thought of leaving the protection of the trench and charging across the open field with nothing between him and the enemies' bullets except one hundred yards of battle-scarred terrain and God's will. He stared at the officer, hoping to gain an ounce of courage from the veteran warrior. If the officer could survive three trips onto no-man's-land, surely the young soldier could survive one. But the officer offered no steely gaze or words of encouragement. His eyes were squeezed shut, and the only words on his lips were panicked prayers.

Blowing into his numb hands one last time, the young soldier lifted his rifle and whispered his own prayer. As if in response to his pleas, the gunfire stopped. The soldier listened for the high-pitched whistle signaling the start of their attack on the enemy position. Word of their imminent charge had reached the men as they'd choked down their morning ration of cold pea soup and dried turnip bread. What little appetite the young soldier had possessed curdled with the news, so he left his ration for another soldier and sat in his dugout, waiting for the signal and praying for courage. Hours later, he'd still received neither.

The howitzer cannons of the enemy fired again, but no explosions followed, only the dull thud of metal falling on sodden soil. The soldier climbed onto the fire step and peered through a narrow hole in the sandbags. Greenish-gray smoke spewed from canisters littering no-man's land. A steady evening breeze carried the chlorine gas, tinged with the scent of pepper and pineapple, across the battlefield, toward the Allied troops.

"Gas!"

Panicked screams raced through the trenches as the poisonous fog spilled over the parapet and into the narrow ditches. The soldier yanked off his helmet and fumbled for his gas mask. He couldn't risk even one breath. Just one lungful of chlorine gas produced coughing and spasms. A second brought confusion and delirium. A third rendered you unconscious. And a fourth delivered death.

They'd run gas mask drills every day since he'd arrived in Ypres, but never had the soldier's hands trembled so violently. The gas settled in the trenches like a toxic river. Soldiers struggled to hold their heads above the poisonous fumes while keeping them tucked below the trench walls as they secured their masks. Enemy snipers picked off those who failed.

A bullet struck the left shoulder of the officer clutching the ladder. Before the soldier could grab him, the officer lost his grip and fell into the deadly fog slithering through the trench. The gas struck like a snake, fast and merciless. The officer clutched his throat and writhed on the wooden duckboards lining the trench floor. His mouth contorted with pain, and his eyes bulged in terror as he choked and coughed. The young soldier looked away. The only help he could offer was a bullet, but the soldier needed all of his for the enemy. Tears streamed down his cheeks, and mucous flowed from his nose as he tucked his head lower and secured his mask. Now, finally, a high-pitched whistle pierced the panicked, agonizing screams filling the trenches. A muffled command followed: "Over the top, boys!"

Muttering one last prayer, the soldier stepped over the officer's motionless body and climbed onto no-man's-land.

TWO

THOMAS SULLIVAN HAD broken two of the Ten Commandments before dawn. Hours later, as he stood in line at Trafalgar Square, sandwiched between men a decade older and a head and a half taller, he prepared to break a third.

Timothy Bennett, March 1, 1899.

Timothy Bennett, March 1, 1899.

Thomas silently rehearsed the lie, burying the truth under constant repetition and an occasional prayer. Having already committed two sins, he worried his prayers might go unanswered, but reminded himself that he'd sinned for a righteous reason, which had to count for something. He whispered another Hail Mary, just in case, and rubbed a hand over his face, hoping to discover that at least one wiry hair had sprouted on his chin during the long train ride from Dover to London, including two disappointing stops in Canterbury and Rochester, but his calloused fingers found only smooth skin. Shielding his eyes from the glare of the late-afternoon sun, Thomas peeked around the man in front of him and counted the recruits standing between him and the wooden table flanked by two of Trafalgar's famed lion sculptures.

Six.

Far fewer than when he'd joined the line three hours earlier. Army officers stood behind the table, asking questions and taking notes. If they accepted your answers, they ushered you to the right. If they rejected them, they dismissed you to the left.

Please, God, Thomas prayed. Let them point right.

As the line moved forward, his stomach complained with a deep growl. He reached into his coat pocket and grabbed the small potato his mother had given him before his eight-mile walk to the coal mine that morning. Despite its dusty, puckered skin and knotty bumps, Thomas hungered for it. His stomach grumbled again. If the men pointed left, the potato would be all that stood between him and starvation.

Timothy Bennett, March 1, 1899.

The month and day didn't matter. Only the year. That was the cutoff. No exceptions—except for the exceptions. Tens of thousands of them, all over Britain. Boys who looked the part and memorized the correct year: 1899. Thomas repeated it again, not out of concern he'd forget, but out of determination that this time the lie would work. This time the recruiting officer would point right.

Thomas had already been rejected twice before reaching London. Once in Canterbury, when a miner from Dover recognized him entering a factory being used as a temporary recruitment office, and once in Rochester, when an officer told him the army didn't have time for children wishing to play soldier. Each failure forced him to spend more of his shillings on another train ride, taking Thomas farther from home. If he was rejected again, he would never get back to Dover before his parents noticed he and the food money he'd borrowed for his train tickets were missing.

Guilt tightened around Thomas's chest. He didn't like disobeying his parents or taking what little money they'd saved, but after his brother had left to join the army and their father's hours in the mine had been reduced due to his failing health, the pittance Thomas made as a pony driver at the mine didn't put enough food on the table. His parents would be better off without another mouth to feed. Besides, he had to find James. The first and only letter they'd received from his brother stated he'd finished training and his unit was headed to the Western Front and a battlefield near the town of Ypres in western Belgium. He'd promised to send word again soon, but word never came.

When news of the Germans using poisonous gas on the Allied troops reached Dover, followed a month later by a B 104-83 form letter from the army stating that James was missing, Dad refused to discuss the matter, and Mum feared the worst and fell into deep despair. But Thomas knew there had to be another reason for his brother's silence.

Perhaps he'd been captured by the enemy and was being held prisoner. Perhaps he was injured and lying unconscious in an Allied hospital. Or perhaps James was working as a spy and had been chosen for a secret mission, so all information regarding his whereabouts was classified.

There were many perhapses to consider, and Thomas was determined to rule out every single one before he'd consider the one he couldn't bear to think of . . .

To rule out the rest, he first had to get to the Ypres Salient, the stretch of battlefield where the Allied line, like a war-ravaged peninsula, jutted six miles into the German-held higher ground. And for Thomas there was only one road to the Allies' front line, and its gatekeeper stood on the other side of the recruitment table.

Thomas reached up and fiddled with two small medals hanging from a tarnished necklace at his throat. He ran his finger over their raised images. His mum had placed the dull chain and Saint Barbara medal around his neck the morning he turned ten and first headed off to the coal mine with his dad and James. Saint Barbara was the patron saint of miners and would watch over him when Mum could not.

James had given Thomas the second medal before he left for the war. The Saint Joseph medal had belonged to their grandad, who gave it to James on his deathbed. Now it belonged to Thomas, but not for long. He pressed both medals against his chest. He didn't care how many broken commandments it took, he would find his brother and return the medal to him. He had to.

The memory of James, dressed in his army uniform, boarding the train in Dover, led Thomas's thoughts back home. The bustling streets of London, crammed tight with tall, soot-covered buildings and swarms of loud people competing for everyone's attention and money, were a far cry from the dirt roads of Dover, where the colliery village residents trudged home too tired from a day in the mines to lift their heads in greeting, much less to gather in the town square to scream about politics and the war.

Thomas shut his eyes against the noise and movement swirling around him and focused on the memory of racing James to the cliffs of Dover. On their days off from the mine, they'd sit atop the cliffs, dangling their legs over the edge, and James would talk about how one day they'd buy their own boat and transport goods across the English Channel.

"Someday, Tommy, we'll have a whole fleet of boats," James would say. "Sullivan Brothers Shipping will be the best shipping company to sail the Strait of Dover. We'll get Dad out of the mines before black lung claims him like Grandad, and we'll never have to crawl beneath the ground again. Won't it be grand, Tommy?" Then he'd reach over and muss up Thomas's hair until every one of his cowlicks stood at attention. The brothers would spend the day talking and laughing as their bare feet rubbed against the silky white chalk of the cliff wall. They'd squint across the Channel, searching for the faint outline of France's coast and dreaming of a future far from the dark and damp of the coal mines.

A phonograph stood on a small table to the left of one of the recruiting officers, playing John McCormack's rendition of "It's a Long, Long Way to Tipperary." Thomas watched the weighted needle bob gently atop the spinning record, marveling at how it pulled music from the etched grooves into the phonograph's large brass horn, amplifying McCormack's voice for everyone in the square to enjoy. Thomas tapped his foot along to the beat to calm the twitchy anxiety building in his muscles.

Not far from the phonograph table, a young gentleman in a fitted suit leaned casually against one of the lion statues and seemed to be watching Thomas. A newsboy cap sat at a jaunty angle atop his head, and he wore a smug smile that made Thomas's palms sweat. It was as if he already knew the lie that Thomas was getting ready to tell.

Thomas had first noticed the gentleman two hours earlier and wondered at the time if he was waiting for the line to shorten before joining it. But as the minutes slogged by, the man made no move from his reclined position against the statue except to light his next cigarette from the dimming stub of his last.

The line moved forward again, and Thomas's view of the man sharpened. What he'd believed to be a fitted suit was on closer inspection a tattered pair of trousers and a discolored coat, two sizes too small. And the cap nesting in his mop of unruly ginger curls was dull with age and frayed with wear. This was no gentleman overseeing recruitment to root out the charlatans hoping to join Kitchener's Army. At best, he was a beggar loitering in Trafalgar Square in search of handouts. At worst, he was a con man sniffing out his next mark.

Eight years earlier, when Thomas's dad moved their family from Ballingarry, Ireland, to Britain in search of mining work, his mum had cautioned him and his brother to steer clear of what she called "street urchins" as they'd made their way across London from one train station to another.

Even at age five, Thomas had sensed something unsettling behind their overly friendly smiles and piercing gazes and he'd pressed closer to his mum. He felt a warning twist in the pit of his stomach now as it occurred to him that his small size made him the perfect mark for such a predator. His hand wandered again to the necklace tucked beneath his shirt, but remembering he was being watched, Thomas shoved his hand in his pocket and wrapped his fingers protectively around the potato. The man might take his food, but he'd never get his Saint Joseph medal. There was only one person worthy of that medal, and it wasn't some London pickpocket.

His concerns about the man lessened as the line moved forward again and he saw that what he'd thought was a thick beard darkening the man's face was not hair, but soot and grime. The beggar was merely a scruffy boy, and though he was taller and undoubtedly older than Thomas, he no more belonged in that line than Thomas did, which was perhaps why he refused to join it.

Between long drags on his cigarette, the street urchin whistled loudly to the music, drowning out the Irish tenor's stirring voice with his shrill, off-key accompaniment. When he noticed Thomas glaring at him, the lanky boy blew out several quick, piercing notes, each carried on a puff of smoke, and winked at Thomas.

Clenching his jaw, Thomas stared at the man standing in front of him. He counted the stitches straining along the seam of the man's coat to keep his gaze from sliding back to the cheeky boy. He had to focus on the tasks at hand: securing the recruiting officer's signal to move to the right, getting to the Western Front, and finding James. But first, he had to remember the correct name and date.

Timothy Bennett, March 1, 1899.

As the man at the front of the line stepped up to the table, Thomas took a deep breath and pulled back his shoulders. He licked his palms and ran them over his hair in an attempt to tame the half dozen cowlicks sticking up in every direction. He failed, but decided for once the disobedient tufts might be a blessing. They easily gave him another quarter inch of height.

While the officer questioned the older recruit, Thomas listened and shifted in his worn boots, trying to find a comfortable position. The scraps of cloth he'd used to line his boots in hopes of gaining some height had bunched into sweaty wads beneath his soles during the walk from Charing Cross to Trafalgar Square. They dug into him like pebbles with each step, and his feet ached from the long journey.

Before Thomas could review his fake identity one last time, the man in front of him stepped to the right, and Thomas stepped forward.

"Name," the army officer stated without looking up from his paperwork.

"Timothy Ben—"

Thomas's voice cracked, and the officer glanced up, taking in the smidge of a boy standing before him. Thomas cleared his throat. "Timothy Bennett, sir."

The officer scribbled down the name. "Birth date?"

"March the first, 1899, sir."

The officer glanced up again. "Today's your birthday?"

"Yes, sir."

"Your eighteenth birthday?"

Thomas pulled back his shoulders and lifted his chin. "Yes, sir. I wanted to join as soon as I was eligible."

The officer's eyes narrowed. Thomas fought the urge to look away from his scrutinizing stare.

After a tense moment, the officer wrote down the date. "Occupation?"

"Coal miner."

"Years in the mines?" the officer asked, his voice deflated by the monotony of his questions.

"Eight."

The officer raised an eyebrow above his bifocals. "Eight?"

"Yes, sir."

"What type of work do you do in the mines?"

"Demolition, sir." Thomas had watched his dad and brother handle explosives in the mine enough to know the basics.

If the officer questioned him further, he was confident he could bluff his way through the answers, but when the boy leaning against the statue chuckled and muttered, "Sure you did," Thomas flushed Union Jack red from his hairline to his collar.

"You handled explosives in the mines?" the officer asked, no longer attempting to disguise his disbelief.

Before Thomas could answer, a frigid wind snaked through the square, scattering the officer's papers. Thomas scrambled after them, fetching each page before returning to the table.

"Thank you." The officer took the papers and shuffled them into an orderly pile. "Your enthusiasm to serve is admirable, son," he said, pushing his bifocals back up the bridge of his long, slender nose. "If we're still at war in five years, come see me, but I'm afraid there's no place for you in the army right now."

Thomas leaned over the table, so no one, especially the nosy ginger, would hear him beg. "Please, sir, I know I'm small for my age, but I'm a hard worker. Just give me a chance. I won't let you down, sir. I promise."

The officer capped his fountain pen and laced his fingers. "I'm sorry, but I'm afraid you just don't measure up to the standards the British Army demands of its soldiers. You'd do well to hurry back home, son. I have no doubt your mother is worried."

Fear and desperation squeezed Thomas's throat, cracking his voice, but he no longer cared who heard. "Please, sir. I have to get to the Western Front. It's a matter of life and death."

The officer sat back and picked up his pen. "Yes, it is." And then he pointed left.

THREE

THE MAN ON Dorset Street had promised George two shillings if he brought him recruits with mining experience. When George spotted the boy in line at Trafalgar Square—Timothy, he'd heard him say—he knew he'd found a mark. Coal dust clung to the boy like a second skin and tinted his blond hair a dingy gray.

George would have bet on his mother's life that the small lad was no older than thirteen—that is, he would have if he had a mother whose life he could bet on . . . or a father, for that matter. But George only had his life, and according to every adult he'd ever met, it held no value worth wagering.

He'd detected in the boy's speech a Kentish accent, but beneath it, there were remnants of an Irish brogue. Either way, the lad was far from home, a fact George would use to his advantage.

As the hours had dragged on, George had considered approaching the young recruit in line, but he knew the boy would never leave if he still held hope the army would accept him, so George decided to wait until the boy was rejected, desperate, and vulnerable.

Watching his mark pace around the square, his head bowed and chin trembling, George almost felt sorry for the lad, but hunger and the damp cold of March kept any tug of pity from swaying him. Two shillings would buy him a hot meal, his first in nine days, so when the dispersing crowd swept the young miner onto the city streets, George followed. As he dodged between carts and motorcars, stalking the boy, his belly warmed with the thought of Mrs. Wellington's mutton broth, potato pie, and duff, that steaming, fragrant pudding with its soft bits of plums and apples, but then a brisk evening breeze cut through George's threadbare coat, and he reconsidered his plan. A hot meal would keep him warm only as long as it took to eat, but a good night's sleep, indoors, under the covers of an actual bed . . .

George sighed at the thought, deciding instead to rent a room in Mrs. Mahoney's boardinghouse for the night. But first, he had to earn the shillings.

. . .

Distracted by thoughts of his latest failure, Thomas shuffled behind the crowd until, one by one, people peeled off from the mob and there was no longer a crowd to follow. He'd assumed the people he'd followed out of Trafalgar Square had been headed to Charing Cross, but when he looked around for signs of the train station, he didn't recognize any of the buildings lining the unfamiliar street. The sun had retreated behind a row of tall tenements, siphoning the buildings and their inhabitants of color and warmth.

Thomas stopped, uncertain how far he'd walked from Trafalgar Square. He entered a shop to ask for help and directions back to Charing Cross, where he prayed a kind soul would give him enough money to cover his fare home to Dover. Seconds later, a clerk's angry voice chased him back onto the street. "If you're looking for charity, find a church!"

Thomas sat outside the shop and yanked the boots from his feet. Hot tears burned behind his eyes as he pulled the wads of damp cloth from his boots and tossed them in the sewer. He needed to find somewhere safe to wait until morning. His mum had warned him of the crimes committed on the streets of London in the light of day. He didn't wish to be a witness to the criminals plying their shameful trade in the dark of night, or worse yet, become their victim.

Wiping his nose on his sleeve, he stood and started back the way he'd come. He hoped to retrace his steps to Trafalgar Square and then to Charing Cross station, but as he passed the shop door, cold dread spilled down his spine, stopping him in his tracks. At the end of the block stood the street urchin from

Trafalgar Square, smoking a cigarette. He smiled at Thomas and waved.

Thomas stumbled back, nearly knocking over the old shop clerk in his escape. He tried to apologize, but the clerk raised a hand to deliver a cuff to the side of Thomas's head. Thomas ducked the strike and ran. When he came to the next corner, he sprinted down an alley, determined to lose his stalker once and for all.

. . .

George stubbed out his cigarette and strolled down the block and past an alleyway to the next street, where he hopped over a small crater in the road and stepped around broken bricks, shards of glass, and splintered wooden beams that had once stood as the front wall of a pub. A German zeppelin had changed that months earlier. Three men, including the owner, had died in the London bombing. The wreckage served as a stark reminder that the battlefields did not wholly contain this war and soldiers weren't its only victims.

The memory of the bombing yanked George's gaze skyward. He scoured the evening sky for Germany's massive silver airships, but found only sweeps of gray clouds hanging over London like a sooty fog. Assured he was safe for the moment, he reclined against the door frame of a tenement building and waited.

It took longer for the lad to appear than George expected, but

George knew the streets of London and there was only one way out of that alley unless the boy backtracked. After several minutes, George started to worry that some other bloke had snatched up his mark, but finally the boy peeked out around the corner and George grabbed him by the back of his collar.

The rejected recruit spun around, his fists and feet flailing, but George kept the boy's punches and kicks at arm's length. Unable to land a hit or break free, the boy clawed at his arm. "Let go of me! Help!"

A cluster of women gossiping in a doorway across the street spared them a fleeting glance before returning to their conversation.

"Help!" the boy screamed even louder, but this time no one looked their way.

"I'm trying to help," George said through clenched teeth as the boy's fingernails drew blood on his forearm. "But you need to calm down."

"Let go!"

"Fine, but first you have to promise you won't run."

The boy stopped struggling.

"Do I have your word?" George asked.

The boy nodded, so George let go and reached into his shirt pocket. The boy scrambled back until his heels hit the brick wall of the tenement.

"Relax," George said, pulling out his last cigarette. He'd earned the pack loading cargo at the shipyard. His blistered hands stung from gripping the ropes all night, and his back, arms, and legs ached from the strain of lifting the crates. He rolled the cigarette between his sore fingers and then held it out to the boy. "Smoke?"

The boy shook his head.

"You're not from around here, are you?" George asked, placing the cigarette behind his ear.

The boy didn't answer. George noticed him start to reach up to touch his throat, but then stop and jam his hands in his pockets, his large blue eyes never leaving George's face.

"I'm not going to hurt you," George said. "I just want to have a little chat. If you don't like what I'm selling, we'll go our separate ways."

The boy's eyes narrowed, but George forged on. "I overheard your conversation with the recruiting officer. I think you got a raw deal being turned away like you were. What do you want to go joining Kitchener's Army for anyway?"

No answer.

"Come on, Timothy," George said, leaning in closer. "Your secret's safe with me."

. . .

Thomas looked down at his worn boots. He was trapped. This con kept digging at him and was now poking around, trying to get at his secrets.

Six months earlier, when James had told Thomas he planned

to join the army, he'd made Thomas swear to tell no one, especially not their mum, until after he'd left for training. Thomas remembered the morning he'd stood on the Dover station platform fighting back tears as he waved goodbye to his brother. Before the train had pulled away, James had leaned out the window, mussed up Thomas's hair one last time, and promised everything would be all right. Thomas hated that James had left them, but he'd kept his brother's secret. When his dad had discovered the truth, he gave Thomas a swatting he would not soon forget.

"A secret can be a friend or a weapon, Thomas," his mum had warned. "Take care how you use it." And then she'd gone into her room and cried. Thomas's backside had stung from his dad's lashing for hours, but the pain of betrayal in his mum's teary eyes still ached in his heart.

Thomas thought about the secret he now kept. His lies hadn't worked with the recruiter. They'd cost him his last chance to find his brother and return him home to his family. It was over. He'd failed his parents again. His secret no longer mattered. It was not his friend or his weapon, but aside from a photograph he'd taken from home, the medals around his neck, and the potato in his pocket, his secret was all he had left. He wouldn't lose that too, not to a lying street urchin.

"Don't tell me you're one of those boys who wants to go fight so he can feel like a real man," the nosy boy pressed.

"No," Thomas said, kicking at a loose pebble on the cobblestone street. "I need the money."

"You and me both. See, we already have something in common. So tell me, *Timothy Bennett*." He said the name through a knowing smile, hitting each *t* with sharp enunciation, as though he and Thomas shared an inside joke. "What's your *real* name?"

Thomas glanced over his shoulder, afraid someone might overhear their conversation, but the boy waved away his concern. "You could call yourself Dorothy around here. No one's gonna bat an eye."

Thomas's lips pressed into a hard line.

"Fine. Timothy it is." The boy pulled the cigarette from behind his ear and held it between his lips as he looked Thomas up and down. "Tiny Tim." He chuckled at his joke.

Thomas didn't. "Don't call me that."

"Tiny or Tim?"

"Either."

"Then what should I call you?"

"Thomas."

"Any last name, Thomas?"

"Sullivan."

The street urchin held out his hand. "Good to meet you, Thomas Sullivan. Name's George."

Thomas stared at George, waiting for him to finish his introduction.

"No last name. Just George."

When Thomas didn't take his hand, George rested it on Thomas's shoulder. "So Thomas Sullivan, I have a proposition for you."

"A propo—"

"—sition," George said. "You know, an offer. I get something I want. You get something you want. Everyone's happy." He leaned forward and placed his hand against the wall behind Thomas's head. "All you have to do is come with me."

Thomas ducked under his arm. "No thanks."

"You haven't heard what I have to offer."

"I've heard enough," Thomas said, walking faster, "and I'm not interested in your kind of help."

George strolled alongside him. "You sure about that, Tommy?"

Thomas broke into a run. No one called him Tommy except his brother, but he had neither the time nor the patience to explain that to George. Distracted by his annoying shadow, he took a left when he should have cut right. Skidding to a halt, he stared at a brick wall at the end of a short alleyway. Cursing under his breath, he spun around and slammed into George.

"You look lost," George said. "Sure you can't use my help?"

"Positive," Thomas said, pushing past him.

George easily kept pace. "What's the hurry, Tommy? Where you headed?"

"Home."

George reached into his pocket. "Tough to buy a train ticket with no money unless, of course, you were planning to sell this."

Thomas stopped. His eyes widened with shock at the medals dangling from the necklace held between George's fingers.

He reached up and felt around his bare neck. "Where did you—? How—? When?"

George shrugged. "Just one of my many talents."

The surprise in Thomas's eyes hardened into anger. He lunged for the necklace, but George pulled it out of reach.

"They don't look to be worth much," he said, inspecting the medals.

"Don't touch those!" Thomas screamed.

George spit on his thumb and worked the saliva in small circles into the raised, tarnished surface of Saint Joseph. "Religious, eh? Well, your prayers have been answered, Thomas Sullivan. Think of me as your guardian angel."

"That's my brother's! Give it back!" Thomas jumped for the necklace, but George lifted it higher.

"Only if you listen to my proposition."

"I don't want to listen to anything you have to say, you lyin' thief!"

George shook his head. "That hurts, Tommy, and here I thought we were becoming mates."

"I'd never be mates with someone like you. Now give me my necklace or I'll scream."

George spotted a bobby rounding the corner. He'd had run-ins with the handlebar-mustached cop many times over the years and couldn't afford to have another today. He had an appointment to keep. Pulling his cap lower, he held out the necklace. "I was just trying to help."

Thomas grabbed it. "I don't need help from the likes of you." Securing the chain around his neck, he hurried in the direction he hoped would lead him back to Trafalgar Square.

"My mistake," George yelled after him as he lit his last cigarette. "I thought you needed to get to the Western Front."

Thomas stopped, and George smiled.

FOUR

TWO WEEKS AFTER he'd arrived in London, Thomas finally made his way back to Charing Cross train station, this time at a full sprint.

He struggled to keep pace with George running ahead of him, but the mustached bobby with the truncheon charging after them kept Thomas pushing through the hitch in his side. The army uniform he wore did little to help his progress. Two sizes too big and three inches too long, it tripped up his every step. Gripping his waistband with one hand and his army kit bag with the other, Thomas hiked up his trousers and hurried to catch George.

He still couldn't believe he was headed to the Western Front. Two weeks earlier, when he'd followed George through the back alleys of London to Dorset Street, he'd feared the street urchin planned to sell him to some factory owner. When they'd reached

Dorset Street, they were greeted by a man in a suit and bowler hat. After George whispered something in the man's ear, the man had dropped a couple of coins in George's outstretched hand, and then, without asking Thomas a single question, the man led the boys into a building where several other recruits waited. Thomas recognized many from Trafalgar Square. Some were old. Some were young. But like him, all had been pointed left by the army recruiter.

That evening, the man with the bowler hat gave Thomas an army uniform and a kit bag that contained a helmet, a gas mask, boots and polish, a blanket, a notebook and pencil, a mess kit, an entrenching tool, a water flask, cigarettes and matches, a bar of chocolate, and several items Thomas couldn't identify. The kit had everything a soldier needed for the front line, except a weapon. Thomas had hoped the man would assign him a rifle before sending him to the Western Front, but during his brief orientation, the man made no mention of what Thomas would be using to fight the enemy or when he'd receive it. He'd simply announced that the recruits now belonged to a special unit under someone he called "Hellfire Jack," and then they lined up for a warm meal of stew, dumplings, and fresh-baked biscuits.

When George slipped out the door that evening after eating two helpings and pocketing several biscuits, Thomas had assumed it would be the last he'd ever see of the street urchin, but George returned the next morning in time for breakfast. He stuck around to watch the first day of training, and when they filed into line for dinner, George joined the queue in front of Thomas with an army uniform tucked under one arm and a kit bag slung over his shoulder.

Thomas had been stuck with a view of George's back ever since. In line for food. On their daily marches. During every drill. Even now, as he sprinted across Trafalgar Square.

"Hurry up, Tommy!" George yelled. "Or we'll miss the train!"

. . .

At Charing Cross station, the army transport train's whistle pierced the din of rumbling trolleys, pounding footsteps, and shouting voices. Pulling his coat collar up to shield his face, Charlie Barnett sank lower in his seat at the back of the train and peeked out the window to the platform, where women and children clung to men in uniforms—husbands, fathers, sons—bidding them teary goodbyes.

For the tenth time since Charlie had boarded the train, he checked the platform's large clock: 5:15 P.M. The train should have left by now. He picked at the torn, dry skin around his thumbnail. He'd never been on a train before, but he'd heard adults say they could set their watches by them. Something was wrong. Charlie switched from picking the skin around his thumb to worrying it with his teeth as a swarm of frightening possibilities buzzed through his mind.

It had been three weeks since he ran away from home. Had his brother, Henry, broken his promise and told their dad of his plan? What if he'd notified the police or the army? What if their dad had sobered up long enough to look for him?

Charlie glanced back at the clock and gnawed a hangnail until it tore free. Blood oozed from the cut and dripped onto the open notebook on Charlie's lap. He tried to wipe the blood off the pencil sketches he'd drawn while waiting on the train, but managed only to smear the drop, leaving a crimson streak across the unfinished image of a soldier hugging a little boy goodbye on the platform. Closing the notebook, Charlie moved on to his next finger.

The conductor hollered the final boarding call, and the soldiers on the platform gently pried themselves from their loved ones' embraces and hurried over to the train. With the last man boarded, the whistle blew out three short bursts. Charlie flinched as memories of the textile-factory whistle twitched through his muscles. He hated the piercing sound, always chastising him and his brother when they were late for their shifts. Each shrill whistle warning them of the punishment that awaited them at both the factory and at home. After echoes of the last whistle faded from Charing Cross, Charlie sagged with relief. The train was finally leaving the station, taking him far from London and his father's reach.

As a group of older soldiers filed past, Charlie inched lower in his seat and feigned sleep. Ignoring the three empty seats around him, the soldiers headed to the front of the car.

A younger soldier with short, tidy black hair, a barely there mustache, round-framed glasses, and a pristine uniform boarded the train after them. His head held high, he strode past, looking down his upturned nose at the train's musty, stained seats and their temporary occupants. His disdainful gaze glided past Charlie like he was part of the worn upholstery.

Charlie was not surprised. There was nothing remarkable about him. His average height, slight build, gray eyes, and dingy brown hair made him forgettable, which was fine with Charlie. He preferred to blend into the scenery, where he could watch, but not be forced to interact with the world. In fact, the only aspect of Charlie that stuck out were his ears, which he was convinced he'd never grow into, even if he lived to be one hundred and two.

When the tidy soldier looked back in his search for a seat, Charlie averted his eyes and pulled his thin, straight hair down over his ears. Thankfully, the soldier chose a seat midway down the car, distancing himself from both the soldiers at the front and Charlie in the back. Charlie watched the soldier wipe the city streets from his shoes with a handkerchief before returning his attention to the world outside the window.

The train shuddered and lurched forward. The people on the platform waved and clutched one another for support while their eyes scoured each window, searching for a final glimpse of their loved ones. Bile rose in Charlie's throat as he scanned the crowd for the one face he prayed to never see again, but only strangers stared back. With a relieved sigh, he rested his head against the back of his seat and watched the station platform inch by. As the cars groaned and tugged against the pull of the engine, Charlie noticed two boys in uniforms running onto the platform with a bobby hot on their heels.

The taller of the two soldiers spotted Charlie watching. "Stop the train!" he yelled.

Charlie sank lower in his seat, praying the train would keep going. He had to get out of London before his father found him. He stared down at his bleeding fingers clutching the scratchy cloth of his army trousers. He shouldn't have looked out the window. He knew better. Make no sound. Make no trouble. Make no eye contact. That was how he'd survived the last fourteen years. He took a deep breath and opened his notebook to a clean page. Drawing always calmed his nerves. He placed the tip of his pencil on the paper and looked around the car for something or someone to sketch. He'd settled on drawing the tidy soldier when a hand slapped against his window, sending him scrambling over his armrest into the next seat.

The banging continued, and Charlie peeked at the window. The tall soldier was running alongside the train. He locked eyes with Charlie. "Stop the train!"

Charlie nodded and glanced to the front of the car, where the conductor was collecting tickets. He started to stand and call out to the conductor, but his legs tingled with numbness and his voice seized in his throat. Sweat blossomed on his upper lip and forehead. He sank down into the seat, swallowing hard before looking back to the window. The soldier was gone.

The train found its rhythm as the engine cleared the station platform, leaving an expanding plume of white smoke in its wake. One by one, the cargo and passenger cars followed the engine from the shadows of the covered platform into the early-evening light. Charlie slid back over to his seat and peered out the window. Both boys were still screaming and chasing the train, but only the taller one kept pace with the last car. As the back platform of the car slid within the boy's reach, he jumped up, grabbed the side handle, and swung himself onto the shallow metal grate, where he waved frantically for his friend to join him. Gripping the side handle with one hand, he leaned out over the back of the train, extending his other hand to his friend. The bobby, still pursuing the pair, kicked up his pace.

Charlie pressed his face against the window, desperate to see if the second boy would make it before the last train car cleared the platform.

. . .

Hanging off the back of the car, George screamed, "Jump!"

The command died beneath the grinding screech of the locomotive's wheels on the steel tracks, but Thomas obeyed. Clutching his kit bag, Thomas reached out for George's hand and leaped from the edge of the platform. The bobby's fingers grazed the cuffs of his trousers but couldn't grab hold. Thomas's body hung suspended in the air for two frantic heartbeats before gravity pulled him toward the steel tracks below.

"Tommy!" George screamed as he thrust his chest out over the railing and grabbed Thomas's arm. Jamming his feet against the base of the grate, he heaved Thomas over the railing and onto the back of the car. Thomas collapsed in a trembling heap while George smiled and waved to the bobby shaking his truncheon and screaming threats at the boys from the end of the platform.

"Told you we'd make it," George said, slapping a hand on Thomas's shoulder. "And you were worried."

Struggling to catch his breath, Thomas shot George an exasperated glare before pressing his lips to his brother's Saint Joseph medal and whispering a prayer of thanks for his protection.

. . .

Inside the train car, Charlie breathed a sigh of relief that the short boy hadn't plummeted to his death. When he heard the creak of the back door opening, he shoved his notebook and pencil in his kit bag and sank lower in his seat. As the footsteps drew closer, he shut his eyes, hoping the tardy soldiers would walk past like the others, but they stopped in the aisle beside him.

"What do you think, Tommy? Did he faint from exhaustion from *not* helping us?"

The only reply was the scrape of a match being lit and the pungent smell of sulfur.

"Leave no man behind. Isn't that what they drilled into our skulls for the last two weeks, Tommy? Guess this one thought that only applied on the battlefield."

Charlie kept his eyes squeezed shut, hoping the boys would find other seats, but a body plopped down in the seat to his right. Opening one eye, he peeked over at the tall, red-headed boy lounging next to him. Blood trickled down his freckled cheek in a broken line from a gash on the bridge of his crooked nose, and a wave of guilt surged through Charlie.

"Hey!" his new seatmate exclaimed. "He's awake! Thanks for giving us a hand, mate."

Charlie scooted away, shifting in his seat until his back was pressed up against the window.

Unfazed by his reaction, the tall soldier stretched out his long legs and rested his feet on the empty seat across from him. "So," he said, staring at Charlie, "how long until we get to Belgium?"

Charlie didn't answer.

The red-headed soldier glanced over at his short friend who remained in the aisle, his face pale and his hands still shaking from his brush with death. "We may have found someone who actually speaks less than you, Tommy." He returned his attention to Charlie. "What's your name?"

Charlie's gaze fell to his lap.

"Blimey, you're quieter than a mouse, aren't you?"

Charlie flinched as the boy slapped a hand on his shoulder.

"Easy there, Mouse. I'm not going to hurt you. That's what we'll call you. Mouse. It's fitting, don't you think, Tommy?"

Tommy, who'd stepped over his friend's legs and taken the seat across from Charlie, shrugged.

"This is going to be a boring trip if I have to talk to myself the whole time," the tall soldier said in a voice loud enough for the whole car to hear.

The tidy soldier, five seats ahead, turned and glared at him like he was filth he wished to wipe from his shoe and discard. The red-headed boy took a long drag from his cigarette and winked at the soldier, who looked away in disgust.

"Think I'll take a stroll and ask the conductor what time we'll be reaching Dover to catch the ferry across the Channel."

The little color that had returned to Tommy's face vanished. "We're stopping in Dover?"

"Of course. Where else are we going to cross the Channel?"

Tommy shifted in his seat.

"What's wrong, Tommy? You afraid of water or something?"

Tommy shook his head, but his color did not return.

"All right then. I'll be back in a bit." The tall soldier looked over at Charlie and smiled. "Don't go having any big, life-changing discussions without me, Mouse."

He paused next to the tidy soldier on his way to the front of the car and blew a stream of smoke over his head. It settled like a fog around the soldier, who coughed and waved a hand before his face.

"Don't mind George," Tommy told Charlie. "He likes to hear himself talk, nonstop, all the time." He held out his hand. "Name's Thomas."

Charlie tucked his bloody fingers under his legs and lifted the corners of his mouth in what he hoped was a passable smile. "I'm Charlie."

Thomas pulled back his hand, surprised by the deep timbre of Charlie's voice. For a mouse, his voice was less squeak and more rumble. "Good to meet you, Charlie."

"You too. I'm sorry I didn't help before. I . . ." Charlie didn't have a good excuse, so his voice trailed off into an uncomfortable silence.

"It's not your fault we almost missed the train. We ran into someone looking for George on our way to the station."

Remembering the cop chasing the pair on the platform, Charlie considered the strong possibility that George might not have suffered his injury during his jump onto the train. As he pondered what type of trouble Thomas and George might be in, Charlie noticed Thomas looking over his uniform.

"You part of Major Norton-Griffith's new recruits?" Thomas asked.

Charlie nodded.

"Us too. I don't remember seeing you with our group at Regent Street."

"I was trained with recruits in West Ham," Charlie said.

Thomas turned and looked toward the front of the train car, where George was enjoying a laugh and cigarette with a group of older soldiers Thomas didn't recognize. "Norton-Griffith's recruiters must be training men all over London, if you can call what we did for the last two weeks training. Did you get a weapon?"

Charlie shook his head.

"Neither did we. Makes you wonder how they expect us to fight the Germans. March them to death?"

Charlie smiled. It felt more genuine. He hoped it looked it. He'd wondered the same thing during his short training. Aside from the uniform, he felt no more a soldier than he had before he skipped his shift at the factory, lied about his age, and joined Major Norton-Griffith's recruits headed to fight on the Western Front.

He looked back out the window as the train pulled away from the crowded London streets. Charlie had never known any place but London. He'd been born there and always thought he'd die there, most likely at his father's hand. As the train snaked its way through the surrounding countryside, London shrank on the horizon until it vanished from view. Charlie wondered what awaited him on the Western Front and what Major Norton-Griffith had planned for a gang of underage, undertrained, unarmed soldiers on the front line of the war they were saying would end all wars.

FIVE

THOMAS JOLTED AWAKE at the sound of the train whistle heralding their approach to the station in Belgium. Stepping over George's outstretched legs, he made his way to the back of the car. He knew James wouldn't be waiting for him at the station, but he wanted to see the country he'd be calling home for the next several months.

He slipped out the door and stood on the grate. It would be hours before the sun rose, but he leaned over the side railing and looked toward the front of the train. The sting of the cold night wind racing along the train drew tears from his eyes, but he kept them open, searching for any sign of the Allied front. Along the horizon, the night sky pulsed with brilliant white and yellow light. A thunderous rumble followed each flash, like a distant storm.

When the train pulled into the station, Thomas hurried

back to his seat, grabbed his kit bag, and followed George and Charlie onto the platform, where a lieutenant ordered them to line up.

George squeezed in between Thomas and the tidy soldier. "I could definitely get used to traveling by train," he said, lighting up a smoke.

He'd been excited to learn the army supplied soldiers with cigarettes. Thomas was certain the free cigarettes and meals were influencing factors in George's decision to join.

"Good smokes, good sleep, and good company," George said, blowing his smoke above their heads.

Beside him, the tidy soldier coughed and fanned the smoke away from his face. "Do you mind?" he asked.

"Not at all," George said with a smile. "That's why I smoke."

"Gutter rat," the soldier muttered under his breath.

"What was that?" George asked, but the soldier didn't answer. He simply stepped to the left, leaving a wide gap between him and the other boys.

. . .

Frederick Chamberlain doubted he'd ever had a worse day. The train was late leaving London, the conductor had refused his reasonable request to be moved to a car with soldiers who behaved in a more civil manner, and he'd been accosted by the boor in a uniform blowing smoke in his face. And that was all before they'd cleared London.

The rest of the eight-hour trip he'd spent failing to ignore the incessant chatter of soldiers with far less intelligence, military experience, and decorum than he possessed; vomiting over the side rail of the crowded ferry that transported them across the Channel to France; and unable to sleep due to the uncomfortable seats and inescapable stench of cheap cigarettes and unwashed masses clogging up the second transport train.

By the time they pulled into the station in Poperinge, Frederick wanted nothing more than to disembark the smelly train he'd been stuck on since their ferry had docked in France so he could distance himself from his traveling companions, but the lieutenant who met them on the platform prior to their transport to the town of Ypres had other plans.

After a quick meal consisting of a bowl of bland stew and a stale biscuit and an even quicker bathroom break, the lieutenant led the recruits to the main road, where Frederick expected to find a row of vehicles waiting to transport them to the front.

"It's rained for over a week now, making the roads impassable by vehicle," the lieutenant announced, "so we'll be marching to Wipers."

"I believe the town's name is pronounced *e-pris,* sir," Frederick said.

The lieutenant's eyes narrowed on Frederick. "I didn't ask for a lesson in linguistics, soldier. Now get marching!"

Frederick's feet sank seven inches into the mud and manure with every step of the eight-mile trek to the Allied front, positioned two miles outside the town of Ypres. His teeth chattered from the frigid early-morning air, and his legs burned with the effort it took to march through the cold, thick sludge. He knew he would never be able to wipe his boots clean, but he held his head high and marched on, always staying several steps ahead of the other soldiers.

George, the ginger soldier with the cackling laugh and big mouth, lobbed taunts like hand grenades at him as they marched, but Frederick refused to let the tall miscreant or the friends he called Tommy and Mouse know any of his insults had hit their mark. To distract himself, Frederick mentally wrote and revised a growing list of complaints, which he was determined to recite to Major Norton-Griffith upon their meeting, starting with the fact that most of the men in this unit were not trained to march in a straight line, much less to fight on the front lines.

Frederick, of course, had been trained to do both at boarding school. He had no doubt that when they arrived at the Ypres Salient, whatever error had placed him with this motley band of ruffians and vagrants would be corrected. A soldier of his caliber was born to lead troops, just as the Chamberlain men had for generations. Of course, the officers would not be aware of his family or his Eton education. He was three years shy of graduating and had been forced to perjure himself to join the army, but surely his impressive lineage, education, training, and experience would be obvious to his superiors the second they witnessed him in action.

Frederick slid his cold hands into the pockets of his greatcoat, where his left hand brushed against the silky vane of a long plume. He'd received the white feather three weeks earlier, when his classmates slipped it beneath his dormitory door after he refused to fight a younger student who'd challenged him. No explanation or message accompanied the feather. It needed neither. Frederick knew its meaning the second he spotted it. Everyone did.

Coward.

He'd kept the feather as a reminder of what he had to do. He'd prove them all wrong. His classmates, the army, his brothers, his father, even the gutter rats trudging behind him. Frederick Chamberlain was no coward. He was born to fight. He was born to lead, and after the war, his name would be engraved on the walls of Eton with the names of the prestigious school's other war heroes. His portrait would hang in the Chamberlain family gallery, alongside his brothers' and his father's. The men and boys marching with him would treat him with respect. And once they heard of his victories against the Germans and saw the medals that would someday hang from his uniform, his perjury at the recruitment table would be forgiven and any difference in age existing between him and the other men fighting for crown and country would be forgotten. Leaving the feather in his pocket, Frederick marched on, determined to catch up to the lieutenant leading the way and distance himself further from those falling behind.

Their unit reached their destination as the sun crested the crooked lines of trenches stretching along the horizon. The lieutenant then divided them into groups. Some of the older soldiers were handed shovels and escorted to the front line to dig trenches and dugouts for the infantry. Others were ordered to report to the Royal Engineers tasked with repairing and reinforcing the muddied roads they'd just traveled. A medic informed a group of soldiers not much older than Frederick that they'd be serving as stretcher bearers at a nearby Regimental Aid Post.

Poor saps, Frederick thought as he watched them leave. *How embarrassing to wear the uniform but not be a real soldier.*

With most of the other recruits headed to their assigned posts, Frederick glanced around to see what officer he'd have the honor to serve. A block of a man with a shaggy gray mustache sprouting beneath a bulbous, ruddy nose that looked like he'd plucked a red potato from the ground and smashed it onto his face was all that remained.

"Guess that means you boys are with me," the man said.

Frederick stepped forward and saluted. "Major Norton-Griffith, sir. It is an honor to meet you. I was wondering if I might have a word with you in private." He cast a disgusted glance back at the other boys. "I have a few concerns I believe you will want to address immediately."

The man adjusted his metal helmet to get a better look at Frederick. "I'm not Hellfire Jack, so you can save your salutes and concerns. I'm Bagger." He then tossed each boy a burlap sack.

Stunned by the man's response, Frederick stared down at the coarse bag and tried to figure out how best to address a superior who refused to tell you his rank.

"Put on your helmets and follow me," Bagger ordered.

He didn't wait for the boys to dig their helmets from their kit bags before plodding in the direction of the reserve trenches, two trenches back from the front line. "First rule in the trenches: keep your head down at all times. You even think of putting a hair above those"—he motioned to the wall of sandbags that lined the top of the trench—"and Fritz will try and give you a close shave. Our front line may be two hundred and fifty yards away from the Germans, but their snipers seldom miss."

The boys jammed on their helmets and, keeping their heads below the top of the trench, scrambled to catch up with their new superior. The squat man lumbered down the long, mud-died stretches and sparse wooden duckboards lining the floor of the zigzag path, his broad shoulders hunched and head low.

Carved into the Ypres farmland, the trench ran ten feet deep and six feet wide, allowing just enough space for two soldiers to pass each other.

Bagger didn't look back as he explained the number of ways one could get maimed or killed on the Western Front. His voice, flat with boredom, droned on as though he were running down a list of items the boys were to pick up for him at the market. "Eggs, bread, milk . . . influenza, tuberculosis, pleurisy, pneumonia, trench fever . . ." Frederick tried to pay attention to the numerous warnings, but the sights, sounds, and smells of the trenches held his senses hostage.

Soldiers, their skin and uniforms caked with dried mud, huddled against shallow wooden benches pressed into the clay walls and took long drags on cigarettes clutched between filthy fingers. They cast the boys the barest of glances as they passed. Between the benches, small dugouts, carved into the trench walls, cocooned sleeping soldiers. Surrounded by dirt, with their eyes closed and bodies still, they looked like freshly buried corpses. Frederick averted his eyes, shaken by the thought.

High above the battlefield, thin smears of clouds inched across a crisp morning sky, yet within the trenches, the air was a sour stew of damp earth, cigarette smoke, body odor, and worse. Frederick pulled a folded handkerchief from his pocket and pressed it to his nose and mouth to stave off the reek of rot and death, but it clung to every breath. He glanced back at the boys pulling up the rear. Tommy held a hand over his nose, but George and Mouse walked along as if unaffected by the putrid odors.

No doubt boys like them are accustomed to such a stench, Frederick thought as he quickened his pace. After several shaky steps, his mockery of their resistance to the nauseating scents turned to envy as he ripped off his helmet and heaved the contents of his stomach into the protective headgear.

George laughed, and Mouse looked away, but Tommy stepped forward. "You all right?"

Frederick waved him off, took one whiff of his vomit combined with the smell of the trenches, and puked again into his helmet.

"Breathe it in, boys," Bagger said with a humorless chuckle. "That's the smell of glory."

When nothing remained in Frederick's stomach, Bagger grabbed the helmet from his hands, dunked it in a puddle at the base of the trench wall, gave the dirty water that filled the helmet a quick swirl, and then dumped the water, along with the vomit, back into the puddle.

"Don't worry, lads," he said, jamming the helmet back onto Frederick's head. "Out here you eventually get used to the stench—or you get killed. Either way, you won't be minding the smell anymore." He chuckled again at the look that flashed across Frederick's pale face before continuing to lead them through the trench.

Bagger navigated the narrow path like he was walking through a minefield, stepping over and around puddles of fetid water oozing up beneath the wooden planks lining the trench floor. "And if you like your feet, watch your step. Keep 'em dry or lose 'em."

Frederick yanked his foot out of a puddle and shook the water from his boot. He'd heard stories of soldiers losing a foot or leg to gangrene. He did not intend to be one of them.

They were quiet after that, even George, whose cocky grin had fallen into an unamused scowl. Frederick tried to keep pace with Bagger as they trudged through a communication trench that connected the reserve trenches to the support and front-line trenches, but a sleepless night and miles of marching through the mud finally took their toll. His feet dragged, and his eyelids drooped.

Bagger led them into a section of the support trenches, where he finally stopped. He turned to face the boys, and Frederick collided with the man's barrel chest.

"Sorry, sir!" Frederick said, stepping back and standing at attention.

"I told you, call me—"

"Yes, sir, Bagger, sir."

"What's your name?" Bagger asked.

Frederick raised his chin and pulled back his shoulders. "Frederick Chamberlain, sir—Bagger."

"What'd you do before joining up, lad?"

"I was a student. At Eton, sir."

Bagger shook his head. "Thought so. Well, Eton—"

"It's Frederick, sir."

Bagger scratched at the gray stubble peppering his cheeks

and chin. "Out here, you'll answer to whatever I call you." He looked past Frederick to address all four new recruits. "Understand?"

"Yes, Bagger," George and Tommy answered. Mouse nodded.

"Understand, Eton?" Bagger stared at Frederick, waiting for his response.

Frederick pursed his lips, fighting the urge to explain the importance of military protocol and decorum to the man standing before him, but decided it wiser to save his breath for a real army leader. "Yes, Bagger."

"Good." Bagger waved a beefy hand behind him. "Welcome to your new home, boys."

Frederick looked around at the narrow trench. Sleeping soldiers already occupied the shallow benches and dugouts.

"Are we to take over the next shift, Bagger, sir? Will we be using their weapons?" He held up his burlap sack. "Is that what these are for? For keeping the rifles dry when we aren't fighting?"

Bagger laughed. "Didn't Hellfire Jack's recruiters tell you? You're not here to fight *on* the front line."

He grabbed Frederick's shoulder and shoved him toward a narrow entrance in the trench wall.

"You're here to work *under* them."

The boys stopped at a doorway framed with thick lumber beams and peered inside. Wooden planks, wedged into the angled clay floor, led to a dimly lit tunnel carved into the ground separating the support trenches, the second line of Allied trenches, and the front line.

Bagger motioned the four young recruits down the hole. "Welcome to the clay kickers, boys!"

SIX

DARKNESS SWALLOWED THE labyrinth that stretched beneath the Allied trenches and burrowed deep under no-man's-land toward Messines Ridge, the higher ground occupied by thousands of enemy troops.

With uncertain steps, the boys followed Bagger into the tunnel. They passed a dugout packed with filled sandbags stacked to the ceiling.

"What are all the bags for?" George asked, breaking the uncomfortable silence closing in on them.

"They're for camouflage. If we get word that the Germans have breached our lines, we use them to seal off the entrance. We don't want the enemy discovering our tunnels."

"Now, when you say 'seal off the entrance,' you don't mean with us in the tunnels, do you?" George pressed.

"That's exactly what I mean. We stay down here and wait

quietly until the threat has passed. When it has, our infantry-men will remove the bags."

"And if the threat doesn't pass?" George asked.

Ignoring the question, Bagger ushered the boys inside a second, larger dugout carved as an offshoot of the main tunnel. Wooden posts and slabs, with wire netting stretched between them, jutted from the walls on either side of the cave-like room, creating eight narrow bunks. Men slept curled up on three of the bunks. Not one woke or even budged when Bagger and the boys entered. In the middle of the dugout, four wooden chairs surrounded an overturned crate, cluttered with flickering candles, dirty tin cups and plates, and a worn deck of cards. A birdcage rested on a square wooden board wedged into a corner near the "ceiling" at the rear of the dugout. Inside the cage, a small yellow canary, a speck of sunshine in the darkness, hopped from its perch to the side of the cage and back, its crisp tweet piercing the silence of the underground barracks.

Thomas knew the flap and scratch of the bird's movement, the clip of its chirp, and the trill of its song meant life to miners. When a canary stopped singing and dropped from its perch, miners knew their deadliest enemy, carbon monoxide, was present and they had minutes, maybe only seconds, to escape.

Without odor or sound, the lethal gas crept upon unsuspecting miners as they worked deep beneath the earth, leaching away their oxygen and suffocating them into wakeless sleep. During his three years in the coal mine, Thomas had learned that explosions, even ones as small as a bullet firing, in confined, unventilated areas, could unleash the miners' deadly foe. If you weren't paying attention, if you forgot to regularly listen for the canary's song, or if you neglected to check whether the bird remained on its perch, you were as good as dead.

As Thomas watched the canary hop around its cage, calling out to them with a rapid, high-pitched greeting, he pulled a long breath deep into his lungs.

"This is our dugout," Bagger said. "We work in eight-hour shifts. One on. Two off. Our crew covers the nine P.M. to five A.M. shift. When you're not working, you can go up top, behind the trenches, for some fresh air and to get some food, but we sleep, eat, and relax in here."

Dread, cold and heavy, pooled in Thomas's stomach. He'd left the coal mines of Dover and traveled to the Western Front only to end up underground again. Reminding himself of his reason for coming to Ypres, he pushed away thoughts of working and, worse yet, sleeping beneath the earth and started calculating how many hours of sleep he could survive on and how much time that would leave him when he was off-shift to search the trenches for his brother.

Now that he'd made it to the Western Front, Thomas couldn't afford to waste any time. He knew finding his brother wouldn't be easy, but he had to try. James would look for him if their roles were reversed. And when Thomas found his brother, they'd make their way home to their family, where they belonged.

While Bagger lectured the boys about storing food to keep rats from infesting the tunnels and explained where in the trenches they'd find the holes they were to use as their latrine, Thomas considered the fact that if he could convince one of the other boys to help him look for James, he would double his chances of finding him. But who could he trust?

His only interaction with Frederick Chamberlain was being on the receiving end of the Eton student's disgusted glares. He'd be no help. Charlie seemed nice enough, but walking through the trenches, the boy had looked like he was about to jump out of his skin. Thomas doubted he could convince him to return to the trenches again on a regular basis. That left George.

Thomas knew him the best, but that wasn't saying much. Despite the fact that he talked constantly, George never spoke about his family or home, and even though he'd been true to his word about getting Thomas to the Western Front, he'd only kept his promise because doing so benefitted George. Even his decision to enlist had nothing to do with Thomas or with helping anyone but himself. The lanky street urchin had only decided to enlist after he saw the contents of Thomas's kit bag and overheard the recruiter say they'd be provided with two meals a day, a place to sleep, cigarettes, and five more shillings a day than the infantrymen.

Despite George's reasons for joining, Thomas was glad he had. He'd distracted Thomas with funny stories on the long train and ferry rides and during their march to Ypres when images of

James lying dead on some foreign battlefield crept into Thomas's thoughts. But he didn't trust George. If there was a chance that sharing Thomas's secret would earn George favor with Bagger or the rest of the crew, Thomas had no doubt the London con would betray him.

No. He couldn't risk telling anyone. He would have to find James on his own.

Bagger nudged Thomas's shoulder with a sausage-link finger. "Take off your boots. All of you. You can leave them in here."

Thomas, George, and Charlie immediately started unlacing their boots.

Frederick, however, did not. "You just warned us in the trenches not to let our feet get wet."

"Boots make noise, Eton. Socks don't. Everyone except our kicker works in socks." He nodded to the largest man snoring away on a low bunk and then turned to walk onward.

"But won't our feet get wet?" Frederick pressed, still refusing to remove his boots.

Bagger stopped in the entranceway. His meaty hands balled into fists the size of sledgehammers.

Thomas stepped away from Frederick, distancing himself as far as he could in the confined space in case Bagger decided to knock some respect into the quarrelsome boy.

Charlie slid behind George, who shook his head and rolled his eyes at Frederick's continued need to question everything and everyone.

But Bagger didn't hit Frederick. He didn't even turn around. His broad shoulders rose and fell as he took a long, irritated breath. "I've been digging tunnels since before you were born, Eton. Mole and I were some of the first tunnelers Hellfire Jack recruited for this war. What we lack in experience on the battlefield, we more than make up for in the tunnels beneath it, so when I tell you to take off your boots, you take off your boots. There are far worse things to worry about than trench foot in these tunnels." Relaxing his fists, he motioned for the boys to follow. "Come on. Time to show you what you'll be doing down here. There's no talking in the lower galleries. Not a sound. The tunnels have ears, and they're always listening. One sound. One word. One small cough can signal your death and the death of everyone in your crew, so I don't even want to hear you breathing, understand?"

Thomas didn't dare nod in case his neck, stiff from the train ride, creaked.

"Got that, Eton?"

"Yes, Bagger, sir," Frederick mumbled as he unlaced his boots.

Thomas, George, and Charlie followed the crew leader down the tunnel to the top of a watertight steel shaft that cut straight down through layers of soil, water, and wet sand to a layer of clay. A minute later, Frederick joined them and, one by one, they descended the shaft ladder to a lower gallery. Thomas was used to working beneath the earth. He'd spent the last three years in a coal mine in Dover, but he'd never feared silence until he descended the tunnels beneath no-man's-land.

The coal mines under the hills of Dover were dark and confined, but they were alive. They hummed with the vibration of pickaxes striking stone, rumbled with carts full of coal pulled by ponies over metal rails, and echoed with men's voices, as deep and gravelly as the earth they dug, shouting out orders, singing Irish tunes off-key, and laughing over jokes Thomas would never dare repeat at home.

The tunnels beneath the Western Front lay deadly quiet. Their silence crept across Thomas's skin in gooseflesh he feared no amount of heat could drive away, and for the first time in two weeks, he wished George would start talking again.

But no one spoke. Not after Bagger's warning.

As they followed the man farther beneath the battlefield separating the Allied trenches from the Germans', approximately a city block away, shadows, cast by candles and electric lanterns burrowed into the narrow clay walls, twitched and scattered down the tunnel like angry apparitions. Timber beams, set three hand widths apart and etched with pencil markings, braced the tunnel walls. Thomas recognized some letters, but he couldn't decipher what they were or what they meant. He had always struggled with reading and writing, and his inability to decipher letters as easily as his classmates had resulted in daily punishments from his teacher. Miss Barry wore a metal thimble on her right pointer finger, which she tapped against Thomas's head every time he mispronounced a word. Thomas went home every day humiliated and with a terrible headache. After five years of such cruel punishment, Miss Barry deemed Thomas unteachable, and Mr. Sullivan pulled his youngest son from school to work with him and James in the coal mine.

Twice, Bagger led them down ladders inside large metal tubes, past pulley systems, deeper into the earth, until they reached the lowest gallery, set one hundred feet below the battlefield. They then began the long walk up a gentle incline in the direction of Messines Ridge. Along the way, they occasionally passed men hauling full sandbags on small rubber-tired trams to the shafts to be transported to the upper galleries. Thomas assumed the bags' final destination was the side room just inside the tunnel entrance. Remembering the sandbags' purpose, his steps faltered at the thought of an enemy breach of the trenches and being walled inside the tunnels with no escape. With a shudder, he pushed the horrific thought from his mind and hurried to catch up with the others.

As they made their way farther beneath no-man's-land, Thomas found himself grateful for his lack of height, for the first time in his life. He didn't have to bow his head or hunch his back like Bagger or the other boys. George hit his head more than once on the timber beams but didn't complain. They all followed Bagger in silence, even Frederick.

Thomas lost count of the side tunnels that sprouted out from the main gallery. He wasn't sure where they led or what the clay kickers were digging for, but it was obvious that like ants, they were creating a maze of tunnels beneath no-man's-land.

After several more minutes of walking, Thomas noticed

that the timber beams bracing the tunnel walls, ceiling, and floor ended. Bagger stopped. Four men worked so quietly at the end wall of the tunnel that Thomas saw them before he heard them. The men gave Bagger a subtle nod and then returned to their work.

The largest man, with legs as wide as tree trunks, lay on his back on a wooden board that rested on a wooden block at a forty-five-degree angle. He wore a pair of boots wrapped in empty sandbags. The other men worked in thick socks so caked with clay their original color could not be guessed. Knees pulled to his chest, the reclining man wedged his feet against the footrests positioned above a finely sharpened spade, then slowly pressed the flat blade into the clay face of the tunnel. Once the blade was deep in the clay, the man pushed up and pulled down on the handle to loosen the cut before slowly withdrawing the spade and the spit of clay.

A second crew member, crouched beside the man cutting clay from the tunnel face, helped ease the slab from the wall and placed it in an empty burlap sandbag. They continued their work without a word. When the bag was full, the second man handed it to the third crew member, who loaded the bag onto a tram, which he pulled to the first metal shaft. There, he transferred the bags of clay from the handcart into a bucket at the end of a pulley system. The bags were then hauled up the shaft by the fourth crew member. Several minutes later, the cart returned below with a pile of timber beams, which the two trammers braced along the newly exposed clay wall. They didn't use hammers or nails to secure the beams, instead carving notches into the clay to wedge the lumber into place before repeating the whole process again.

Push, pull, bag, drag, raise.

Nine inches at a time.

Thomas followed their movements, in awe of the precision and silence with which they worked, operating more like machines than men. He thought about how before the war his brother and he would pass the long hours digging for coal by listening to the old miners' stories of their youth. Even after James left to join the army, Thomas had relied on the miners' voices and tales to keep loneliness and boredom from pressing in on him from all sides. When he led Morty, one of the company ponies, from the mine with a cart full of coal or rock, Thomas would regale the pony with the miners' tales, often changing the names to include his own and those of his family. Morty listened, occasionally tossing his head or whinnying. The hours underground passed faster with the distractions. Here, in the tunnels, Thomas would feel every second of silence-imposed solitude.

SEVEN

MUFFLED BATTLE CRIES preceded the first wave of soldiers climbing out of the trenches, their rifles and voices raised in a common goal—break the enemy line. The Germans answered with machine-gun fire, mowing down dozens before they reached the top. Some fell back into the trenches. Others collapsed over the edge of the parapets. Those who escaped the first barrage climbed over those who didn't and charged onto no-man's-land.

They squeezed through holes cut in the barbed wire stretched between spiked posts. The rusty steel barbs tugged at the young soldier's wool greatcoat as he crawled through an opening. An infantryman, sent out before the assault to clip the wire, lay near the jagged hole, the wire cutters still clutched in his lifeless hand.

The young soldier yanked his coat free, raised his rifle,

and rushed across the barren field with his battalion. A line of bullets carved a path within inches of his feet, kicking up mud and rocks. The soldier dove into a large crater gouged into the battlefield by an artillery-shell blast. He landed in a cloud of chlorine gas pooling in the bottom of the crude hole. It scattered before his boots like weak fog as he tripped over large chunks of earth and slipped in patches of mud. Pressing his mask to his face, the soldier hunkered down as the battle raged on around him.

He tried to take in a full breath through his nose, but the mask held his nostrils clamped shut. His breaths came fast and short. What little air he managed to siphon through the mouthpiece was tinged with charcoal from the respirator-box filter. His skin grew slick with a clammy sweat, and his vision began to go black. If he didn't regain control, he would pass out in the crater. Closing his eyes, he tapped a beat against his rifle and hummed a song from home—one his mother sang to soothe him when he was a child and frightened. By the second verse, his breathing had slowed, and the light-headedness receded.

Above him, masked soldiers rushed past, firing their rifles and waving the troops behind them forward. Smoke thickened the air, cloaking the setting sun in a sooty shroud. The sky howled with cannon fire and artillery blasts. The ground trembled beneath the bombardment. A fellow infantryman spotted the young soldier and jumped down to join him, but a bullet caught the man beneath his left ear before his head cleared the edge. His limp body slid into the large hole, coming to rest in a twisted pile at the soldier's feet.

Blood seeped beneath the dead man's masked head, pooling under the haze of gas lingering in the crater. The young soldier choked back vomit rising in his throat. He couldn't get sick in his mask, but he also couldn't risk taking it off. He had to move. He glanced back in the direction of the Allied trenches. If he returned, against military orders, he'd be shot at dawn for cowardice. But if he remained, whether it be by bullet, bomb, or gas, death would find him.

He had one chance: cross no-man's-land and pray what was left of his battalion could break the enemy line. Clutching his rifle, the soldier climbed from his hiding place and rejoined the firefight. Seventy pounds of uniform, equipment, ammunition, and weapons slowed his pace, and the muddy battlefield tripped up his steps, but the soldier pressed forward. He took cover behind sparse trees, stripped of bark and limbs by bullets and blasts. He ducked into craters to shield himself from the shrapnel of mortar- and artillery-shell blasts, but he never stopped. To stop was to die.

The enemy increased their fire as the battalion neared their trenches. The young soldier's ears rang with the deafening blasts. Through the eyepieces of his mask, he squinted against the blinding flash of artillery shells exploding and spotted the front-line trenches and helmeted heads of the enemy. The soldier aimed his rifle at a machine gunner and pulled the trigger.

He didn't wait for the man to fall before running forward and aiming his rifle at another German soldier.

As he pulled the trigger, an explosion ripped into the ground before him. The blast tore his rifle from his hands and heaved him into the air. He slammed back to the battlefield with teeth-shattering force. His lungs seized, and his vision blurred. The world around him faded. The gunfire and screams evaporated, and the ringing in his ears quieted, until all that remained was the frantic, uneven beat of his own heart.

It was the last sound he heard.

EIGHT

BAGGER LED THE boys back to their dugout, where the three men they'd left sleeping now sat around their makeshift table, drinking tea, smoking, and playing cards.

"'Bout time you got back, Bagger," said a large man. He had long auburn sideburns, a scattering of teeth, and no neck. His voice grated through his throat like a spade against gravel. "Where's Max?"

"He's running messages," Bagger replied.

"Command better not wear him out. We need him well rested for later."

"Don't you worry about Max. He'll be ready."

"He better be." The large man motioned to the empty chair beside him. "We're getting ready to play pontoon. You in?"

"No chance, Mole. You chaps took all my earnings last time we played. I've got nothin' to wager."

George stepped forward. "I do." He reached in his pocket and threw a couple of shillings into the small pile on the table, eager for a bit of card-playing to relax—and to relieve these fellows of their money.

"Who are these lads?" asked a slip of a man with watery eyes magnified by lenses twice the width of George's thumb.

Bagger motioned to the boys. "Say hello to our new attached infantry, Bats. Hellfire Jack thinks we need a few more beasts of burden." He glanced back at Frederick. "Though I don't think Eton here's seen much burden in his life."

Frederick's nostrils flared with indignation, but he kept quiet.

"These boys will be hauling clay and timber and shadowing us while they learn the ropes," Bagger continued.

Mole pushed back from the table. "Beasts of burden? More like babes of burden." He circled the boys in slow, disapproving steps before stopping in front of Thomas. "How old are you, lad?"

"Eighteen."

Mole leaned down so he was eye to eye with Thomas. When Thomas didn't step back or look away, he smiled with the same crooked grin, sparse teeth, and glint in his eyes as the jack-o'-lanterns Thomas and James used to carve from turnips and potatoes to scare their little sisters. "Eighteen what? Months?"

"Let 'im be, Mole," Bagger said, waving him back to the table. "If Hellfire Jack's not questioning his age, neither are we. Besides, we need all the help we can get. I was in a meeting at the command center with Major-General Harington and the other crew leaders before picking up these lads. Jones's crew is almost finished with the Kruisstraat Four chamber, which leaves only Banning's crew working on the Ontario Farm gallery and us."

"If Jones's crew is almost done, why doesn't command send us their tunnelers?" Bats asked as he shuffled the cards.

"They're being sent to Vimy along with most of the hundred and seventy-fifth to help the French with dugouts for the Second Army."

Bats passed Mole the deck. "So we're to finish two galleries and chambers while Banning's crew just has one to dig?"

"Major-General Harington ordered that we abandon the Wytschaete Wood chamber, so we're down to one."

Mole slammed a hand on the table, causing Charlie to jump back. "What? Why?"

"There's not enough time to finish both," Bagger explained. "He wants us to focus on finishing the gallery and chamber at Maedelstede Farm. It's a race to the finish line, chaps, and we're currently losing."

"Not exactly a fair race when our gallery has to be almost one hundred and ten yards longer than Banning's," Mole grumbled, "especially if they're sending us children to help."

"Doesn't matter," Bagger said. "Harington commanded that all twenty-four chambers be completed and ready by June, so we're accepting any extra hands he sends our way." He tossed a fleeting glance at Thomas. "Even if they are small."

Thomas tucked his hands in his trouser pockets.

"What happens in June?" George asked, retrieving his two shillings and snatching an extra while the men weren't looking.

"Nothing you need to know about now," Bagger said. "You just concern yourselves with packing bags with clay, hauling the spoil up top, and keeping your mouths shut."

"What are we digging all these tunnels and chambers for anyway?" Frederick asked. "Coal?"

The men laughed.

"Coal?" Mole said. "Under no-man's-land? No. We're the Allies' first line of defense and offense."

"It was *my* understanding the infantry was the army's first line of defense and offense in the war," Frederick said.

Bagger shook his head. "Eton, we could fill a million graves with what boarding-school soldiers *think* they know about this war."

Mole sat back and smiled.

"But for now," Bagger added, "all you need to know is that down here, you follow my orders and obey my rules." He ticked them off on his beefy fingers. "No talking in the lower galleries. Between shifts, sleep is not optional. Tired tunnelers make mistakes, and down here, mistakes cost lives. In the dugout, no cheating at cards or stealing." He gave George a hard look and held out his hand. A blush tinted George's freckled cheeks as he fished the extra shilling from his pocket and dropped it into Bagger's open palm. The crew leader tossed the coin onto the pile on the table. "And lastly, you can go in the reserve and support trenches, but stay away from the front-line trenches. There's a reason we had spots to fill on our crew, and it's not because the lads before you were promoted."

The smirk that had remained on Mole's face as Bagger lectured the boys disappeared at the mention of their former crew members.

"Follow my rules, and we'll get along fine," Bagger said. "Break them, and I'll have you transferred from my crew and Ypres Salient. You'll be digging trenches in France before you can utter 'I'm sorry.'" He leaned forward. "Have I made myself clear?"

The boys nodded.

"Now that that's settled, what do you lads bring to our merry crew?" asked the fourth clay kicker, a short stump of a man with more hair coating his knuckles and arms and sprouting from under his shirt collar than on his head. He held a pipe firmly between his teeth. Only his lips moved when he spoke. "Any of you have mining experience?"

"I do," Thomas said.

"What kind?" the man asked.

"Coal. In Dover."

Smoke streamed from the man's nostrils as he scrutinized Thomas. "I worked the coalfields in South Wales. Thirty-five years. Any work with explosives, Dover?"

Remembering Thomas's lie to the recruiter at Trafalgar

Square, George smiled. "He's got loads of experience, right, Tommy?"

Thomas's face flushed scarlet. "I used to watch my dad and brother set the explosives."

The man with the pipe nodded. "Dover can work with me."

"Leave it to Boomer to grab the only recruit with any experience underground," Mole said, dealing out two cards to the other men. He motioned to George. "How about you, Shillings? What experience do you bring our fine crew?"

George took a seat in the only empty chair around the table. "I've done a bit of everything. You name it: dockworker, chimney sweep, army recruiter." He shot a quick wink at Thomas before turning his attention back to the men at the table. "I've seen and done it all."

"Not yet, you haven't," Bagger said, pulling him out of the chair by his ear. "But you will. Shillings is with me bagging spoil. How about you, Bats? Which one of these fine British soldiers do you want shadowing you? Eton or—" Bagger craned his neck around Thomas to find Charlie, standing as far away from the men as the cramped dugout allowed. "What's your name, lad?"

Charlie stared at his stockinged feet. "Charlie."

"What'd he say?" Mole asked.

"Charlie," George answered, "but we call him Mouse."

"Not all of us," Frederick corrected under his breath.

"And what special skills do you bring our crew, Eton?" Bagger asked.

George reclined on one of the lower bunks. "I believe Eton's special skill is complaining."

"I'll have you know," Frederick said with a huff, "I have a great many abilities that will no doubt prove far more beneficial to this crew than anything you could offer."

As Frederick began listing his numerous, invaluable skills, Bats took off his glasses and massaged the deep impressions on either side of his nose. "I'll take Mouse," he said in a slow, measured voice. "I don't need anyone talking while I'm trying to work."

"Bats is our ears in the tunnel," Bagger told Charlie. "When you're not hauling spoil with the others, you'll be helping him listen for the enemy."

"And with those ears," Mole said with a laugh, "Mouse can help you monitor the movement of every Fritz in Berlin."

Charlie ducked back behind Thomas and tugged his hair down over his ears.

Frederick saluted Mole. "I guess that means I'm with you, sir."

"Sorry, Eton," Mole said, lighting a new cigarette, "but those spindly legs of yours couldn't push through a wall of wet sand, much less a tunnel face of packed blue clay."

George snorted.

Frederick tried to ignore him by keeping his attention glued on the large clay kicker, but the flare of his pinched nostrils told George he was getting to the snooty, eager soldier, so George laughed harder.

"Then who *am* I working with?" Frederick asked.

Boomer slapped him on the back, knocking the helmet from his head. "Eton, you get to work with the most important member of our crew."

"Who might that be?" Frederick asked, bending down to fetch his helmet.

Boomer walked over to a corner of the room, retrieved the birdcage from its post, and handed it to Frederick. "Meet your partner. Feathers."

. . .

After the men finished their card game and fed the boys a cold meal of bully beef, a tinned corned beef, and K-Brot, a bread sometimes made of such things as dried potatoes, oats, barley, and pulverized straw, Bagger and the other men exited the dugout, leaving the boys with one order—get some rest before their first shift. Thomas hoped the other boys would go to sleep right away so he could start his search for James, but as exhausted as everyone was, no one appeared eager to close their eyes and sleep underground for the first time.

George, lying on the wire bunk above Thomas, regaled his captive audience with stories about life on the streets of London, occasionally asking Charlie to verify his description of London's seedy underbelly. Every time his voice would start to quiet and the silences between his words stretched long, Thomas hoped he was finally falling asleep, but then George's head would pop out over the edge of his bunk, his red hair dangling in messy curls like a mane of fire, and he'd begin his next tale.

Seated on the bottom bunk across the dugout, Frederick seemed to grit his teeth against George's ramblings and scribbled furiously with a fancy fountain pen in the notebook from his kit bag.

Charlie sat in the bunk above Frederick, sketching pictures of Feathers with the nub of a pencil. As he drew, he fed the canary pieces of the bread he'd tucked in his pocket during dinner through the bars of the cage on a shelf in the dugout's corner. He didn't speak, but nodded in agreement any time George asked, "Ain't that right, Mouse?"

After an hour, George's story about running messages for some man named Grugar trailed off until the only sounds coming from above Thomas's bunk were stuttered snores.

"I thought he'd never shut up," Frederick mumbled, taking his glasses and setting them on the top corner of his bunk. Tucking his book and pen under the coat he'd rolled as a pillow, he adjusted the scratchy wool army blanket from his bag and turned toward the wall.

Thomas peeked up at Charlie's bunk. He couldn't see Mouse's face, but the shy boy lay still, his fingers resting against Feathers's cage. Thomas listened for the slow, steady breaths of deep sleep before slipping off his bunk, grabbing his boots, and tiptoeing out of the dugout.

Muted light glowed at the entrance to the tunnel. Before ascending the incline, Thomas wedged his stockinged feet into his boots and pulled a photograph from his pocket. The edges were soft with wear, and the image yellowed with time. Six faces stared back at him. His mum, her hair pulled back in a tight bun, sat in a chair holding his twin sisters, Charlotte and Letitia, in her lap. Behind the chair stood his dad, a hand resting on his wife's shoulder. Thomas and James stood on either side of their mum and sisters. Thomas ran his thumb around the creases lining the edges of the photograph, imprints of the frame that had protected it for the last four years, a frame that now stood empty in his parents' bedroom.

Mum had kept the framed photograph on her nightstand next to a candle that she lit every night for James before saying her rosary. The frame held the only photograph of their family. It was Mum's most cherished possession, the first thing her eyes sought out when they fluttered open each morning and the last image they held before they drifted closed at night. Like Thomas's St. Joseph medal, the photograph kept Mum connected to James. It was her lifeline when grief threatened to drown her, and Thomas had severed it and left home, abandoning her to face the crushing waves alone.

For the thousandth time since he'd snuck into his parents' room on the morning he'd run away to London, Thomas questioned his decision to take the photograph. He knew it was a sin to steal, especially something worth so much to his mum, but staring at James's face, he knew he'd had no choice. His parents' letters to the army begging for any information on James had gone unanswered for four months. Thomas had to leave Dover to find James. He would question every infantryman on the Western Front if he had to, and Mum's photograph would help. There would be plenty of time for apologizing after he brought his brother home.

Tucking the photograph carefully back in his pocket, he exited the tunnels. The midday sky, heavy with clouds, provided little more light than the lanterns in the tunnels as Thomas made his way into the support trenches. No-man's-land lay quiet between the Allied and Central Powers, but Thomas knew lack of artillery fire didn't mean the enemy wasn't watching. He looked down the communication trench that led from the support trenches to the front-line trenches, but, remembering Bagger's rules and the consequences for breaking them, he kept his head down and scrambled along the communication trench in the opposite direction toward the reserve trenches. Thomas couldn't afford to be transferred from Ypres, not until he found James.

He searched the reserve trenches for any soldier who was awake, but every infantryman he passed was taking advantage of the brief reprieve from artillery fire. Some lay curled up in muddy dugouts. Others slept sitting upright, leaning against sandbags and one another, steel helmets strapped to their heads, weapons within reach. Thomas crept past, studying as many faces as he could. He knew how desperately they must need the rest and he didn't want to risk startling an armed soldier.

After forty minutes of searching, he realized if he didn't head back to the crew's dugout soon, Bagger and the other men would return to find him missing. The clay kicker had been very clear about his expectations. The new recruits were to get as much sleep as possible, so they'd be rested and alert for their first shift. Not wanting to anger Bagger, Thomas made his way back to the communication trench that led to the support trenches and tunnel entrance. When he reached the last stretch of trench before the tunnel opening, he decided he couldn't leave with no information about his brother, so he cut left instead of right. He stopped by a sleeping soldier and cleared his throat. The man didn't stir. Thomas stepped closer and coughed, but the soldier remained motionless.

Thomas coughed louder.

Nothing. Not a twitch of his eyelids, no annoyed groan.

If it weren't for the shallow rise and fall of the soldier's chest, Thomas would have thought him dead. Thomas shook his head. No amount of coughing was going to wake a soldier who was used to sleeping through artillery fire. Disappointed, he had turned to leave when he heard voices and laughter in the distance. He glanced toward the tunnel entrance and then reached up and grabbed hold of his medals. "Just five more minutes," he whispered to himself.

The voices led him down another section of the support trench that zigged and then zagged its way farther from the tunnel entrance, where a cluster of soldiers gathered. Their backs to

Thomas, they taunted one another and placed bets on two pairs of soldiers working at the far end of the trench. As Thomas drew closer, he recognized the voices of his crew among the infantrymen.

"Bagger and Max have it this time," Boomer boasted.

"You tunnel rats are crazy," an infantryman with a hard, square jaw said as he stubbed out a cigarette on the duckboards.

"Get it right, Harry," Mole said. "We're sewer rats."

Harry laughed. "Digging beneath the streets of Manchester, you may have been sewer rats, Mole, but out here, you're tunnel rats. Not that it matters. Either way, you're losers. Johnny and Dan are undefeated."

"Double or nothing, they lose today," Mole challenged.

"You're on," Harry said, and the men shook hands.

"Count me in with Mole," Boomer said, tossing five shillings into the waiting hands of an infantryman with a steep forehead and weak chin.

"Anyone else?" the infantryman asked.

Thomas looked for Bats, but the clay kicker's listener was not among the cluster of men.

A few more soldiers tossed coins to the infantryman, all placing their bets on Johnny and Dan for the win. Thomas inched closer to see what game the men were playing and to catch a glimpse of Bagger's partner, Max, the crew member who Bagger had said was running messages two hours earlier.

Bagger stood with his back to the others, yelling to his

partner hidden beyond the corner at the far end of the trench. "Come on, Max! We got this! Just one more!"

"Shut up, Bagger," an older infantryman crouched on the floor of the trench warned. "You're gonna scare 'em off."

"What's wrong, Johnny?" Boomer called out. "You afraid of losing?"

Johnny motioned to a soldier at his side. "Give me another piece, Dan." His partner, a husky infantryman, not much older than George, handed him a hunk of bread. Johnny speared the bread on his rifle's bayonet, laid the weapon flat on the ground, and slowly backed up. "You tunnel rats haven't beat us yet."

"First time for everything," Bagger said, turning his attention back to his partner working around the corner.

Thomas was so engrossed in the strange competition between the tunnelers and the infantrymen, he didn't notice the creak of footfalls on the duckboards behind him. Then a hand grabbed his shoulder, and a slow, measured voice asked, "Just what do you think you're doing out here, Dover?"

NINE

THOMAS'S STOMACH DROPPED. He'd let himself get distracted and hadn't asked one soldier about James. At best, he'd be reprimanded and sent back to the dugout until their shift started. At worst, he'd be sent to dig trenches in France. Either way, he'd failed his brother and his parents.

Several lame excuses stumbled through his brain as he turned to face his punishment, but when he raised his eyes to meet what he expected to be the stern glare of the crew's listener, he was instead met with the amused smirk of the London street urchin who'd followed him to the Western Front.

"Good God, Tommy." George chuckled. "You should see your face. You'd think a Fritz had snuck up on you." He dropped his voice to mimic Bats. "You didn't wet yourself, did you, lad?" His gaze dropped to the front of Thomas's trousers.

Thomas bristled at George's continued use of James's nickname for him. "Stop calling me Tommy."

George rubbed the patchy stubble on his chin and cheeks and cleared his throat to imitate Bagger. "Out here, you'll answer to whatever I call you. Understand?"

Thomas shoved him away from the cluster of soldiers and back toward the path to the tunnel entrance. "No. And you didn't scare me. You surprised me. What are *you* doing out here anyway?"

"I saw you sneaking out. Thought you were hitting the latrine, but when you didn't come back, I figured I should come looking for you and make sure you hadn't decided to catch the next train back to London. Brought Mouse along to help drag you back if you had."

Behind George, waiting at the corner of the trench, Charlie gave Thomas a timid wave, then returned to gnawing on whatever was left of his nails.

George leaned in closer. "You're not thinking of leaving, are you, Tommy? 'Cause I hear they shoot deserters."

Thomas started to explain that he just needed some air, when a soldier called out. "Two minutes!"

"What's going on here?" George asked, peering past Thomas to the gathering of men clogging up the trench.

"Some kind of competition."

George pushed forward to get a better look. "This I need to see."

Johnny and Dan had climbed onto a wooden plank lining the trench wall, careful to keep their heads below the sandbags. Everyone's attention was fixed on the piece of bread on Johnny's bayonet. Suddenly, a long brown rat scurried along the trench floor.

"There's one!" a soldier yelled.

The rat stopped, and Johnny shot the soldier a threatening glare, silencing him.

"I sure hope that's not dinner," Thomas groaned.

"Wouldn't be the first rat I've eaten," George whispered. "Bet you've had a few too, eh, Mouse?"

Charlie, whose curiosity had lured him closer, didn't answer.

"Don't worry," George said, when he noticed the embarrassed blush tinting Charlie's face and ears. "Norton-Griffith's recruiter promised real food for our work."

The rat's head swept side to side, nose twitching. Its beady black eyes locked on the hunk of bread. Perched on the bench, Johnny nodded to Dan, who tossed a clot of soil at the trench wall behind the rat. It exploded in a spray of dirt, and the rat bolted forward, picking up speed as it neared the bread. The clay kickers and soldiers leaned in, blocking Thomas's view. He ducked down to peer between their legs just as the rat, its mouth wide open to snag the bread in its retreat, impaled itself on the bayonet. Johnny jumped down and jammed the blade deeper, and the infantrymen cheered.

Boomer kicked at the ground, and Bats groaned as Johnny lifted his weapon for everyone to see. Blood dripped from the speared rat's mouth and its legs twitched twice before falling limp.

"What's the count now?" Johnny asked.

Two soldiers lifted the ends of a wooden beam. A line of dead rats hung below the board, like prisoners dangling beneath a tiny gallows.

"That one makes nine!" Dan yelled. "We're up by two."

"Pay up, boys!" Johnny shook his weapon, sending the dead rat's legs into a drunken jig. "Our undefeated status lives on!"

The infantrymen cheered louder.

George reached into his pocket and pulled out two shillings. "I've got to get in on some of this action."

"You can't," Charlie whispered, his voice tight with panic.

"Sure I can. Coin is coin. These chaps won't care who places a bet as long as he can pay, which I can." He jingled the shillings in his hand. "And if I play the odds right, which I always do, between my wages and winnings, after the war, I'll be strolling back into London with enough coin to pay off my debts and buy myself off the streets."

He started toward the men but stopped when Charlie grabbed his arm. George's eyes narrowed on Charlie's hand clutching his sleeve.

Charlie let go and tucked his hands in his pockets. "Sorry," he mumbled, backing away.

"Charlie's right," Thomas said. "If Bagger catches you, he may never let us out of the tunnels again."

With a frustrated groan, George shoved the coins back in his pocket. "What good is finally having money if I can't enjoy it?"

Up ahead, Johnny plucked the rat from his bayonet and tossed it to Dan. "You ready to surrender, tunnel rat?"

"Clay kickers never surrender," Bagger replied.

In the excitement, Thomas had forgotten the crew leader was still standing at the end of the trench.

"How much time left, Richard?" Bagger asked.

A soldier holding a pocket watch answered. "Twenty seconds."

Bagger smiled and turned his attention back to his partner. "Plenty of time."

"Best you can do is tie us," Dan said as he strung the rat up by its neck next to the other dead rats. "Might as well give up now."

Bagger ignored him. "Come on, Max! You've got this! That's it!"

"Ten . . . nine . . . eight . . ." Richard's voice grew louder with each second.

Bagger knelt on the trench floor and pounded his fists on his thick thighs. "Come on, Max! Get 'im!"

Thomas tried to catch a glimpse of Bagger's partner, but the trench wall blocked his view.

"Seven . . . six . . . five . . ."

"Yes!" Bagger yelled.

"Four . . . three . . . two . . ."

"Come on, Max!"

"One."

Bagger reached out his hands, and a small blur of white-and-brown fur flew into his arms. Bagger had told the boys that the rats in the trenches could grow as large as cats. By the size of the animal squirming in his arms, not only had the clay kicker not been exaggerating, but Max also had not killed the rat. Bagger's rule about keeping any food stored as high as possible moved up Thomas's list of warnings to heed in the tunnels.

"Time!" Richard yelled.

"Good boy, Max!" Bagger said. He turned around, but it wasn't a large rat squirming in his arms. It was a small dog. The white terrier, with brown spots encircling its eyes and covering its small, floppy ears, wagged its tail with pride over Bagger's praise. Clamped in its teeth was a dead rat. Bagger patted the dog's head, and Max dropped the rat into Bagger's hand. The clay kickers cheered.

"Settle down," Johnny said, re-counting Bagger and Max's haul, including the new rat. "You're still down by one."

Bagger smiled and held up two more dead rats. "Make that *up* by one."

As the clay kickers and soldiers settled their wagers, Johnny spotted the boys watching. He turned, seeming about to say something to Bagger, but just at that moment Dan handed him his rifle and pulled him into a conversation about their hunting strategy.

"We better go before anyone else sees us," Charlie whispered to George.

"Fine," George said. With a disappointed groan, he followed Charlie toward the tunnel entrance, but Thomas stayed behind. He still hadn't asked anyone about James and hoped an infantryman would break off from the group before the rest of the crowd disbanded.

"Hey," George called out to him softly from a corner of the trench. "You comin'?"

Thomas hesitated.

"Your funeral, Tommy."

Thomas pressed a frustrated fist to his chest until he felt the hard edges of his medals burrow into his skin. *I will find my brother*, he vowed. Then he turned and trailed George back to the crew's dugout.

TEN

THOUGHTS SCURRIED THROUGH Thomas's weary brain like trench rats, numerous, insatiable, and each one chased by death. When exhaustion finally claimed his mind, guilt and fear plagued his sleep, and his family haunted his dreams.

Dad. Working in the coal mine. Fighting for every breath. Coughing into his bloodstained handkerchief.

James. Clutching at a wound. Writhing on the battlefield. Lying unconscious in a hospital.

Charlotte and Letitia. Crying out in hunger. Begging for scraps on the streets. Shivering in the cold.

Mum. Nursing her ailing husband. Praying for her missing sons. Weeping over an empty picture frame.

Thomas felt her tears on his face. He tried to wipe them away, but they continued to fall. He rolled over and burrowed his face in his coat, desperate for a few more minutes of sleep, but her tears persisted. This time dripping down the back of his neck.

Thomas lifted his head to tell Mum everything would be all right, but instead of staring into her pale blue eyes, he found himself face-to-face with Max, Bagger's rat-catching partner from the trenches. The terrier gave him a lick on the tip of his nose. Remembering how many rats the dog's mouth had killed the day before, Thomas pulled his wool blanket over his face before the ratter could land another lick.

"Rise and shine, Dover!" Bagger said, yanking off the blanket. "It's 8:40. Our shift starts in twenty."

Cold, damp air flowed over Thomas, and Max scrambled forward to continue his lick assault on Thomas's neck and chin.

"I'm up. I'm up," he said, scratching Max behind the ears. "So you're a ratter *and* a rooster."

The dog's stubby tail thumped against his leg.

"Max has many jobs down here," Bagger said, picking up the dog. "He runs messages for command, keeps the rat population under control, wins me money in the trenches, and wakes soldiers when they're almost late for their shift." He plopped the terrier onto the upper bunk, where the furry alarm clock went to work rousing George.

When Max had finished waking all four boys, Boomer gave them ten minutes to visit the latrine, grab some food, and join him in the tunnel for the start of their shift. At the table, George and Charlie scarfed down strips of dried meat and dunked hard biscuits into cups of water to make them edible while Frederick sat on his bunk, sipping a cup of weak tea and reading the copy of Aeschylus's play about Prometheus that he'd brought with him from Eton. Thomas picked at his food.

George reached over and grabbed one of Thomas's biscuits. "Aren't you eating, Tommy?" he asked, dipping the hard army ration into his water before popping it in his mouth.

Thomas snuck Max a small piece of meat under the table. "I'm not hungry."

"You sick?" George asked, lighting a cigarette.

"No."

Max nudged Thomas's hand for more food. He broke off a small chunk of biscuit for the dog before pocketing the rest in case he managed to find his lost appetite in the lower galleries.

"Were you hoping for some rat instead this morning?" George said with a chuckle. "I'm sure Max can chase one down for you."

Frederick looked up from his book. "The British Army would never feed its men rat."

"If you hadn't noticed, Eton," George said, motioning around the dugout with a cigarette, "the British Army is not serving us crumpets with jam. We're living corpses digging our own graves. If things get bad enough, we'll be eating whatever they give us."

"I'd never eat rat," Frederick said.

"That's because you've never been hungry," George retorted.

"Yes, I have," Frederick said, returning to his reading.

George's smile soured. "*No*. You haven't." He tore at a strip of meat with his teeth and turned his attention back to Thomas. "What's wrong, Tommy?"

"Nothing," Thomas lied.

"He's probably tired from your escapades in the trenches," Frederick said.

Thomas shot George a worried glance. He'd been certain Frederick was asleep when he left the dugout to look for James, and when George, Charlie, and he had returned an hour later, Frederick had been in the same position as when he'd left, snoring loudly.

"You spying on us, Eton?" George asked.

Frederick closed his book and stood. "Just paying attention."

"Pay attention to this," George said. "What we do is none of your business."

"I disagree," Frederick argued, plucking a biscuit from the table. "Like it or not, we're all part of the same unit now. I'm here to make sure you don't get in any trouble that could reflect poorly on the rest of us."

"Bagger didn't say we couldn't leave the tunnels," George said.

"He said we could leave to get some food or use the latrine, not to muck about in the trenches."

"What's wrong, Eton?" George teased. "You afraid if you go back in the trenches you might vomit again or get some dirt on those shiny boots of yours?"

Frederick nudged his boots farther beneath his bunk with

his heel. He'd spent the hour after the boys had snuck out cleaning the mud, clay, and manure from them.

"Just because you take no pride in your appearance or in the British Army uniform you're wearing doesn't mean the rest of us have to lower ourselves to your abysmal standards."

Charlie climbed onto his bunk and huddled close to Feathers's cage. While the quarrel continued, he turned his back to the boys and sketched in his notebook.

"Who died and made you head of the crew?" George asked, his voice growing louder.

Thomas glanced toward the dugout entrance. "Keep it down. Bagger'll be back any second now."

Ignoring Thomas, Frederick looked down at George with disdain. "I have five years of military training, which is five more than any of you or the rest of this crew can claim. If you want to survive this war, you'd be wise to follow my lead."

George stood so abruptly, he toppled his chair. It crashed against Bagger's bunk, startling Charlie, who pressed closer to the dugout wall.

Thomas remained in his seat, sneaking Max pieces of meat under the table. He'd seen enough arguments between miners back home to know they rarely ended in a throw-down fight. Tensions always ran high underground.

George walked around the table. "You think you can teach *me* to survive?" He stopped before colliding with Frederick, who took a step back. "When you were four years old, learning your letters and numbers and which silver fork goes with which food, I was learning to scale chimneys."

"You're a liar," Frederick said. "The government outlawed climbing boys years ago."

"You think the man who snatched me off the streets or his customers looking for a cheap chimney cleaning cared about any law?"

Frederick didn't answer.

"By the time I was five, I was sweeping chimneys just like the ones in whatever manor your kin calls home."

Frederick's face flushed a purplish red. "You know nothing about my family or my home."

George poked him in the chest. "That's where you're wrong. See, all those chimneys I climbed for all those years were in the homes of spoiled rich boys just like you."

Frederick didn't answer. He seemed intent on refusing to acknowledge anything the London street rat said about him or his upbringing, no matter how close to the mark it hit.

George shook his head with feigned pity. "It must have been *so* difficult living under such horrific circumstances. Tell us, Eton, how *did* you survive?"

Frederick crossed his arms over his chest so George couldn't poke him again. His lips pinched tight with muted outrage.

"My master liked to light fires beneath me to keep me climbing. Nothing like the fear of falling to a fiery death to keep a five-year-old moving, though the smoke did make it difficult to breathe during the climb." George took a long drag of his shrinking cigarette and blew the smoke in Frederick's face.

Frederick didn't blink or wave it away, but his eyes watered and he began to cough and sputter.

"That's what I thought," George said, taking another drag. "While you and your Eton chums were playing soldier, boys like Mouse, Tommy, and me were fighting to survive another day." Without taking his eyes from Frederick, he questioned Thomas. "Tommy, what time did you get up in the morning to walk to work in the coal mines?"

"Three," Thomas answered.

"And how many hours were you in the mines?"

"Twelve."

"Mouse," George called out. "The peeling skin on your hands, that's from the lime powder used to bleach the fabrics at the textile factory, right?"

Charlie pulled his sleeves down over his hands.

"And the scars lining your back," George continued, "those were from punishment for being late or making a mistake."

Charlie's face and ears burned bright red. He looked back to the wall and his notebook to hide his shame.

"Don't worry, Mouse," George said. "I've got a matching set on my back from my short employment in a factory. After the supervisor beat me unconscious for fainting from the chemical fumes, I ran, but the scars never leave, do they?"

Charlie stretched one of his peeling fingers into the birdcage and stroked the canary's soft feathers.

"You boys ever see someone die?" George pressed.

Thomas's head bowed with the memory of the night Grandad Sullivan's persistent, phlegmy cough quieted forever. Neither Charlie nor he answered George. Their silence was affirmation enough.

"How about you, Eton?" George said, snuffing out his cigarette under his boot.

Frederick's response was barely audible. "That's none of your business."

"What's that?" George asked, leaning closer.

Frederick lifted his chin and stared George in the eye. "That's none of your business."

"Finally, something we agree on." George dusted off the shoulders of Frederick's uniform. "You can save your lectures on survival. We've already been well schooled on the subject." He snatched the biscuit from Frederick's hand, righted his chair, and sat back down at the table as Bagger appeared in the doorway.

"Let's go, ladies!"

The boys scrambled to their feet.

"You remember what I told you yesterday. No talking in the lower galleries. We communicate through hand signals." He reached out, and Max jumped into his arms. "Our shift ends at five, before sunrise. You have until then to move as many bags of clay out of these galleries as possible. You boys are to haul the bags our crew fills and the bags the other two crews filled in the shifts before ours."

"Why do we have to haul their bags too?" George asked. "Don't their crews have trammers?"

"Yes, but we don't move spoil out of the tunnels during daylight."

"Why not?" Frederick asked.

"The less movement seen coming in and out of these tunnels, the better, so sandbags are hauled out of the tunnels at night, which is during our shift. PBIs will meet you at the tunnel entrance."

"What are PBIs?" Frederick asked. "I've never heard of that rank before."

"Poor bloody infantry," Bagger answered. "When they're not dodging bullets in the trenches, they're helping us haul spoil. Give them the bags. They'll use some of the bags to fortify the forward and back walls of the trenches, but most of them will be put in the storage dugout near the tunnel entrance or taken far beyond the trench lines. We don't want many visible changes to the trenches. The Germans are always watching. We need to keep our mission a secret."

"What *is* our mission?" Frederick asked.

"Eton, your mission is to haul spoil and watch Feathers."

Before Frederick could ask another question, Bagger motioned for the boys to follow. "The gallery we're working is deep. We don't want the Germans seeing us moving bags of clay, especially blue clay, or they'll know we're not digging new trenches or dugouts and they'll shell the hell out of us. That's why we need to remove as much clay from these tunnels as possible at night. Get the full bags to the PBIs and then get back to the crew with timber beams to support the newly dug portion of the gallery and empty bags to fill. Any other questions? Ask 'em now or save 'em until after the shift." His heavy-lidded eyes scrutinized each boy's face, searching for uncertainty or confusion.

Thomas shifted from one stockinged foot to the other. How was he to know if he was doing his job if Bagger didn't tell him what that job was? And why keep the mission a secret, especially from the soldiers ordered to carry it out?

A secret can be a friend or a weapon, Thomas. Take care how you use it.

Staring up at Bagger, Thomas had no doubt the secret of their mission was a weapon; he just hoped he wouldn't find himself on the wrong end of it.

Bagger stood before Frederick. "What about you, Eton? Any more questions or commentary?"

"No, sir—Bagger."

"Blimey, Eton! King George hasn't knighted me yet. Call me Bagger if you want me to respond."

George failed to stifle a laugh.

Frederick's cheeks bloomed bright red, but he bit back any retort.

"The rest of the crew is already at the tunnel face. When we get down there, you're to help haul spoil and timber. When you're not hauling, watch and learn. Follow your supervisor's lead. I'll signal when you can break for a quick bite or to use the latrine. Otherwise we're working straight for eight hours, so I hope you got plenty of rest. You're going to need it."

Frederick glared at George, and for a moment Thomas feared he was going to tell Bagger about them sneaking into the trenches, but Frederick said nothing.

"All right, ladies. Follow me."

As the boys trailed Bagger into the tunnel toward the first shaft, George called over his shoulder. "Don't forget your supervisor, Eton."

Cursing under his breath, Frederick returned to the dugout to fetch Feathers.

ELEVEN

THOMAS HATED WORKING in silence. It squeezed the tunnel and stretched the hours, but he started praying for silence when the first artillery shell hit. The explosion aboveground echoed like distant thunder in the gallery and trembled through the earth, shaking loose clots of clay that rained down from between timber beams onto the tunnelers' bowed heads and hunched backs.

Frederick let out a startled squeak and ran for the shaft ladder at the first blast, but George, who had returned with a timber beam, blocked his escape. Charlie covered his ears, and Thomas dropped his sandbag and threw his arms over his head. He remained in that position, waiting for the explosions to stop, but they continued to pound the battlefield. He had no way of knowing whether the artillery shells were being fired from the cannons of the Central Powers or the Allied forces, but he knew it didn't matter. If a shell hit directly above them, whether it be English or German, French or Austro-Hungarian, the explosion would inflict the same amount of damage.

As the barrage of artillery fire increased and the tunnel walls and ceiling continued to tremble, Bagger handed Thomas his dropped sandbag and motioned for the boys to keep working. Thomas quickly filled his bag and ran to the ladder. He hurried up the shafts to the tunnel entrance, eager to be free of the quaking gallery. When he handed a sandbag to one of the PBIs, the soldier told him it was the Allies who'd started the firefight and that they tended to last for hours.

The PBI was not exaggerating. The shelling continued well after the boys' shift ended. Poor Feathers was so agitated by the constant noise, Charlie couldn't coax him to eat when they returned to the dugout. The boys made quick work of the cold stew Bats spooned into bowls for them. Exhausted from their first shift, they collapsed onto their bunks with pained groans. Thomas wondered if he'd be able to lift his arms by their next shift, much less lift full sandbags.

Max pawed at Bagger's leg, trotted over to the dugout doorway, glanced back at Bagger, and whined.

"Not now, boy," the clay kicker said, pressing his hands into the small of his back and stretching. "I'm too sore to take you for a walk."

Max whined again, but when Bagger made no move to get up from his chair, the dog trotted over to where Thomas lay, jumped onto his bunk, and curled up next to him.

As the men sat at the table playing cards, Thomas stroked the short fur on the dog's back, his weary eyes following the lines and angles of the metal mesh of George's bunk above him, fighting to stay open. He had to return to the trenches, but first he had to wait until the rest of his crew fell asleep.

Charlie had climbed up onto his bunk as soon as he finished eating. Resting on his stomach, his face inches from Feathers's cage, he sketched the men playing cards. He whispered to the canary as he drew, but the voices of the men buried whatever secrets he shared.

Frederick also retreated to his bunk, where he turned his back to the room and wrote in his notebook. Thomas couldn't see what he was writing, and even if he could, he wouldn't know what it said, but it was obvious by how fast Frederick scribbled and how hard he pressed down his fountain pen that whatever words Frederick was writing were angry, and, Thomas suspected, about George.

George didn't notice. His full attention seemed focused on the card game. He perched on the edge of his bunk with his long legs dangling above Thomas, hoping the men would invite him to play.

But they extended no invitation, and after three hands of cards, they dimmed the lamps and retired to their bunks, a clear signal that the boys were expected to sleep now too.

Max leaped from Thomas's bunk and curled up on top of Bagger's rounded belly. Thomas missed the dog the second he left, taking his warm body and calming presence with him.

After several minutes of bodies shifting in search of comfortable positions, the dugout quieted, and the snoring began. It started with Frederick. Exhausted from his first stint of manual labor, the Eton student fell asleep almost as soon as the room darkened. His mouth hanging open and drool dribbling down his chin, he snored, assuring Thomas that Frederick would not be monitoring his movements today. The men and George soon joined Frederick, slumber rattling through their throats. Even Max's sleep rumbled with soft snores. Only Charlie remained quiet. Either he was still up, or he was as quiet asleep as he was awake. To be safe, Thomas waited a bit longer before attempting to leave.

Ten minutes later, Thomas stepped from the shadows of the tunnels into the glaring light of day. Squinting his eyes until they adjusted, he raised his face to the sky and drew in a deep breath to purge the stagnant stench of the tunnels from his lungs. He coughed at the smell of smoke hanging thick in the morning sky, a hazy reminder of the artillery fight that had raged during his shift. Thomas hesitated at the mouth of the communication trench that would take him left to the reserve trenches or right to the front-line trenches. The firefight had ceased for now, but the Germans could renew their assault at any moment. He shoved his hands in his pockets, and his fingers grazed his family photograph. He'd made a promise that he would find the answers to what had happened to James. It was a promise he wouldn't be able to keep if he stayed cowering in the tunnels. As he stared down the trench leading to the front line, searching for the courage to move, something butted against his calf. He looked down to find Max staring up at him.

He knelt to pet the dog. "What are you doing out here? You should be asleep with the others." He glanced back at the tunnel entrance, expecting to find Bagger lumbering toward him, but the entrance was empty.

"Go back to bed," he ordered Max.

The terrier licked Thomas's hand and wagged his stubby tail.

"Go on." Thomas stood and waved him away, but Max barked and wagged his tail faster.

"Shhh." Thomas hushed the dog, afraid his barking would draw unwanted attention. "Fine. Come on then." He motioned for the dog to follow, grateful for the company.

They walked the support trenches for two hours. Most of the soldiers they encountered were sleeping. Those who were awake did not recognize James in Thomas's photograph. Frustrated by another unsuccessful search, Thomas headed back to the tunnel entrance with Max trotting along beside him. When they arrived at the intersection where the communication trench crossed the support trench, Thomas once again stared down the path leading to the front line. Distant voices and laughter rumbled through the forbidden trenches. He stopped and looked down at Max, sitting at his feet.

"What do you think? Should we head back to the dugout,

or see if any of the soldiers in the front-line trenches know what happened to James?"

The dog stared up at Thomas and then stretched a hind leg to his head to scratch behind his right ear. Thomas glanced back at the tunnel entrance. No movement stirred within its shadows. No sounds echoed from its cavernous throat. "We'll just go for a minute," he told Max. Keeping his head low, he turned right and hurried down the communication path.

When Thomas and Max entered the front-line trench, they came upon a group of soldiers sharing a tin of bully beef, slicing pieces of the congealed, shredded pink meat with a bayonet.

"Pardon," he said. "I was wondering if you could help me."

The men looked up from their food but kept eating. "Depends on what kind of help you're looking for," one of the soldiers mumbled through a mouthful of beef.

"Have you seen this soldier?" Thomas pulled the family photograph from his coat pocket and pointed to his brother. "His name is James Sullivan."

The men licked off their fingers and passed around the photo.

"Can't say I have."

"Doesn't look familiar."

"Sorry."

The same scene played out over and over during the next

two hours. Most soldiers he asked were nice enough to look at the photograph, but not one recognized his brother.

Drained from his work in the tunnels and from the disappointment in the trenches, Thomas had decided to head back to the dugout when Max let out an excited yip and ran around the corner to the next trench segment.

"Come on." Thomas groaned. Bagger would have him digging trenches in France if he learned Thomas had snuck out to the front-line trenches, but the burly clay kicker would bury him beneath no-man's-land if Thomas returned to the tunnels without his ratter. He stepped around the corner and spotted the terrier trotting toward a trio of soldiers. Thomas recognized the men from the rat hunt the day before. Two of them, Johnny and Dan, had been the team Bagger and Max had beaten. The third had kept time.

Thomas ducked back behind the corner, hoping the men hadn't noticed him. He was certain Johnny had seen him at the rat hunt. He couldn't take the chance that Johnny or his friends would tell Bagger they'd seen him sneaking around the front-line trenches.

"Max," he whispered.

The dog stopped and glanced back at him. He knelt and patted his thighs quietly, like he'd seen Bagger do during the hunt. "Come here, Max."

Max cocked his head.

"Good boy. Come on."

Max took a couple of steps toward him.

"That's it," Thomas whispered, patting his thighs faster.

Max took one more step toward Thomas, lifted his nose, sniffed the air, and turned tail back toward the soldiers.

"Stupid dog," Thomas hissed. He hid behind the corner, watching and waiting for the terrier to return.

Max sat begging at the feet of Johnny, the oldest soldier.

"Do the tunnel rats know you're out here begging for food, Max?" he said, patting the dog's head.

Max sat up on his back legs. His stubby tail thumped against the duckboards.

"I don't have anything to feed you, boy. Barely have enough to feed myself." Johnny fished a biscuit from his pocket and tapped it on the wooden bench. "And what I do have is barely edible."

"Dunk it in some tea," Dan said. "They soften up right fast." Unwrapping his own biscuit, he dipped one end of the stale ration in his tin cup. "Tell him, Richard."

"That's not tea," Richard argued. "It's weak, cold, and smells like piss."

"Just like the rest of us," Dan said with a chuckle.

Johnny bit down on the hard biscuit, but it didn't break. "Take it," he said, dropping it in front of Max. "Maybe if you crack some teeth, you won't catch so many rats."

Max snatched up the hard treat and trotted away with his prize.

“What? No thank-you?” Johnny called after him.

“You think Bagger and his crew have hot tea in those caves they’re digging?” Dan asked.

“Don’t know. Why don’t you ask ’im?” Johnny jutted his grizzled chin toward the corner of the trench, where Thomas hid. “Bagger’s sent one of his new rats to spy on us.”

TWELVE

THOMAS COULDN'T TALK his way out of this one. They'd never believe that he'd been assigned to the front line, and he was too far from the tunnels to claim he'd become lost looking for the latrine. He was considering making a run for it when Johnny called out, "We know you're there, son. Might as well come out and introduce yourself."

Cursing his luck and Max, Thomas stepped out from behind the wall.

Dan pushed back his steel helmet. "You one of Bagger's crew?"

"Yes, sir."

Dan smiled. "You hear that? He called me sir."

"Don't let it go to your head," Richard said, lighting a cigarette. "It's already the size of an overripe pumpkin. Get any bigger and it'll be an easy target for snipers." He looked Thomas up and down, his thick brows knitted in confusion over the rims of his glasses. "How old are you, son?"

"Eighteen, sir."

Johnny laughed. "And I'm the King of England."

"Be nice, John," Richard said. "No need to accuse the boy of lying."

"Eighteen," Johnny scoffed. "I've got hair on my backside older than this lad." He looked past Thomas, expecting to see Bagger or one of the other clay kickers. "You out here alone?"

"Yes, sir."

"Did Bagger send you down here with his mongrel to taunt us, or is he looking for a rematch?"

"Neither, sir."

"Then what are you doing wandering the front trenches with his ratter?" Johnny asked.

"I'm looking for someone. Max tagged along."

"You won't find any of your tunneling buddies out here," Richard said.

"Actually, I'm looking for an infantryman." Thomas handed him his family photograph and pointed to his brother. "Do you recognize him?"

Richard flicked the ash from his cigarette as he studied the photograph. He looked up when he recognized a younger version of the boy standing before him in the family portrait. "Is he your brother?"

Thomas nodded.

Richard handed the photograph to Dan, who gave it a fleeting glance before passing it to Johnny.

"What battalion is he with?" Richard asked.

"I don't know."

Richard took a drag from his cigarette. "Do you know where they were headed?"

"The Western Front."

"You're going to have to be more specific than that, son," Johnny said, examining the photo. "The Western Front covers over four hundred miles, with over twelve thousand miles of trenches weaving along it."

Thomas paled. He'd never be able to search twelve thousand miles of trenches. He'd barely searched one. "In his last letter, all James said was they were headed near Ypres."

"When was that?" Dan asked.

"Seven months ago, sir. The army sent word two months ago that he is missing."

Johnny shook his head and handed him the photo. "I'm sorry for your loss, son."

Thomas carefully tucked the photograph back in his pocket. "My brother's not dead, sir. He's missing."

"Same difference out here, I'm afraid," said Johnny.

Richard flicked the remnant of his cigarette at him. "Let him be, John."

Johnny pressed the smoldering stub into the duckboards with the toe of his boot. "What? Am I lying?"

Richard pulled a new cigarette from his pocket but didn't answer, and Dan suddenly became very interested in his cup of cold tea.

"No," Thomas said. "You're wrong. If James were dead, the

army would have said as much in their letter, but they didn't, which means there's a chance my brother's still alive."

"Of course there is," Richard said. He looked pointedly at Johnny and Dan. "Right?"

Johnny sighed. "Son, there are thousands of missing soldiers in this war, and the army knows exactly where they are."

"They do?" Thomas tried to catch Dan's eye for confirmation, but the young soldier refused to look at him. "Where are they? In field hospitals? Where can I find them? I know my brother is with them. He has to be."

Johnny stood and motioned for Thomas to join him.

"John, don't," Richard warned.

"Richard's right," Dan said. "He's just a boy looking for his brother. Let him be."

"He may have been a boy before he raced his friends to the recruiter's table, but the second he put on that uniform, he became a soldier. If he can't handle the truth, he doesn't belong on the front line, or under it." He led Thomas to the front wall of the trench and pointed to a periscope fed through a small opening in the parapet. "Most missing soldiers are out there."

Climbing onto the fire step running along the front wall of the trench, Thomas pressed his face against the periscope. The mirrors inside the rectangular tube reflected images of no-man's-land, the same battlefield Thomas had been digging beneath just six hours before. Twenty yards in front of the Allied trenches, two rows of wooden posts extended along the battlefield in both directions. Miles of barbed wire, which the infantry called devil's rope, stretched between the posts in tangled curls, like giant metal thorn bushes. On the other side, large craters pocked the earth. Hazy smoke drifted up from the deepest of them, and a chill stole through Thomas at the thought of how close those artillery shells had come to reaching his crew in the tunnels. The only remnants of what must have once been rich Belgian farmland and countryside were splintered trees, stripped of their bark and branches, jutting from the soil like wooden stalagmites.

Life no longer existed on no-man's-land, except for the flies swarming over the dead and the maggots feasting on the bloated carcasses of horses and men, mowed down by machine guns or torn apart by artillery. The field was littered with them, no matter which direction Thomas looked. The uniforms, caked with dirt and blood, camouflaged the fallen soldiers' allegiances. Friend or foe? Ally or enemy? It no longer mattered. Only the dead remained.

Hands shaking, Thomas pushed back from the periscope and climbed down from the fire step. "Those soldiers aren't missing. They're dead."

"Yes. But until they're identified, the army can't verify their deaths," Johnny explained.

"Why don't they retrieve their bodies?"

"We can't," Richard said. "Raise even a finger over that parapet, and a sniper will shoot it off." He took a long drag from his cigarette. "Until both sides agree to a ceasefire to retrieve their dead, there's nothing we can do. And if we get many more nights like last night, it won't matter."

"What do you mean?" asked Thomas.

"Explosions from heavy artillery bury most of the dead before we can get to them—or to what's left of them," Richard explained. He lit a cigarette and offered it to Dan, who took it between his trembling fingers.

Echoes of the artillery shells striking the earth above the tunnels shuddered through Thomas's memory. How many dead or wounded soldiers had lain on the battlefield as the shells fell? How many now lay beneath it, and was James among them?

"I pray you find your brother," Dan said, taking a drag, "wherever he may be. If there's one hard truth I've learned on the Western Front, it's if we don't bury our dead, the war will, and us with them."

THIRTEEN

DARKNESS PRESSED DOWN on the young soldier as he lay on his back. His body ached, and his head thrummed with pain. A thick paste of bile and something else, something metallic, coated his tongue. Blood. He blinked, but the darkness did not soften or clear. The soldier didn't know how long he'd been unconscious or where he was, but he sensed something was very wrong.

He listened for gunfire and explosions, but the only sound he heard was a low, ringing noise like a distant alarm. Cries for help tore from his throat but suffocated in the darkness, never reaching his ears.

The musty, charcoal-tinged air from his gas mask had been replaced with the sharp, burning smell of chemicals. The memory of charging across no-man's-land and an artillery-shell blast came back in a rush. He took a shuddering breath. It scratched like hot sand in his nose and throat, triggering a violent coughing fit that pulled fluid from his lungs.

Had he lost his mask in the explosion?

He had to get away. He tried to roll over but couldn't move. His head lolled to the side. He opened his eyes wide but saw only darkness. The coughing continued. He couldn't get enough air. The dark world, holding him hostage, tipped. He could no longer tell if he was flat on his back or falling. He tried to scream for help again as more questions assaulted his muddied mind.

Am I still on the battlefield? Why can't I see or hear? Why can't I move?

Adrenaline surged through his veins, burning off the fog of confusion clouding his thoughts. He choked on the fluid pooling in his throat. His stomach convulsed, forcing vomit into his mouth.

Breath one produces coughing.

Breath two, confusion.

Breath three renders you unconscious.

Breath four, death.

How many breaths had he taken?

The memory of the officer, eyes bulging and body contorted in pain on the trench floor, surged forward in the soldier's panicked thoughts as another wave of vomit flooded his throat. His body tensed, and in his mind he screamed, *Please, God! I'm not ready to die!*

Hands grabbed his shoulders and legs. In his tomb of darkness and silence, he couldn't see who it was. As he continued to heave and choke, he fought to pull free, but their grip was too strong. In one clean jerk, the hands thrust him onto his side. Vomit spewed from his mouth and burned through his nostrils. He coughed and sputtered until he drew a wheezy breath. Hot tears streamed down his cheeks as more memories of the war flashed before his unseeing eyes.

Machine guns firing. Soldiers falling.

Shells exploding. Comrades burning.

Gas clouds descending. Brothers drowning.

Brothers—the young soldier clung to the word like a life raft.

When the retching stopped, the hands eased him onto his back again and wiped his mouth and face clean with a cool cloth. His heartbeat and breathing calmed.

A hand took hold of his arm. The prick of a needle and the heavy pull of morphine followed the gentle touch. As the young soldier slipped back into unconsciousness, images of the battlefield receded like the tide, revealing calmer memories.

Of chalk-white cliffs and clean sea breezes.

Of a brother, a plan, and a promise.

FOURTEEN

THOMAS DIDN'T RECALL the walk back to the tunnels. He got lost twice and had to backtrack to find the path to the support trenches and tunnel entrance. Max sensed the tension in Thomas and stayed at his heels the whole way, his ears and tail low. He didn't even give chase to the rats scurrying along the trench floor.

His mind numb with shock, Thomas passed other soldiers on the way, but did not stop to ask them about his search. His thoughts were seized with grief for his brother as he surrendered to the truth Johnny had shown him.

As he neared the turn for the tunnel entrance, Thomas could feel the dam he'd constructed to hold back his tears begin to crack. He reached down for Max. "Come here, boy."

Max jumped into his outstretched arms and licked his face.

Thomas fed him a piece of biscuit from his pocket. Max gulped it down in one bite. "You don't even chew, do you?" He hiked Max up higher in his arms and stepped through the tunnel entrance. He paused several yards inside to allow his eyes time to adjust to the darkness. Max squirmed in his arms, anxious to get down, but Thomas held him tighter. "Sorry, boy. I can't have you running ahead and waking the others." Thomas hurried toward the dugout but stopped at the sound of a voice behind him.

"Sneaking out again?"

George pushed off from the tunnel wall near the entrance, where he and Charlie had been waiting. He sauntered toward Thomas. "And here I thought I was the rule-breaker of our merry band. I underestimated you, Tommy." He scratched Max behind his ears. "How much did you pull today?"

"Pull?"

"Don't play stupid with me. How much did you win?"

"I didn't win anything."

"That's tough luck. It'll probably take a few goes before you and Max work well together. Does Bagger know you borrowed his ratter?" George looked down at Thomas and smiled. "I thought about sneaking out too, but never considered taking Max." He glanced back at Charlie. "Mouse, how come I didn't think of that?"

Charlie shrugged.

Thomas shook his head. "I didn't take Max anywhere. He followed me."

George's smile widened. "I like that. Sneak the dog some

scraps, and you don't have to *take* him anywhere. He'll follow you wherever you go. Seriously, why didn't I think of that?"

"I didn't . . . it's not like that."

"You're telling me you didn't take Max to compete in rat hunts?"

Thomas adjusted his hold on Bagger's dog. "No . . . I mean, yes, that is exactly what I'm telling you."

George lit a cigarette. "You're getting a little flustered, Tommy. What're you hiding?"

"Nothing."

"Then where have you been for the last four hours?"

"Nowhere." Thomas turned to escape to the dugout, but George slung an arm over his shoulder and steered him back to the tunnel entrance. Charlie followed a few steps behind.

"Look," George said. "I just want you to tell me next time you sneak out to the support trenches with Max, so I can come along and place a few bets of my own."

"I wasn't in the support trenches."

"What? You went to the front-line trenches?" He smiled at Thomas. "I'm impressed, Tommy. I thought for sure I'd be the first of us to break one of Bagger's rules. So, Mr. Rule-Breaker, when are we sneaking out with Bagger's ratter again?"

Thomas sank against the wall of sandbags until he was seated on the duckboards lining the trench floor. "I'm not sneaking out again."

Charlie's shoulders dropped as he gave a relieved sigh and sat down beside Thomas.

"Why not?" George asked, sitting on Thomas's other side. "We'll be careful and make sure Bagger doesn't find out. Mouse'll be our lookout, won't you Mouse?"

Charlie swallowed hard.

"As for the others," George continued, ignoring Charlie's obvious discomfort with his plan, "they won't care where we go as long as we show up for our shifts and work hard. The only one we'll have to worry about is Eton and his big mouth, but I can handle him."

Thomas shook his head. "I'm not worried about Frederick."

"Are you afraid of losing your earnings? Because with me at your side, you're guaranteed to walk away with money."

Charlie reached over and petted Max. The dog rolled onto his back in Thomas's lap and offered up his tummy for a rub.

"I wasn't in the trenches looking to make money," Thomas said.

"What do you need? Cigarettes?" George pulled a pack from his pocket and offered it to Thomas.

"I don't smoke."

"Then what has you sneaking out?"

Thomas was too tired, too shattered, to lie. "Not what. Who."

"Who?" George shot Charlie an amused look and nudged Thomas in the ribs with his bony elbow. "You got a girl you're visiting in one of the neighboring villages? You cad, you."

Thomas pushed him away. "No. I wasn't visiting anyone. I was looking for someone."

George smiled. "Aren't we all?"

"It's not like that!"

"Calm down, Tommy. I'm just teasing."

"Who are you looking for?" Charlie asked.

Thomas handed Mouse his photograph. "My brother."

George's teasing smile withered into a confused frown.

"Your brother's here?" Charlie asked, not looking up from the photograph.

"He was."

Charlie handed the photo to George. "What happened to him?"

"He's missing."

"I'm sorry," Charlie said. "You look like him."

Thomas felt the prickle of tears building in his eyes and tried to steer the conversation away from James. "Do you have any brothers?"

Charlie nodded. "One. Henry. He's eleven."

"Does he know you're out here?"

"I couldn't leave without letting him know where I was going. He swore he wouldn't tell, but my father has a way of making you reveal your secrets." His voice and eyes trailed off to a distant point beyond the trenches, and Thomas thought back on the promise James had made him keep.

George handed Thomas the photograph. "Your necklace.

The one with the old medals." He pointed to James in the photo. "He's the brother you said you had to return the necklace to—before you called me a lying thief?"

"Yes." Thomas grimaced. "And sorry about calling you that."

"Why? It's accurate. Those two skills kept me alive. I don't apologize for them, so why should you?" George took a final drag from his shrinking cigarette. "What's so special about those medals anyway?"

Thomas pulled on the chain until the medals toppled over the collar of his shirt. He held up the Saint Barbara medal. "This one my mum gave me." He dropped the medal and held up the Saint Joseph one. "This was my brother's. He gave it to me before—"

His voice choked off. His tears were still too close to the surface. He waited until he'd regained some control before continuing.

"He gave it to me before he left for the war." He ran his thumb over the medal. "He said it would keep me safe, but he should have taken it with him. He was the one who needed protecting. Not me." He tucked the medals back under his shirt.

"Let me get this straight." George stubbed out his cigarette on a damp sandbag. "Your brother left you and your family to fight in the war, then he went missing, and you thought it was a good idea to risk not only your freedom but also your life to join up so when you're not digging tunnels under a battlefield, you can search the trenches for him?"

Hearing someone else explain his plan made it sound so much more foolish. "Yes," Thomas admitted.

"I'm all for playing the odds, Tommy, but the odds on this bet are pretty long."

Thomas's head dipped forward. "It's stupid, I know. I didn't realize how many miles of trenches there were."

George stared at Thomas as though he were a puzzle he couldn't solve. "Then why do it?"

Thomas looked up at George. Tears welled in his pale blue eyes. "It's what brothers do."

FIFTEEN

PHYSICALLY EXHAUSTED AND emotionally drained, Thomas could feel his body begging for sleep, but his mind refused to rest. Hours after George, Charlie, and he had snuck back into the crew's dugout, Thomas lay awake on his bunk, listening to the discordant rumblings of his crew's sleep and replaying the numerous mistakes he'd made since the day James had told him of his plans to join the army. With every secret he'd kept, every lie that he'd told, he'd dug himself deeper, yet as he stared up at the bottom of George's bunk, it wasn't the many lies he'd told that he feared would bury him, but the one truth he'd shared.

Sleep was a skittish visitor, sneaking in for short stays, only to scurry away when frightful memories of no-man's-land and anxious imaginings of when and how George would tell Bagger about Thomas breaking his rules returned. Thomas tried to convince himself that George wasn't selfish enough to want Thomas transferred just to win some bets using Bagger's ratter, but by the time the rest of the crew woke, George sat at the table feeding Max pieces of dried meat and smiling at Thomas.

When George asked Bagger if he could have a word with him, anxiousness roiled through Thomas's stomach in nauseating waves, and when they exited the dugout to talk in private, Thomas began to pack his bag. They returned minutes later, and Thomas stood, prepared to face the consequences of his mistakes.

"I hear you've been keeping a secret, Dover," Bagger said.

Thomas swallowed hard and shifted in his stance.

"Might as well fess up, lad. Shillings already let the cat out of the bag."

Thomas glanced at George, who had the nerve to smile. He'd expected George to snitch on him, but was surprised, and a little hurt, that George found such amusement in the betrayal. He looked to Charlie, seated on his bunk next to Feathers's cage. Charlie had a brother—he had to understand. Charlie kept his eyes locked on his sketch pad.

Bagger reached down, and Max jumped into his arms. "Or should I say he let the *dog* out of the bag?"

Unable to meet the old clay kicker's disappointed gaze, Thomas stared at his boots and silently scolded himself for letting down his guard around George. He never should have trusted the London street urchin, but the damage was done. All that was left was to face his punishment.

He tightened his grip on his bag. "Are you sending me to France to dig trenches?"

Bagger's bushy eyebrows knit in confusion. "For what? Sneaking out to take Max for a walk?" He pressed a hand to his lower back and stretched. "You've saved me the hassle of taking him topside."

Thomas's head snapped up. He glanced at George, whose smile widened. Before he could respond, Bagger took Thomas's bag, tossed it back on his bunk, and handed him the small dog.

"Just tell me before you go, so I know the little guy is with you," the grizzled clay kicker said. "Understand?"

Thomas nodded.

"Good." Bagger turned to face the rest of the crew. "Let's head to the trenches and see if we can scare up something better to eat."

Thomas watched in stunned silence as Bagger, Frederick, and the men filed out of the dugout. When only Charlie, Max, and Thomas remained, George clapped his hands.

"So what are we waiting around for, Dover? Let's go find your brother and return his Saint Joe medal."

"We?" Thomas asked.

"Why not? Like I said, I like playing the odds. Big risk, big reward. Besides, Mouse and I have nothing better to do. Right, Mouse?"

Charlie lowered himself from his bunk and handed Thomas three sheets of paper. "I drew some sketches of your brother, so we each have a picture of him to show when we look."

Thomas stared in disbelief at the drawings. "Thank you."

Charlie gave him a meek smile.

"See, Tommy. We're all in." George leaned closer and whispered as though he were divulging sensitive military plans. "It'll be our secret mission."

"You really want to help me find James?" Thomas asked.

"Sure. It's not like I'm going to be participating in any rat hunts." George shot a disappointed glare at Bagger's dog. "Even if I had more scraps, it doesn't look like I'd be able to lure Max away from you." He took one of the drawings of James. "So, let's get started."

"Now?" Thomas asked.

"No time like the present. Besides, thanks to me, we no longer have to wait until the crew's asleep to sneak out. They'll just think we're taking ol' Max here for a walk." He patted the dog's head. "Won't they, Max?"

Thomas stared up at the boy who, just minutes before, he'd been certain had betrayed him. "Thank you, George."

"No problem," George said, heading for the doorway. "Now let's go find Jim."

"James," Thomas corrected.

"That's what I said, and don't worry, Mouse and I promise we won't say a word about your secret trips to the front lines. I may be a lyin' thief, Tommy," he said with a teasing smile, "but I'm a lyin' thief who keeps his promises."

. . .

George kept his word. He and Charlie accompanied Thomas into the trenches after each shift. With Max trotting ahead of them, the boys showed Charlie's sketches to soldiers in the front-line and support trenches and asked if they'd seen James. Some ignored them. Others chased them off with language so colorful it tinted Charlie's ears. Those who did answer, did so with an apologetic shake of the head.

Unaware of what Johnny, Richard, and Dan had shared with Thomas about the true fate of missing soldiers, George's optimism about their secret mission never dimmed. He walked the trenches whistling and greeting every soldier they passed, but as days stretched into weeks, Thomas's hope faded. He started to look forward to their shifts in the tunnels, away from the trenches and the constant stream of disappointment awaiting him there.

SIXTEEN

AFTER THREE WEEKS with the clay kickers, the boys settled into their monotonous routines. Frederick helped Bagger load the sacks of spoil on a trolley, which George, the unit's trammer, pulled to the tunnel entrance.

While they waited for George to return with the trolley and timber, Frederick sat on the tunnel floor next to Feathers's cage. The team's canary was the only member of their unit foolish enough to make any sound, except for George, of course, who somewhere along his trip to the entrance and back always forgot about the crew's silence rule and offered some ridiculous comment or uncouth joke on his return. His forgetfulness was answered with an icy glare from Mole and a swift slap to the head from Bagger.

Frederick was convinced that if George didn't learn to keep his big mouth shut, he'd end up with a permanent impression of

Bagger's large hand on his skull. Not that Frederick thought it would matter to George. The London street rat would probably boast to anyone who'd listen about his misshapen, hand-imprinted head like it was a badge of honor.

While Frederick waited for George to return with the lumber, he ignored Feathers's tiny chirps and watched Bats and Charlie huddle close to the tunnel wall. Armed with a notebook, pencil, compass, and geophone, Bats used the two mercury-filled disks attached to a stethoscope to listen for and track enemy movement beneath the battlefield. One hand signal from Bats, and the entire unit froze. No one dared breathe while they waited for the listener to indicate where the enemy was: to their right, their left, above their heads, or below their feet.

The moment Bats pointed out the direction, Boomer and Thomas abandoned their work helping Bagger fill sacks and quietly bored a hole into the clay wall in the direction of the enemy. The rest of the crew, including Feathers, retreated to a safe distance to protect themselves should the blast fire back into their gallery instead of through the wall into the enemy's. With the hole finished, Boomer eased a cylinder charge called a torpedo into the opening. Thomas would then pack the opening behind the explosive with sandbags to direct the blast toward the enemy and away from the crew. Work was performed swiftly and silently—that is until the torpedo exploded, and everyone prayed their gallery would hold and the enemy's gallery would collapse. When the dust settled, Bats and Charlie would listen for proof that the explosion had hit its mark. Silence meant success. Noises meant failure and that Boomer and Thomas had to quickly bore another hole before the Germans detonated their own torpedo.

After one such explosion, Bats thought he heard movement beyond the tunnel wall. Boomer gave Thomas a quick hand signal, and Thomas started to silently bore a second hole in the wall several feet to the left of the first hole. When he'd drilled deep enough, Bats listened again at the wall to determine whether they needed to load another torpedo. From his position farther down the gallery, Frederick watched Bats's face for any hint of what he heard on the other side of the clay wall. His muscles tensed, ready to run should the listener signal that an explosion was imminent.

After several torturous minutes, Bats mouthed "False alarm" and gave the crew the all clear. Breathing a sigh of relief, Boomer signaled Thomas to remove the drill and start packing the hole while the rest of the crew resumed their work at the tunnel face.

Frederick, who'd returned with Feathers's cage to his position behind Mole and Bagger, watched the small boy work, cursing the fact that Thomas would get to return to his family after the war and tell them he'd protected the Allied front by killing dozens of the enemy with explosives. All Frederick would be able to tell his family was that he'd carried sacks of clay, lugged lumber beams, and watched a stupid canary flit about its cage. That would be Frederick's total contribution to Britain's war effort—army ornithologist.

He nudged the cage with his elbow, sending Feathers into a flurry of flapping and chirping before the canary settled back onto its perch. *Some war hero I've turned out to be,* Frederick thought, returning his attention to Thomas. *At this rate, my father will be too ashamed to let me in the house, much less hang my portrait in the family gallery.*

Frederick had contemplated writing to his father and requesting he use his influence to have Frederick transferred to a unit of real soldiers. He felt confident his father would agree and go along with Frederick's deception, not wanting a son of his tarnishing the family name by having to reveal he'd left school and lied to a recruiting officer, but Frederick wasn't as certain about his mother. If she saw Frederick's letter and learned where he was, she would move heaven and earth to bring him home. He'd be an Eton dropout, a military embarrassment, and the shame of his family.

No, he'd have to remain under no-man's-land with these tunnel rats until he came up with a better plan. Sweat trickled down his face and back as he sat, hating everyone and everything connected to his unbearable situation. He pushed his glasses up for the millionth time, but they slipped down again the second he let go. Adding the stagnant heat and his poor eyesight to the never-ending list of things Frederick loathed, he left his glasses perched on the tip of his nose and returned to plotting new ways to get himself transferred from the clay kickers unit.

When George finally returned with a trolley stacked with timber and a new question for Mole, Frederick stood to help unload the trolley at the exact moment Bagger swung out a hand to cuff George for talking. This time George dodged the blow by jumping back, a move that drove the timber beam he held into Frederick's gut.

Everyone stopped their work and watched as Frederick clutched his stomach and sank to the ground, unable to draw a full breath. Thomas, still removing the drill from the hole for Boomer, giggled. Frederick glared at him, and Thomas covered his mouth to stifle the laughter.

Sorry, Eton, George mouthed, putting the beam back on the trolley and extending a hand to help Frederick up.

Frederick slapped his hand away. "Don't call me that," he whispered, "and pay attention to what you're doing before you get someone killed."

"No need to get all poked up about it," George whispered, an amused smile tickling at the corners of his mouth. "It was an accident."

"Accident," Frederick spat, drawing Bagger's attention, once again, from helping Mole at the tunnel face.

Now it was Frederick who got whacked in the side of the head.

Back to work. Now, Bagger mouthed.

With a roll of his eyes, George returned to the trolley, but Frederick followed him.

"You and your friends," he whispered, stabbing a finger in the direction of Thomas, who was now clutching his stomach in a fit of stifled giggles, "have mocked and insulted me every chance you get."

George shoved Frederick, knocking the glasses from his

face. "That's because you've looked down your nose at us like we're gutter rats since the second you saw us on the train."

Boomer shot the boys a warning look.

Frederick plucked his glasses from the floor and cleaned the smudged lenses with a handkerchief he pulled from his pocket. Putting the glasses back on, he leaned in close, so only George could hear. "That's because you *are* gutter rats."

George grabbed the front of Frederick's shirt and cocked back his fist. "Well, this gutter rat is gonna bash in that uppity nose of yours until you're breathing through your eyes."

Boomer grabbed Frederick while Mole restrained George before a punch was thrown.

"Knock it off," Bagger said through clenched teeth. "Both of you."

Frederick struggled to break free from the miner's grip. "He started it."

"And I'm gonna finish it," George sneered, spitting in Frederick's face.

"Get them out of here," Bagger ordered in a harsh whisper, "before they give away our—"

"Shut up!"

Everyone stopped and looked at Charlie.

"What is it, Mouse?" Bats whispered.

"Do you hear it?" Charlie asked.

Bats held up his hand, signaling for quiet. Frederick and George stopped struggling, and Boomer and Mole released their holds on the boys. Frederick closed his eyes and held his breath, trying to pick up the noise Charlie heard. Fear trickled like ice water down his spine at the possibilities. Was it digging? Had his fight with George given away their position? Were the Germans packing their own torpedo into the wall separating them? Panic took hold, and he was turning to run when Bats said, "I don't hear anything."

"Neither do I," whispered Charlie. "That's the problem."

Before he could explain further, Thomas bent over and vomited. After the second heave, his eyes rolled back, and he fainted.

Boomer rushed over to his apprentice's side. George, Mole, and Bagger joined him, but Frederick's attention remained fixed on Charlie, whose trembling finger pointed to the birdcage behind him and the lifeless canary lying on the cage floor.

SEVENTEEN

OUTSIDE THE TUNNEL, Thomas woke to Bagger shaking him so hard his teeth chattered. Pain throbbed through his head with every violent jostle.

"Please stop. I'm all right." His voice echoed through his skull, sharpening the dull edges of the growing ache.

Despite Thomas's insistence that he just needed to rest, the old clay kicker carried him to a Regimental Aid Post in a reserve trench dugout to be examined by a medic. The doctor was busy patching up injured soldiers and returning them to the trenches or, for the more serious cases, sending them on to the Advanced Dressing Station for further treatment.

When Bagger explained that Thomas had been exposed to carbon monoxide, the doctor ordered that he be taken to the ADS in an abandoned church in the village of Ypres for examination. Thomas claimed he could make the walk himself, but the doctor ordered two stretcher bearers to carry Thomas. George, Charlie, and Max accompanied their friend to the church, while Bagger returned to the tunnels to help the next crew seal off the leak by filling in the hole Thomas had drilled.

During the two-mile walk to the village, waves of dizziness and the rocking motion of the stretcher tempted Thomas to close his eyes and sleep, but his close call in the tunnel resurrected long-buried nightmares of men dying in the coal mines and sparked renewed fear that Thomas would one day die the same way, without warning, beneath the ground. To stay awake and avoid revisiting those fears, he focused on George's voice regaling the soldiers carrying Thomas's stretcher with tall tales Thomas could now recite as he watched the scenery slide by on both sides of the dirt road.

Three weeks earlier, when Thomas and the other boys had arrived at the Poperinge train station and marched the muddy roads to the Allied trenches, darkness had hidden the towns between the train station and the battlefront. Now, as he was carried through Ypres, the early-morning sun exposed the Belgian village caught in the war's crosshairs.

Ypres lay in ruins. Medieval structures that had stood tall and strong against time and weather for hundreds of years, had bowed down beneath two years of artillery fire. Crumbling walls, mountains of rubble, abandoned homes, and charred building frames were all that remained. As they neared the ruined church, Thomas gripped his medals and said a prayer that the recent zeppelin strikes over Dover had spared his home and family such devastation.

The church buzzed with voices and movement. Where pews once held worshippers, now hundreds of cots held ailing, injured, and dying soldiers. Damaged statues of Jesus, Mary, and several saints kept a silent vigil over the soldiers as field doctors and nurses, with red crosses stitched on the fronts of their white smocks, tended to patients. While Thomas waited to be examined, the morning sun peeked through the large, round stained-glass window behind the altar and above the sacristy. Its rays broke through the glass, scattering colors across the church floor.

The smell of disinfectant burned Thomas's nostrils with every inhale. Beneath the strong chemical scent lived other smells. The metallic scent of blood. The nauseating stench of rotting flesh, diarrhea, and vomit. No matter how much bleach and ammonia the nurses scrubbed into the instruments, bedsheets, and surfaces, the smells lingered.

Thomas was thankful for George's incessant talking to distract him from the moaning, crying, and screaming coming from the other cots, occupied by soldiers suffering from trench fever, gangrene, or injuries sustained in the latest volley of gunfire from the enemy.

After Boomer and the others helped the next crew seal the hole, they checked in on Thomas. Frederick did not join them. Boomer explained that the explosion in the German tunnel had created a pocket of carbon monoxide that Thomas accidentally tapped into when he burrowed too deep in the wall to set their next torpedo.

"I'm sorry," Thomas said.

Boomer patted his shoulder. "It's not your fault. There was no way to know the wall was so thin at that point."

"I could have gotten you all killed," Thomas added, recalling the men, young and old, whose lives were stolen by carbon monoxide in the coal mines back home.

"That's why we bring canaries in with us," Mole said.

At the mention of Feathers, Charlie excused himself to go get some fresh air. He didn't return until the men were leaving for the dugout. Thomas told George and Charlie to go with them to get some rest, but they refused.

Two hours later, a doctor examined Thomas and told him he was lucky his crew carried him out of the tunnels when they did. A few more minutes' exposure, and they would have been carrying out a corpse. He ordered Thomas rest and fluids, then released him back to active duty.

George and Charlie accompanied Thomas back to the tunnels. As they neared the entrance, Thomas noticed the crew's birdcage tucked in the corner beside the door frame. Feathers's lifeless body still lay at the bottom of the cage.

Charlie knelt beside it. "I'd hoped the fresh air would bring him back too."

"I'm sorry about Feathers," Thomas said.

Charlie reached a finger through the wire frame and stroked the canary's tiny head. "It's not your fault."

"No. It's Eton's," George said. "And he knows it. That's why he didn't come see you, Tommy. I hope Bagger's kicking him off the crew as we speak before the idiot gets us all killed."

"He didn't know about the leak any more than the rest of us," Thomas said.

"No, but he should have. He was supposed to be watching Feathers. If he had been doing his job, he would have been able to warn us as soon as the bird started acting funny."

Thomas's head throbbed with pain. He was too tired to argue with George that Frederick might have noticed the bird sooner if he and George hadn't been fighting.

"What will they do with Feathers?" Charlie asked.

Thomas knew the answer. It was the same thing the miners in Dover did with dead canaries. Toss out their bodies, replace them with new birds, and get back to work. But the truth seemed too harsh to speak as Charlie continued to pet the dead canary. Apparently, George did not feel the same way.

"They'll replace him, just like they do when a soldier dies on the front line or a miner in the tunnels."

Charlie's chin trembled. "He deserves to be remembered. Everyone does."

"Just because he deserves it doesn't mean it will happen," George mumbled.

Thomas caught George's eye and shook his head.

"What?" George said. "It's the truth, and Mouse knows it. The bird is disposable, just like the rest of us. It was no different in the factory, right, Mouse? A worker gets killed in an accident or falls sick, and the next day a new worker is standing in his spot. There's no time for mourning or memorializing. There's work to be done."

"There's time now," Thomas said.

"You want to bury the bird?" George asked.

Charlie looked up at Thomas. Tears welled in his eyes.

"Why not?" Thomas said. "He was part of our crew. His death saved my life. It saved all of us."

George took off his helmet and ran a hand through his messy hair. "Sure. Why not?"

The boys carried the cage to a field beyond the reserve trenches. The cold, wet March weather that had greeted the boys the morning they'd arrived in Ypres had lingered into April, leaving the abandoned farmlands behind the Allied lines as lifeless and muddy as the battlefield that stretched before them.

"I never thought any place could make me miss the streets of London," George said as he knelt below a large elm tree. The leafless branches offered the boys huddled beneath them little protection from the rain that had begun to fall in earnest again during their walk from the tunnel entrance. George sank his fingers into the mud beside the trunk of the tree and started to dig a small hole. "But when this war is over, I never want to see mud again."

"Bats told me in another month or so all of these fields will be covered in poppies," Charlie said.

Thomas knelt to help George. "That sounds nice. I'll be happy to see any color other than brown." He pulled a handful of cold, wet soil from the hole George had started.

"Bats said after shifts last summer he'd come out here and sit among the poppies to remember that even in the middle of all this fighting and death, beauty still exists and life continues." Tears brimmed in Charlie's eyes as he stared at Feathers's still body. "I hope I get a chance to see them."

"You will," George said. "We all will."

When George and Thomas finished digging, Charlie wrapped Feathers in a handkerchief and placed him in the grave, which George covered with the removed mud. No one spoke. Any prayers offered or thanks given were done so silently.

As Thomas stood before Feathers's grave, he thought back to the bodies strewn across no-man's-land. Each dead soldier had been replaced without a funeral, without a proper burial.

If we don't bury our dead, the war will, and us with them.

As they walked back to the dugout with Feathers's empty cage, Thomas thought of James. If his brother was among the dead on or under no-man's-land, he deserved to be laid to rest. They all did. Whether James was dead or alive, Thomas would find his brother and bring him home.

When they arrived at the dugout with Feathers's empty cage, they found a new cage sitting on the corner shelf, and a new canary chirping from its perch.

EIGHTEEN

FREDERICK LOOKED UP from his notebook when Thomas entered the dugout. He was relieved to see Thomas alive and well, but his shame over neglecting his duties in the tunnel and nearly costing Thomas his life strangled the apology he knew he owed.

After reassuring Bagger and the rest of the crew that he was fine, Thomas collapsed on his bunk with Max curled up next to him. He was asleep before the others finished eating. George glowered at Frederick as he hopped up onto his bunk, and Charlie refused to look Frederick's way as he placed the old cage on the floor by the wall before climbing onto his own bunk, where he silently stared into the new birdcage. Charlie only looked up once, when Mole announced they'd call the new canary Feathers.

"He should have his own name," Charlie said, dropping a biscuit crumb into the cage.

“Fine,” Mole said. “We’ll call him Feathers the Second.”

“Actually,” Boomer said, ticking off numbers on his stubby fingers, “he’d be Feathers the Seventh.”

“You’ve lost six canaries?” George asked.

“I think so. This is our seventh, right, Bagger?”

Bagger shrugged.

“He *deserves* his own name,” Charlie said between clenched teeth.

Bagger smiled. “Look at little Mouse standing up for himself. You might have to give him a new nickname, Shillings.”

George stared at Charlie with an expression of shock and amused admiration. “I just might.”

“Call the bird what you want, Mouse,” Mole said, opening a can of bully beef. “But down here, it’s wise not to get too attached.” The words of advice, spoken with kindness, struck Charlie like a punch to the gut. Turning away from the advice and the rest of the crew so they wouldn’t see his tears, Charlie fed the new canary another crumb.

. . .

The next morning, Frederick woke to the sound of crying. Disoriented, he jolted up and slammed his head on the bottom of Charlie’s bunk before scrambling to his feet. Rubbing the knot swelling on his forehead, he put on his glasses and looked for the source of the sobs. Except for George’s loud snoring, the dugout was silent. The men were not on their bunks, and Max was no longer snuggled up next to Thomas.

At first, Frederick thought the crying was coming from Charlie, who he'd heard sniffing back tears before Frederick fell asleep, but when he peeked at the upper bunk, he found Charlie sleeping quietly, his fingers resting against the birdcage.

Convinced he'd dreamed the noise, Frederick had started to lie back down when he heard more panicked whimpers and incoherent mumbling from across the room. He crept over to the lower bunk where Thomas, in the grip of a nightmare, twitched and thrashed in his bed.

"Thomas," he whispered.

"No," Thomas mumbled in his sleep.

Frederick shook his shoulder. "Thomas."

Thomas's eyes sprang open. "James, no!" He flinched away from Frederick's hand. Except for a couple of stubborn cowlicks, his blond hair stuck to his sweaty forehead in dark clumps, and his chest heaved with stuttered, panicked breaths.

"It's okay," Frederick whispered. "You were having a nightmare."

His eyes wide and unblinking, Thomas stared at Frederick. "Where am I?"

"In the dugout. There was an accident. Do you remember?"

"An accident?" Thomas repeated, his voice hollow and his brow furrowed in thought. He squeezed his eyes closed and kneaded his forehead with unsteady fingers.

"Yes, but we're safe now."

Thomas nodded as lingering images from his nightmare vanished and memories of the day reemerged. "Feathers died."

Guilt squeezed around Frederick's chest at the memory of Charlie's face as he pointed to the small canary lying motionless at the bottom of the cage. "Yes. But the important thing is you're all right. You just need rest." He grabbed a flask of water from the table. "And something to drink." He offered the flask to Thomas.

Thomas took a small sip and handed it back. "We buried him."

"Who?" Frederick asked. "Feathers?"

Thomas nodded again, shaking the last cobwebs of poisoned sleep from his brain. "He was part of our crew, so George, Charlie, and I buried him."

"Oh." Frederick glanced up at Charlie asleep on his bunk, his hand still resting against the new canary cage. With a heavy sigh, he placed the flask back on the table. "Thomas, about what happened down in the gallery—"

The bunk above Thomas creaked beneath George's shifting weight. "We all know what happened in the gallery," George said, swinging his legs over the edge of his bunk and landing beside Frederick. "You almost got Tommy killed."

"I didn't—"

"Do your job? We know, so why don't you go back to your bunk and leave Tommy alone?"

"He was having a nightmare. I was just trying to help."

"He doesn't need your help, Eton."

Charlie sat up, awakened by the heated conversation.

"George," Thomas said, "leave it alone."

"No. He nearly got you killed. He almost got us all killed. Someone needs to tell Eton what he is."

"Enlighten me," Frederick said, bracing himself for another fight with the London orphan. This time there'd be no clay kickers to stop them. "What am I?"

George leaned forward until his freckled nose almost touched Frederick's. "You pretend to be a tough British soldier, but I've met guys like you before. All talk and bluster, but when things get rough, when it really counts, you run away because under all that talk, you're nothing but a coward."

Frederick's eyes narrowed. "Take that back."

"Bagger and the crew know it," George continued.

"That's enough, George," Thomas said.

George motioned to Charlie and Thomas. "They know it, and I've known it since Charing Cross."

Frederick's hands began to shake. "I said take it back!" He shoved them into his pockets, where his fingers brushed up against the white feather he kept hidden there.

"What's wrong, Eton?" George pressed. "No one in your pampered little life had the nerve to tell you how spineless you are before?"

Frederick turned to storm out of the dugout—just as Bagger stepped through the door.

"Are you two at it again?"

"I was just making sure Thomas was all right—"

George plopped down on a chair at the table and lit a cigarette off a candle. "You wouldn't have to make sure Thomas was all right if you'd done your job in the first place."

"If you hadn't hit me with that beam—" Frederick had started to retort when Bagger grabbed him by the ear.

"That's it!" the clay kicker roared. Still gripping Frederick's ear, he strode over to the table and grabbed hold of one of George's ears.

"Hey!" George yelled, dropping his cigarette as Bagger yanked him to his feet. "What are you doing?"

"Ending this," Bagger announced. Stubbing out George's cigarette with his boot, he dragged both boys out the doorway, toward the trenches. Thomas and Charlie scrambled off their bunks to follow.

"Let go!" Frederick yelled, trying to pull his ear free from Bagger's hold. "Where are you taking us?"

"Where you can settle this without getting the rest of us killed." Tightening his grip, Bagger led them through the communication trench toward the reserve trenches. Soldiers, playing cards and resting in their dugouts, pointed and laughed at the spectacle. A few abandoned their games to follow.

Frederick's face burned with humiliation at being disciplined like a schoolboy. "Let go!" he demanded again.

Bagger didn't answer. He didn't speak again until he'd dragged both the quarrelsome boys out of the trenches and behind the

Allied lines, to a field outside the town of Ypres, where sniper bullets and artillery shells couldn't reach. Only then did he release their ears. "Now, you two will settle this feud like gentlemen."

George rubbed his sore ear and motioned down the field to a group of soldiers kicking a ball toward a makeshift goal. "You want us to play football?"

"No." Bagger bent down and plucked two pairs of dusty brown leather gloves from the ground. He tossed a pair to George. "Put these on." He tossed Frederick the other pair.

"You want us to box?" George asked with a chuckle.

"That's how we end arguments on the Western Front," Bagger said. "Settle them in a fair match off the battlefield, so you don't get someone killed on or *under* it." His hard gaze settled on Frederick.

"Sounds good," George said.

"This is ridiculous," Frederick scoffed. "I am not going to box with *him*."

"Why not, Eton?" George asked. "Scared you'll lose?"

"Scared?" Frederick huffed. "Of losing to you? I bet you've never even held a pair of boxing gloves before, much less worn them."

"You're right," George said, pulling on a glove. "I've always boxed bare-knuckled."

Frederick's smug smile crumbled under the amused laughter of the soldiers who'd gathered around the boys.

"Enough talking," Bagger said. "Get your gloves on and let's get started." He tossed two more pairs to Thomas and Charlie.

"We're all boxing?" Thomas asked.

"A few rounds in the ring will get rid of the nerves and anger you lads have built up in the tunnels. You'll feel better after. I always do."

Thomas shrugged and started pulling on the gloves, but Charlie didn't move.

"What's wrong, Mouse?" Bagger asked. "Gloves don't fit?"

"No, they're fine. It's just—" Charlie swallowed hard and, without looking up at Bagger, handed the gloves back to the clay kicker. "I'd rather not fight, if that's all right."

Bagger huffed and shoved the gloves back into Charlie's hands. "You're a soldier, Mouse. This is war. You need to be ready and willing to fight at all times."

Charlie stared down at the gloves. "But I don't know how."

"All the more reason for you to get in the ring." Bagger pointed back toward the trenches. "Because when we come across the enemy in those galleries, which we will, if you don't fight, you're dead, and you'll probably take some of us with you. Now put on the gloves."

Minutes later, Bagger stood in the center of a large circle of soldiers eager to place bets on the next fight.

"We've got some rookies here today, fellas," he announced. "So I'm gonna give them a few pointers before we get started." He motioned to Charlie. "You first, Mouse."

Charlie tried to step back, but George shoved him inside the circle of soldiers. "Go get 'im, Mouse!"

"Keep your hands up at all times." Bagger said, grabbing Charlie's gloved hands and lifting them in front of the boy's chest and face. "You drop your hands, you give your opponent a target." Releasing the gloves, he stepped back into a defensive stance, facing Charlie. "Don't plant your feet. Keep moving." He began to bounce on the balls of his feet, dancing around his terrified opponent. "A moving target is harder to hit."

"Come on, Mouse!" George yelled. "You can outmaneuver that old man!"

Bagger shot George a warning glance. "Watch it, Shillings. You're next."

George smiled. "Looking forward to it, sir, Bagger, sir." He gave him a cockeyed salute before winking at Frederick.

Frederick glared back.

Bagger addressed the boys as he started dancing around Charlie again. Hands shaking, Charlie pivoted in a circle, following the crew leader's movements and shrinking into himself like a scared turtle.

Bagger placed his gloved hands on Charlie's shoulders and gave him a rough shake. "Stay loose, Mouse. It looks like your ears are trying to eat your shoulders."

Everyone laughed except Charlie, whose face turned sallow and clammy.

Bagger bobbed to the right, then weaved to the left. Charlie struggled to keep up with the quick changes in direction.

"While you're moving, throw some fakes to get your

opponent to drop his guard and give you a target." Bagger threw two short jabs. One high. One low.

Charlie's eyes widened. He failed to block the jabs and stumbled over his own feet in a panicked retreat.

The laughter around the circle grew louder as Bagger pressed forward, continuing to throw fake jabs, while Charlie scurried back.

"Always look for an opening." Bagger threw another jab to Charlie's chest, and Charlie dropped his guard.

"Then strike!" Bagger lunged forward and threw a reverse to Charlie's head, stopping inches from his nose.

"No!" Charlie dropped to the ground and covered his head with his arms. "Please don't hit me again. Please. No more."

The laughter stopped, and Thomas rushed to Charlie's side. "Mouse, you all right?" He placed a hand on his friend's back.

Charlie recoiled from his touch.

"I didn't hit him," Bagger said. "I swear. I didn't even touch him."

Slowly, Charlie looked up from the protection of his arms. The soldiers standing around the circle stared down at him with expressions ranging from confused concern to unabashed amusement. A mortified blush burned away all traces of Charlie's ashen complexion.

George knelt before him. "What happened, Mouse?"

His hands still trembling, Charlie struggled to take off the gloves.

"Are you hurt?" Frederick asked.

Charlie threw his gloves aside. "I don't want to talk about it!" Pushing to his feet, he shoved his way through the crowd and ran back to the tunnels.

Worry creased Bagger's forehead as he watched Charlie leave. "I think we're done for today, boys."

"I don't get to fight Eton?" George asked.

"Not today," Bagger answered, taking off his gloves.

"Come on, Bagger," George pleaded. "We'll be fast, I promise. It'll only take two hits. Me hitting Eton, and Eton hitting the dirt."

"I said, *not today.*"

NINETEEN

TENSION IN THE crew's dugout worsened after Bagger's failed boxing lesson. Charlie refused to talk to anyone but the crew's new canary, and everyone's mood soured when heavy rains kept them trapped in the tunnels for the next two days. George couldn't sit still. When he wasn't pacing the length of the small dugout, his fingers drummed on the table like they were sending out frantic messages in Morse code.

"Can't we just box in here?" he asked Bagger on day three of their weather-imposed confinement.

"There's not enough room," Bagger answered without looking up from his breakfast.

"If we move the table into the tunnel, there would be."

With an exasperated sigh, Frederick glanced up from his notebook. "Would you please just shut up?"

George stopped pacing. "What's wrong, Eton? You afraid to fight me?"

"No. I'm just tired of hearing your mouth run."

"Then why don't you try and stop it?" George tapped a finger to his chin. "Come on. I'll even give you the first hit."

Frederick shook his head. "I don't have time for this." Grabbing his coat and boots, he exited the dugout, but George's voice chased him out of the tunnels.

"You've got plenty of time," George yelled. "We all do! What you lack, Eton, is the courage!"

Frederick didn't stop until he reached the front-line trenches. He didn't care if Bagger caught him and transferred him from Ypres. In fact, he hoped Bagger did. Digging trenches in France would be preferable to working alongside George and the others for one more minute. At least in France he'd be above ground with real soldiers and have a chance to serve his country like a true Chamberlain. The thought quickened his pace and reinforced his resolve to get himself kicked off Bagger's crew.

He came across a lone soldier standing sentry on a fire step in a parapet, watching the enemy lines through his rifle's telescopic sight. The soldier's profile looked familiar, and as Frederick drew closer, he recognized the sniper as William Gentry, an Eton graduate and the older brother of Edward Gentry, one of Frederick's classmates.

"William?"

The soldier turned to face Frederick. He'd grown a mustache since Frederick had last seen him, but it was definitely the oldest Gentry brother. William smiled. "Frederick? What the bloody hell are you doing out here?"

"Fighting for crown and country, just like you."

William scrutinized Frederick's uniform. "I have to admit, you're the last person I thought I'd ever see on the Western Front."

The admission stung, far more than all of George's barbs, but Frederick schooled his expression. He was an Eton student. He was a Chamberlain. And despite his age and lies, he was a British soldier.

William abandoned his rifle and held his hand out to Frederick. "Bloody good to see you, Chamberlain."

Seeing a familiar face, a *friendly* familiar face, infused Frederick with a confidence George and the clay kickers had worked hard to stomp out of him. Frederick grabbed hold of William's outstretched hand. "Good to be seen." He squeezed tight and tugged William toward him with a quick, firm jerk.

William stumbled forward a step, but quickly recovered. With a shake of his head, he chuckled and looked Frederick up and down. "Does your father know you're out here?"

"No. And I'd like to keep it that way—for now."

"I understand. You're not the first undergrad I've seen on the front line, and if this war continues to drag on, you won't be the last. What unit are you with?"

"It's classified. My unit is working on a top-secret mission." It wasn't really a lie. The clay kickers' mission was a secret. So secret, in fact, even Frederick didn't know what it was.

William's eyebrows rose in surprise. "I guess it doesn't hurt to be a Chamberlain, even at the front."

Before William could question him further, Frederick pointed to the older boy's rifle. "I see the army recognized your marksmanship. I'm not surprised. Edward was always bragging about how you were the best marksman in your class."

"Was he now? Sounds like Edward. He didn't join with you, did he?"

"No," Frederick said. "Last I saw him, he was still at Eton."

"Good," William said. "That's good."

Frederick motioned again to the rifle. "How many kills have you recorded?"

"Marked my thirty-second this morning. Had thirty-three in my crosshairs when you arrived. How about you?"

Frederick sighed. "Like I said, it's top secret."

William nodded. "Right."

"Mind if I take a look?" Frederick asked, motioning again to William's rifle.

"Not at all." William stepped aside, and Frederick climbed up on the fire step. "Keep your head low," William warned. "The Germans have snipers too. Bloody good ones."

Frederick ducked down and pressed his right eye against the scope. His view of no-man's-land was magnified. The enemy line appeared close enough to reach out and touch.

"See the trench corner, to the left of that high ridge?"

Frederick adjusted the angle of the scope. "Yes."

"There's a tall Fritz whose head keeps slipping above the parapet. See him?"

Frederick's pulse pounded with anticipation as he scanned the lip of the trench, but there was no movement. His eyes swept back along the edge again, and he saw it. The domed helmet of a German soldier. "There he is! Wait. He's gone again."

"Give it a second."

A minute later, the helmet reappeared. "He's back!"

"Do you have a shot?" William asked.

"I think so."

"Take it."

Frederick pulled back from the scope. "I don't want to take your thirty-third kill from you."

"Go ahead. Another Fritz will find himself caught in my crosshairs soon enough."

"Are you sure?"

"Anything for a fellow Eton."

Frederick's nerves crackled with excitement. This was his way out of the tunnels. He could feel it. If he killed the German with one shot, William would undoubtedly recommend he be transferred from the tunnels to the infantry, where he belonged. Frederick couldn't help but smile as he pressed his right eye back up against the scope. The steel helmet was still visible above the trench line, but now Frederick could also see the profile of the soldier's face. He didn't have a mustache like William or Bagger, and his cheeks were round with youth.

"Can you still see him?" William asked.

"Yes."

The soldier was talking to someone below the trench wall.

"Do you have a shot?"

"I think so."

The German soldier's hands and face were animated with broad movements and exaggerated expressions. Frederick wondered if he was telling a story or perhaps a joke. Frederick's hands, slick with sweat, struggled to maintain a firm grip on the weapon.

The soldier laughed. His broad smile swelled his cheeks, making him look even younger. Frederick flexed his fingers to break up the tension building in his muscles.

"Don't hesitate if you can take him out," William said.

Frederick wiped one hand and then the other on his trousers, grateful for the first time in days for the terrible weather. He hoped William would assume his hands were wet from the rain and not from nervousness. He repositioned them on the rifle, but they were already damp with sweat again.

Still laughing, the soldier turned and looked out over no-man's-land.

Frederick curled his pointer finger around the trigger and took a deep breath. He lined the crosshairs of the rifle between the soldier's eyes. It was the perfect shot. His ticket out of the tunnels. All Frederick had to do was squeeze his finger.

But Frederick was in no danger. The laughing soldier wasn't aiming a rifle at him. He didn't even have a weapon in his hands. In that moment, he wasn't Frederick's enemy.

Frederick's finger eased off the trigger, and he backed away from the scope.

"What's wrong?" William asked.

Frederick climbed down from the fire step. "He ducked."

"Not to worry," William said, climbing onto his perch and pressing his face to the scope. "He'll be back."

"I better return to my unit," Frederick said, but William's full attention was focused on the enemy trenches.

"There you are, thirty-three."

Frederick did not say goodbye or look back. As he walked away from William and his chance to get out of the tunnels, he slipped his hand into his pocket and wrapped his fingers around the white feather. He crushed it until he felt the spine snap.

Behind him, a bullet exploded from William's rifle.

Across no-man's-land, a laughing boy died.

TWENTY

TRAPPED IN DARK silence, time lost its form. The only markers of its passage for the young soldier became the gentle pressure of a cup to his chapped lips, which brought a trickle of water on his parched tongue, and the prick of a needle.

Sleep brought little rest and no comfort. The morphine numbed his physical pain, but the nightmares forced him to relive every terrifying second of his time on the Western Front.

He ached with exhaustion but dreaded the morphine injections. He fought back against the hands holding his arm, but his strength had not returned. He had no choice but to surrender to the needle and the nightmares. They were his penance, his punishment for all he had done and all he had failed to do. His deeds on the battlefield were etched in his mind and soul like epitaphs on tombstones. In sleep, he revisited them, carving their lines deeper.

TWENTY-ONE

WHEN GEORGE CALLED Frederick a coward, Thomas had expected Frederick to slap George with a glove and challenge him to a duel. He couldn't believe the Eton boy's pride would allow such an insult to stand, but hours after Frederick had stormed from the dugout, he returned without a word. He demanded no apology, nor did he offer one. His head bowed, he took off his muddy boots and, without wiping them clean, tossed them aside. He then lay down on his bunk and scribbled in his notebook until Bagger ordered the boys to the lower galleries for their next shift.

The feud between George and Frederick appeared to have reached a stalemate. Everyone embraced the reprieve, no one more than Charlie. The constant tension between the two boys had strained his already frayed nerves. His frustration over their petty arguments had curdled into anger over the weeks, and when Boomer had carried Thomas's unconscious body from the tunnels, Charlie had wanted to scream at George and Frederick until his throat bled. He knew which words to use. Which words would stun into silence and which would leave scars so deep they became part of you, as familiar and identifying as your name. But they were Charlie's secret to keep, passed down from grandfather to father, and from father to son. He refused to continue the cruel tradition. No matter how hot his rage boiled. The secret might someday kill him, but it was a secret he was determined to take to his grave.

So Charlie said nothing. Instead, he scratched his thoughts and anger into drawings in the notebook George had given him from his kit bag, along with an unused pencil after Charlie had worn down his own. He'd offered to pay George for the items, but George waved his pence away. "Take them," he'd said. "They're no use to me." But Charlie had insisted on paying him something, and when he'd offered George his cigarettes, George gladly accepted the trade. "Now those I can use."

When the boys weren't working the galleries, searching the trenches, or sleeping, Charlie passed the long, boring hours capturing life on the Western Front in his drawings. He drew soldiers sleeping in dugouts, husbands and sons writing letters home, rat hunts and card games in the trenches, and football and boxing matches in the fields far behind them. He sketched snipers on fire steps, injured soldiers on gurneys, and bodies on the battlefield. He drew every member of their crew, including Max and the new canary that Charlie, despite Mole's warning about getting too attached, had given a new name.

"Don't forget Feathers," Bagger would remind Frederick every time they left the dugout.

"Her name's Poppy," Charlie would correct.

With a pitying shake of his head, Bagger finally gave up, and the crew started calling the new canary Poppy.

. . .

A few days after Thomas's carbon monoxide poisoning, Charlie woke to find himself alone in the dugout. It was the first time he'd been alone since he'd joined the army. At first, he thought he should look for the others, but instead he lit a hunk of solidified alcohol in Mole's Tommy's Cooker, a small, smokeless portable stove, and made himself a cup of tea from the tunnelers' rations before climbing back onto his bunk. Ever since he'd drawn the sketches of James for Thomas, Charlie had longed for a picture of his own brother, Henry. Taking advantage of the quiet, he opened his notebook and started to draw.

An hour later, Thomas and George returned to the tunnels after watching a raucous football match between several tunneling crews. As they neared the dugout, they heard a scream and rushed inside just as Charlie hurled a tin cup across the room. Thomas jumped back, and George ducked as it struck the beam above his head.

"Blimey, Mouse! What was that for?" George picked up the

cup and attempted to reshape the dented side. "We all know the tea is rubbish, but no need to take it out on the cups."

Charlie's face blanched. "I'm—I'm sorry," he stammered. "I didn't mean to . . ."

Thomas stepped into the dugout. Dozens of crumpled balls of paper littered the floor. Charlie jumped down from his bunk and, apologizing again, scrambled to pick them up. "I didn't mean to make such a mess."

"What is all this?" George asked, snagging one before Charlie could. He straightened out the paper. Dark scratch marks partly obscured the image of a boy's face.

Charlie snatched the sketch from George. "It's none of your business!"

George held up his hands in surrender. "Sorry, Mouse."

Clutching the paper, Charlie slumped down in a chair at the table and stared at the ruined sketch. "No, I'm sorry. I didn't mean to snap at you like that. It's not your fault."

George and Thomas pulled up chairs next to him. "What's going on, Mouse?" George asked. "Who's the boy in the sketch?"

Charlie placed the drawing on the table. "It's supposed to be my brother, Henry, but I can't get it right."

"What's wrong with it?" George asked.

"It doesn't look like him."

Thomas grabbed two more tin cups and poured tea. "You'll get it right, Mouse. You're an amazing artist. You did a great job with the sketches of my brother."

"But I had your photograph of James to look at."

"Do you have a photograph of Henry you can use?" George asked.

Charlie shook his head. "My father never had any taken."

Thomas placed a cup in front of Charlie. "That'll make it harder, but you'll get it right. It's just going to take some time."

Charlie pushed the cup away. "You don't understand. I don't have any more time. I should have drawn him as soon as I got here, but thinking about him was too hard." Charlie grabbed the sketch and tore it in half. "I waited too long."

"Nonsense," George said. He fetched Charlie's notebook and pencil from his bunk and placed them on the table. "You can still draw him."

Charlie slammed his fist on the table, snapping the pencil. "I've tried, but it's too late!" He dropped his head into his folded arms on top of the notebook. "I've already forgotten what he looks like."

. . .

Listening to Charlie, Thomas stared into his cup of pale tea. He knew how painful it was when the memory of someone you lost started to fade. It had happened to him shortly after his grandad died. One day he could remember the sound of his grandad's voice, and the next it was gone. It was the same with James. A week after James enlisted, Thomas could no longer recall how his brother's laugh sounded when Thomas told him a corny joke. It was like losing them twice. "I'm sorry."

"Me too, Mouse," George said, patting Charlie on the back.

Charlie looked up. A tear slid down his cheek. "I knew when I left it would happen someday. I just never thought it would happen so soon."

Thomas pushed back from the table and walked over to his bunk. A few seconds later he returned with the unused pencil from his kit bag. "Talking to you and George about my brother helped me remember things about him I thought I'd forgotten." He placed the pencil on Charlie's notebook. "Tell us about Henry."

TWENTY-TWO

AFTER THEIR LATEST argument in the dugout, George and Frederick ignored each other's existence, except to pass filled sandbags and timber beams back and forth. When Thomas, George, and Charlie snuck out to search for James, Frederick watched them leave and was always awake when they returned hours later from another fruitless search, but he kept his lectures to himself.

With each shift, they extended the gallery toward the location for the Maedelstede Farm chamber, bracing the newly dug sections with timber. Nine inches at a time. While pulling the heavy bags of spoil to the tunnel entrance and dragging the unwieldy beams back to the tunnel face, Thomas often thought of his pony from the coal mine and wished he had Morty's help in the tunnels. Thomas would distract himself from the burning pain in his back and arms by remembering his time with James and his dad while he worked. The memories helped pass the time until artillery fire rumbled through the gallery walls, like a giant clearing his throat, and Thomas's thoughts snapped back to where he was and why he was there.

James.

Even with the additional help of Charlie and George, Thomas had found no information about his brother. The closest they'd come was a soldier who said James looked familiar, but then he admitted that after several months in the trenches, all soldiers had started to look familiar.

After weeks of digging, the boys hoped with every bag of spoil they hauled that the gallery was almost complete, but Bagger kept pushing the crew to dig farther and faster.

"How much longer are we going to make this tunnel?" George whispered to Bats during a shift, but the listener held a finger to his lips and set back to work at the wall.

When they retired to the dugout five hours later, hungry and worn to the bone, George asked again. Bagger did not look up from his food. "Until I tell you to stop."

"And when will that be?" George pressed.

Bagger arched his back. It cracked with every twist and stretch. "When we've completed our mission."

"What mission?" George asked. "The one you haven't told us about?"

"Watch your tone, Shillings," Bagger warned. "I haven't had my tea yet."

George poured a cup and sat down across from the crew leader. Bagger reached for the tea, but George pulled it away.

The rest of the crew stopped what they were doing and watched to see how Bagger would respond. Even Frederick paused in his writing and looked up from his notebook.

Bagger set down his ration.

"We've earned an answer," George said. "Thomas almost died on our mission, doing our job. The least you can do is tell us why."

"The boy's got a point," Mole said.

Bagger stared at George for a hard minute, then pushed away his plate. "Fine, but what I'm about to tell you doesn't leave this dugout, understand?"

George nodded, and the other boys gathered around the small table.

"That goes for all of you," Bagger added. "No one outside the tunneling crews can know. Not even the infantrymen hauling our spoil beyond the trenches. The success of our mission depends on its secrecy."

"We're digging behind enemy lines, aren't we?" Frederick asked. "So we can ambush them from behind?"

"Wrong again, Eton," Bagger said.

"Then what's our mission?" George asked.

Bagger waved the boys closer. "To earthquake the ridge."

"What's that mean?" Frederick asked.

"I know." Thomas looked at their crew leader. "We're not just digging galleries. We're digging mine chambers."

Bagger nodded.

Frederick adjusted his glasses. "I don't understand. I thought you said we're not mining for coal."

The mention of coal brought Thomas's thoughts back to Dover. He remembered watching Dad and James work, carefully pouring black powder into cartridges and inserting the cartridges into drill holes to blast the mine walls. "We're not," he answered. "We're digging mines to charge with explosives"—he locked eyes with Boomer—"beneath enemy lines."

Stunned by Thomas's statement, the boys looked to Bagger and the others for confirmation.

"The Germans hold Messines Ridge," Bagger explained. "They are completely entrenched on the higher ground. Our men don't stand a chance against such a fortified position. The army is depending on us to end this stalemate. It's gone on far too long and claimed far too many lives."

"Their trenches stretch on for miles," George said. "One mine of explosives isn't going to break their line."

"No," Mole said. "But twenty-four will."

"We're digging twenty-four mines?" Frederick asked.

"Us and twenty thousand other tunnelers," Bagger said. "We've got miners and sappers from all over Britain, as well as Canadian and Australian miners helping with the mission."

"I don't know about you chaps," George said, "but I'm not too comfortable putting my life in the hands of a bunch of saps."

Frederick shook his head. "Sappers are combat engineers," he said, correcting George before Mole could reply. "They specialize in fortification and demolition, and the British army has the best. We are fortunate to have them overseeing our work."

"You're right, Eton," George said. "We're so lucky to be digging their tunnels beneath an active battlefield."

"How close are we?" Thomas asked Mole before Frederick and George could get in yet another squabble.

"The mines have to be dug and packed to blow by early June."

Thomas paused in his petting of Max, who looked up at him from the comfort of Thomas's lap. "That's less than eight weeks away." Less than eight weeks to finish the mines, which meant less than two months to find James. "Are we using black powder or dynamite?" he asked Boomer, not happy about the prospect of working underground with either of the two unstable explosives, especially in galleries and mines that were periodically shelled with artillery fire.

"Neither. We're using ammonal. It's cheaper and more stable."

"How much?" Thomas asked.

"Close to one million."

"Pounds?" Thomas asked, unable to hide his shock.

Mole smiled and leaned back in his chair, resting his large feet on the edge of Frederick's bunk. "The Germans won't know what hit them."

"One million pounds?" Frederick asked. "That's almost five hundred tons of explosives! That's unheard of!"

"Yes, it is," Bagger said, "and we want to keep it that way

until we blow those mines. If the Germans suspect what we're up to, they'll rain hellfire on our heads before we finish digging."

"One million pounds," Frederick repeated, sitting down next to Charlie.

"Now do you understand why we keep our mouths shut about our mission?" Bagger asked. "If we succeed, we could change the course of the war."

Boomer laughed. "Who'd have thought the Great War would be in the filthy hands of a bunch of clay kickers and miners?"

"Certainly not any of your school chums, eh, Eton?" Mole tossed a biscuit at Frederick's chest. It bounced off and landed on the dugout floor. Max scurried off Thomas's lap and snatched it up before Frederick could retrieve it. "All these weeks you've been moping about, wishing you were on the front line, fighting like a real soldier. And all this time, you *were* a real soldier."

"I'm not a real soldier," Frederick said.

"Sure you are," Mole said. "We all are. We just can't tell anyone."

"We're secret soldiers," George said with a smile.

"And if we fail?" Charlie asked, speaking for the first time since they'd entered the dugout.

Bagger finished the last of his tea and placed his cup back on the table with a loud thud. "Failure is not our mission."

TWENTY-THREE

HIS CARETAKER'S hands became the only proof that a world existed beyond the darkness and silence. They soothed the young soldier when he woke in a cold sweat, screaming for help. They stayed to wipe his tears and hold his hand when he couldn't forget or stop crying.

After one such episode, the hands slowly unwound a strip of cloth encircling the soldier's head. Dull light filtered through his closed eyelids, and fingers gently pried open one eye and then the other. A blinding light flitted between them. The young soldier yanked his face away, and the bright light disappeared, but it took several minutes and many rapid blinks to clear the tears and spots crowding his vision. He shielded his stinging eyes with an unsteady hand to take in his surroundings for the first time.

Everything appeared unfocused, like the world had been

submerged in cloudy water, but the young soldier's weak eyes could make out shapes and shadows. Dozens of medical beds, identical to the one he lay on, crowded a narrow room with a vaulted ceiling. Patients occupied every bed. He didn't recognize the field hospital. Its stone walls didn't match his memory of the medical hospital behind Allied lines, where he'd often visited sick and wounded comrades. His heart raced. Where was he, and who had brought him to this strange place?

He squinted, trying to focus his vision enough to see anything familiar. The frightened eyes of the man in the next bed captured the young soldier's blurry gaze. Beefy red burns distorted the man's features, and the young soldier wondered if he'd known the man. Had they charged across no-man's-land together? Had he been standing near the man when the artillery shell hit?

The man spoke, but the soldier heard only the low buzzing always humming in his ears. He tried to read the man's charred, swollen lips, but their movement was too fast and frantic to follow.

I'm sorry, he mouthed, and then turned away, shaken by the thought that the artillery blast might have left him looking just as monstrous. He reached up and touched his face. His nose felt swollen and tender beneath his fingers, and a sticky trail of small, raised bumps ran across his forehead like tiny, crooked train tracks. He focused on the fuzzy silhouettes of nurses and doctors weaving between hospital beds, checking vitals and administering drugs in the form of pills and through syringes. His anxiety eased with the care with which the medics treated their patients. No matter where he was, he was in kind, capable hands.

A prism of soft light spilled through a window behind the soldier's bed. He lifted his arm and watched the rainbow of colors glide across his hand, and a weak smile twitched on his lips. He didn't know where he was or the extent of his injuries, but he did know one thing. He had crossed the dark abyss. He had survived no-man's-land, and once he fully regained his sight, hearing, and strength, he would never have to step foot on another battlefield. He would keep his promise and return home to his family.

No longer able to hold up his arm, he let it fall to his chest. A nurse rushed over, her brow lined with concern. He studied her as she checked his forehead. Dark shadows, hollowed from endless hours of caring for the injured, outlined kind hazel eyes in a soft, pretty face. Long blond hair hid in the coil of a tight bun tucked beneath her white nurse's cap. A few strands had fallen loose and hung down her slender neck in lazy curls. She smiled when she caught him staring. He knew he should look away. It was not polite to stare, but he couldn't stop. He was desperate to memorize every line and curve of her face, hoping it would join the others in his sleep. Praying it would bring him comfort in his nightmares.

Her lips moved. He shook his head and pointed to his

ears. Giving him an understanding pat on his shoulder, she took hold of his hand. He smiled, grateful for her kindness, but his smile fell when she reached for a needle. He shook his head.

"No!" The word clawed through his throat as he pulled his hand away. The nurse turned and called out to someone. Seconds later, a doctor grabbed hold of the soldier's arm and pinned it down. The soldier struggled to pull free, but the doctor tightened his grip. The young soldier stared up at the nurse, his eyes begging her not to put him back to sleep. With a sympathetic smile, she pressed the needle into a vein in his arm and depressed the plunger.

One heartbeat. Two heartbeats. Three.

The morphine loosened fear's grip on the soldier's muscles and tugged at his eyelids, dragging him back into the darkness. *At least this time,* the soldier thought, *I know I'm safe. Soon, I'll be better, and they'll let me go home to my family.*

Comforted by this thought, he stopped fighting sleep, but before his eyes fluttered closed, they landed on a medal pinned to the doctor's uniform. The young soldier's drugged mind screamed in recognition of its blackened center and silver trim. He had seen it on no-man's-land—pinned to the uniforms of the enemy. The Iron Cross.

TWENTY-FOUR

FOLLOWING THOMAS'S CLOSE call, Bagger had insisted the crew carry their gas masks in the galleries at all times. Before shifts, he ran drills to test how fast the boys could secure them. The masks were cumbersome. The eyepieces offered limited range of vision, and the heavy material, though effective at keeping out poisonous gas, also trapped the wearer's breath, turning the air inside the mask hot, humid, and foul. When not wearing the masks, the crew carried them in pouches strapped around their waists. The large pouches impeded their movement in the tight confines of the galleries. After Thomas's pouch caught on a beam and came unfastened during a shift, he tossed it in the corner, out of the way, but still in reach.

"Dover, where's your mask?" Bagger hissed in Thomas's ear.

Thomas pointed to the abandoned pack.

"Get it on, now."

"It's too big. It keeps falling off."

"Now," Bagger grunted before handing Thomas a full sandbag.

By early May, the Kruisstraat Four chamber was completed and charged, leaving only the Ontario Farm and Maedelstede Farm mines unfinished. After nearly two years of digging, the Allied tunnels spread out like fingers burrowing beneath the battlefield, the hands of the Grim Reaper, reaching for the enemy, waiting to deliver death's touch. The clock ticked down with every press of the spade. Second by second. Inch by inch. The crew clawed their way toward the enemy line. Always listening.

For the warning scratch of picks and the muffled voices of the enemy whispering orders in foreign tongues and digging toward their position.

For artillery fire that might tear through the fragile ceiling of dirt, sand, water, and clay above their heads.

For the hush of death that would suffocate Poppy's reassuring chirp and steal into their lungs on every labored breath.

They were grave diggers, but the farther they crept beneath no-man's-land, the deeper uncertainty crept into Thomas's weary mind. Were they digging their enemies' graves or their own? As they inched closer to the German trenches, he worried they were digging both.

. . .

The crew made good progress on the new gallery until late one shift when Bats heard the scratch of picks and the scrape of shovels on the other side of the wall where they were working.

"They're trying to undermine us," he whispered to Bagger. "If we keep on our projected path, they'll intercept us by the week's end."

"We'll angle our dig a bit higher," Bagger said, "but we have to stay in the clay and we have to gain enough distance to avoid a breakthrough, or we'll be fighting them in these here tunnels, which is a fight I'm not looking to have."

The rest agreed. Guns were not an option underground, where the firing of one bullet in such an enclosed space would put the whole crew in danger of carbon monoxide poisoning. Not even Mole, with all his big talk about what he'd do to the enemy should they ever come face-to-face, liked the idea of hand-to-hand combat in a dark space with barely enough room to swing a pick, much less a punch. They worked in tense silence, widening the distance between them and the sound of the Germans closing in on their position. After a couple of days, the scratch of enemy picks and the scrape of enemy shovels grew fainter. When Bats felt they'd evaded danger, they turned their tunnel forward again toward the enemy trenches.

After a week of digging, Bagger signaled them to stop. They were below enemy lines. He motioned for Mole to start widening the end of the gallery to carve out a chamber that, when finished, would be packed with explosives, creating a time bomb buried deep beneath the feet of the unsuspecting German soldiers huddled in their trenches.

While Bats listened for the enemy, Mole and Bagger worked the tunnel face, and Boomer and the boys removed bags of spoil and placed timber beams. Focusing on the top corners of the face, Mole kicked the spade into the clay and pressed down with his feet to work the clay free. As he pulled back, sand and water gushed from the narrow cut.

He scrambled up from his board. Everyone stopped their work and watched as Mole and Bagger rushed to plug the hole with the slab of clay they'd just removed, but wet sand continued to seep in around the edges of the cut.

Frederick dropped the beam he and George were carrying and stepped back as a growing puddle of water crept toward his stockinged feet.

In sharp, urgent hand gestures, Bagger signaled for Thomas and Charlie to bring him the full sandbag they'd been carrying to the shaft ladder.

Thomas and Charlie rushed forward with the bag, which Mole tore open. The kicker shoved two slabs of spoil into the boys' hands. "Plug the holes," he whispered.

The boys obeyed without question, frantically pressing chunks of clay into the widening cracks outlining the cut, but water and sand continued to leak from the tunnel face.

George and Frederick sprinted to the shaft to retrieve more bags to help. Hoisting two full bags of spoil they'd left by the ladder onto their shoulders, they hurried back, splashing through the rising water that was cresting above their ankles. They squeezed in beside Charlie and Thomas, dropped the bags at the tunnel face, and started packing the hole. Poppy chirped and flapped in her cage on the floor. Gently stroking the agitated canary's head, Charlie lifted her cage from the water and hung it from an exposed nail on the shaft's entrance before returning to help the other boys.

"It's not working," George whispered, as a jet of water sprayed out from the hole.

Max barked and bit at the stream.

Bagger scooped up Max and clamped a hand over the dog's muzzle. With Max silenced, Bagger removed his hand and motioned for the men in his crew to join him at the base of the shaft.

Thomas inched closer to overhear their urgent whispers.

"There's too much pressure behind those leaks," Mole said. "Packing them with clay is a temporary fix at best."

"The section's a loss," Boomer added. "Even if we stop the flow, we can't dig any farther. We angled too high and broke back through the water table."

Bagger kicked at the water creeping up the cuffs of his trousers. "So we abandon the chamber?"

"Not until we stop the water," Boomer said. "If we don't, this whole gallery will flood."

"We've got to dam it," Bats said. "We'll need enough bags to wall off the face."

Scratching his mustache, Bagger glanced back to where the other boys stood at the tunnel face as he considered the men's assessment of the situation. Inhaling deeply, he nodded and then signaled to the men to climb the shaft to the upper gallery to fetch more filled sandbags. Once Mole, Bats, and Boomer had started their ascent, Bagger grabbed hold of the ladder to heft himself onto the bottom rung. Thomas moved to follow, but the crew leader held up a hand to stop him. With Max tucked under one arm, Bagger shook his head, jabbed a finger at Thomas and then pointed toward the other boys waiting at the tunnel face before pressing the finger to his lips. Though he didn't speak a word, his orders were clear. Thomas and the boys were to stay in the chamber and keep the leaks as contained as possible, and they were to do so quietly.

Max whimpered as Bagger hauled the dog up the shaft and into the upper gallery. Thomas watched with envy. He'd been caught before in a gallery that flooded back in Dover. It was not an experience he wished to repeat. Water was unforgiving in mines.

When Thomas rejoined the boys at the tunnel face, Frederick lifted a soaked foot from the rising water. "So much for keeping our feet dry," he whispered to Thomas.

Thomas didn't answer. Wet feet were the least of their worries. With the chamber flooded, they'd wasted days, if not weeks, of digging, but if they lost the gallery too, they'd be pushed further behind a deadline they were already struggling to meet. He passed Frederick another slab of clay, which Frederick pressed into a new crack. The plug held, and Frederick stepped back to scan the wall for any other leaks. Only the hole George struggled to plug remained.

Charlie handed George the last slab in his sandbag. George pressed it into the growing cracks, but the water pressure eroded the edges. Chunks of clay broke free, and water gushed from a gaping hole, soaking his shirt and trousers. "Mouse!" he whispered through clenched teeth. "Tell Bagger we need those bags now!"

Charlie hurried over to the shaft, but hesitated at the bottom of the ladder.

Thomas grabbed George's arm. He knew if the wall broke, the chamber and gallery would flood in seconds. They needed to escape before it was too late. He pulled on George's arm and pointed to the shaft ladder, but George yanked his arm free and covered as much of the hole as he could with his hands. "Go," he mouthed to Thomas. "Help Mouse." He looked to Frederick. "You too."

Frederick squeezed in beside him and covered the rest of the hole with his hands. "This is no time to play the hero, George," he whispered. "You need our help, or this wall will fall."

"I don't need help," George said, his whispers growing in volume and annoyance. "What I need is you to get those bloody bags down—"

Before he could finish, the crumbling tunnel face collapsed. Water and sand surged through the opening, knocking the boys off their feet. Thomas tumbled end over end and slammed into one of the beams lining the tunnel wall. The force knocked the air from his lungs. He opened his eyes and tried to get his bearings, but the water had doused all light and sound in the tunnel. Finding his footing, he pushed off the floor, praying to find an air pocket near the ceiling.

TWENTY-FIVE

BARELY SIX INCHES remained between the tunnel ceiling and rising water. Thomas lifted his chin as high as he could and took a deep breath before his heavy clothes dragged him under again. He kicked harder, propelling himself upward to keep his face above the water. Unable to see in the darkness, he screamed for the others. "Charlie! Frederick!"

"I'm here," Frederick whispered, his voice so close Thomas flinched. "You shouldn't scream. The Germans could hear you."

"Who cares? If they blast their way into this tunnel, they'll drown with us," Thomas said.

"Fair point. Can you swim?"

"Yes," Thomas answered, thankful for the summer days James and he had snuck into St. Margaret's Bay, where James taught Thomas how to swim. He kicked to keep his face in the shrinking pocket of air, and his nose scraped against a beam in the ceiling. He knew he should swim for the ladder, but he couldn't leave the others behind. "Can you?"

"Yes, and I can still stand." Frederick pushed up on the tips of his toes to keep his face in the pocket. "But we've got to get out of this chamber before it fills."

"Where are George and Charlie?" Thomas asked, angling his head to lift an ear from the water to hear Frederick's response.

"Charlie!" Frederick yelled, no longer worried about the enemy hearing. "George!"

The sound of loud, panicked splashing drew the boys' heads in the direction of what had been the tunnel face.

"Over here!" George yelled.

His reply was echoed in the opposite direction, by the shaft. "Help!" Charlie called out with a gurgled plea. "Help!"

"Get George," Thomas ordered Frederick, realizing the Eton student's size would help in rescuing George. "I'll help Charlie."

With no time and little air left to argue, Frederick swam in the direction of George's voice, careful to keep his arms stretched out in front of him, so he wouldn't run face-first into George or a fallen beam. When his hands found George, Frederick lifted his face to the ceiling for air. "This way. Follow my voice." He started back in the direction of the shaft, but George didn't move.

"Come on!" Frederick yelled.

George answered from the darkness. "I can't swim, and even if I could, half the tunnel face is on my right foot."

"You're stuck?"

The frustrated sigh that followed felt heavier in the darkness.

"Right," Frederick said. "I'll swim down and see if I can free it."

George struggled to keep his face in the shrinking pocket of air. "Hurry. I can't stretch any higher, and this water is rising fast."

Frederick ducked beneath the water. His hands followed the line of George's leg until they reached the mound of clay and sand pinning George's foot to the floor. He dug around his leg but couldn't remove enough to free George. Unable to hold his breath any longer, he resurfaced. "I need to get help."

"There's no time. You *are* the help." Water lapped over George's lips, and he began to choke. "Try again," he said between coughs.

"The water's coming too fast." Frederick looked back in the direction of the shaft. In school, he'd been taught that junior officers were the first over the top and the last to retreat, but Frederick had no choice: George needed more help than he could offer, and if he stayed, they'd both drown. "Keep trying to work your foot free. I have to get help."

"No!" George lunged in the direction of Frederick's voice. "Please don't leave me here!" His fingers grasped at Frederick's shirt, but Frederick splashed out of reach. "Eton!"

"I'm sorry. I can't do it by myself. I'll be back with help. I promise."

As Frederick swam back to the shaft, he heard George scream one word.

"Coward!"

And then he heard nothing at all.

. . .

At the other end of the tunnel, Thomas had freed Poppy from her submerged birdcage and swum for the shaft, where Charlie stood on the third rung of the ladder. "Take her," Thomas said, handing Charlie the canary.

Clinging to the ladder with one hand, Charlie stroked Poppy's wet feathers, and the little bird released a string of loud chirps. As Thomas turned back toward the tunnel face, Frederick lunged from the water with a desperate gasp and grabbed hold of the ladder.

Hunched over and pulling in fast, greedy breaths, he pointed back down the tunnel. "George's foot is trapped. Hurry."

Before Thomas or Charlie could respond, Frederick dove back under.

"Go up and get Bagger and the others," Thomas told Charlie. "Tell them George is in trouble." Taking a deep breath, he followed Frederick.

When they found George, he was no longer fighting to get free. The chamber had flooded, and his body floated motionless beneath Thomas's hands. Thomas feared they were too late.

Pushing the thought aside, Thomas dove down and clawed at the clay trapping George's foot, tearing away chunks and pushing aside heavy slabs while Frederick pulled at George's leg, moving it back and forth to help dislodge it. Thomas's chest burned. Frederick and he would need air soon, but to get any, they'd have to swim back to the ladder, and any chance of saving George would be lost.

Thomas dug faster and harder, ignoring the cramping in his muscles. Though he couldn't see Frederick, he could feel his frantic tugs on George's leg. Just as Thomas began to fear all three of them would drown under no-man's-land, he felt the clay around George's leg give way. So did Frederick, who yanked the leg free. Wasting no time, the boys grabbed George's limp arms and kicked with their waning strength for the ladder.

When the two boys reached the rungs, pulling George along with them, large hands grabbed hold of their arms and hauled all three of them up the ladder. Mole laid George's unconscious body on the floorboards of the upper gallery. George's head hit the board with a dull thud. Clutching Poppy, Charlie winced at the sound, but George did not move.

. . .

George's last word echoed in Frederick's memory. George was right. He was a coward. A real soldier would have fought harder to free George's foot before the water filled the mine. A real soldier would have stayed with his comrade until help arrived. A real soldier would have stayed even if help had never arrived. But Frederick was no real soldier.

He backed away from the group while the others huddled around Mole. The clay kicker took George by the shoulders and shook him. "Come on, Shillings! Wake up!"

George's head lolled to the side. His eyes remained closed, and his lips fell open.

"Is he breathing?" Bagger asked.

Mole placed a large hand on George's chest and shook his head.

Holding Poppy, Charlie began to pace while Thomas stood behind Mole, clutching his medals and whispering the Our Father.

"Come on, George," Bats whispered. "Breathe."

Mole and Bagger each grabbed one of George's arms and legs. Holding his limp body between them, they lifted his legs toward the ceiling, so his head hung just above the floor. Securing their grip, they shook George up and down three or four times. "You're a scrapper, Shillings!" Mole said. "You're not going to let a little water claim you, are you? Bloody breathe!" He pounded a fist on George's chest.

The jostling shook water and sand free from George's mouth and nose. He suddenly sucked in a sharp breath, and his eyes sprang open. He coughed violently, choking on the sand and water swamping his lungs. Mole and Bagger quickly eased him onto the floor, and Thomas sank against the wall.

"That's it, Shillings," Mole said, slapping his back. "You're all right."

George continued to cough, spewing water on the floor-boards. "What happened?" he asked, when at last he found his breath.

"The tunnel face collapsed and trapped your foot," Thomas said. "We thought you'd drowned."

"You did drown," Bagger said. "When we pulled you from the mine, you were as lifeless as a corpse. But it takes more than a little water to stop us, eh, Shillings?"

"You're lucky your mates got you out when they did," Boomer added, mussing up George's hair.

George's accusing gaze found Frederick standing back against the wall. "Yeah. Lucky."

TWENTY-SIX

BAGGER ORDERED GEORGE to rest in the dugout while he and the others began the difficult task of sealing off the flooded chamber and section of the gallery with sandbags and a dam of steel mesh and concrete. Aside from Mole telling the boys the job would take several shifts and the help of rotating crews to complete, no one spoke as they worked. When the next crew arrived, Bagger and the other men headed into the trenches, while the boys shuffled back to the dugout. George was sleeping quietly when they arrived, so they ate in silence, too exhausted to form thoughts or words, and then they retired to their bunks.

Thomas woke an hour later to the creak of George lowering himself off his bunk and the padding of his stockinged feet leaving the dugout. When George didn't return after five minutes—the time it usually took him to smoke a cigarette—Thomas rolled off his bunk and went looking for him. He found George just outside the tunnel entrance, seated on the ground with his bony knees pulled to his chest and his face cradled in his hands.

Thomas took a tentative step toward him. "George? Everything all right?"

George lifted his head and looked up at Thomas. The confident smirk that normally curled his freckled lips sagged, and the mischievous glint that always shone from his green eyes had dimmed. "I'm alive, which is as good as it gets out here, eh, Tommy?" He took a cigarette and match from his pocket. Cuts and splinters from clawing at the timbers in his desperate attempt to escape the flooded tunnel covered his hands. On his right hand, the nail of his pointer finger was missing. He tried to strike the match against a floorboard but dropped it when his raw fingers grated against the wood.

Thomas picked up the match, struck it on a beam, and lit George's cigarette.

George took a long drag and let his head fall back against the sandbags. "Thanks."

"What are you doing out here?" Thomas asked, sitting down beside him.

George stared unblinking at the opposite wall. "I couldn't sleep, and that is crazy because I don't think I've ever been more tired, which if you knew my life, is saying a lot."

"It's not crazy. After my carbon monoxide poisoning, I couldn't sleep either," Thomas admitted. "I was afraid if I closed my eyes, I'd never wake up. I guess it's normal to fear death. Everyone does."

"Not me." No pride or arrogance bolstered George's claim. He stated the words as calmly as if he'd just told Thomas the sky was blue. "Only people like you, who have something to lose, fear death."

Thomas remembered the small potato he'd carried in his pocket from Dover to Trafalgar Square on the day he'd met George. If George hadn't convinced him to meet Norton-Griffith's recruiter, Thomas might have starved on the streets of London. "I'm a coal miner from Dover. I've never had much to lose."

The tip of George's cigarette glowed bright red as he pulled another drag deep into his lungs. "You have everything, and you don't even know it. You should go home to your family while you still can. Leave before this war kills you, Thomas."

George's use of his real name cut through Thomas with a chill, more disturbing than his warning of the possibility that the war would claim his life. He clutched his saints medals. He wanted to believe they would keep him safe and help him find James, but each night in the tunnels and every day in the trenches carved away at the foundation of his faith, inch by inch, until all that remained now was a gutted hole, cold and empty. He traced the raised image of Saint Joseph with his thumb. "I can't. Not until I've found my brother."

George turned to Thomas. "You've almost died twice already. What if you coming here to find your brother ends with your parents mourning two sons?"

Thomas shook his head. "It won't. I *will* find him. And I *won't* die."

"And if you don't find him? And if you do die?"

The questions had scratched at Thomas's thoughts night and day since Johnny had shown him the bodies of missing soldiers strewn across no-man's-land, but hearing them spoken aloud by George gave his own doubts a voice he could no longer dismiss or ignore.

"You know the chances of your brother having survived this war are about as good as our chances of surviving it," George said, "which, if you haven't noticed, are getting slimmer by the minute."

Thomas tucked the medals under his shirt. "I have to find him, George."

George sighed. "I know, and I hope you do."

Silence hung between them like the smoke lingering around George's head.

Thomas combed his fingers through his hair. "What about you? Isn't there anyone in London wondering where you are?"

"Aside from the men I owe money?" George shook his head. "No. I'm sure no one's even noticed I'm gone. You could have let me drown in that tunnel today, and no one would have mourned my death."

An aftershock of the panic Thomas had felt when Mole had said George wasn't breathing shuddered through him. He'd come to not only rely on George, but to trust him with his life. "That's not true."

"That's nice of you to say, but let's be honest, if I die under this godforsaken battlefield, no brother will come looking for me. No father will bring my body home. No mother will cry over my grave. I will leave this world the same way I came into it, forgotten." His voice weakened as the truth in his words settled heavy around them. "But in the end, aren't we all."

"You won't be forgotten," Thomas said as George stubbed out his cigarette. "I promise."

"Don't make promises you can't keep, Tommy. Even in our crew, I wouldn't be missed. Blimey, Eton would probably do a jig on my grave."

"Frederick doesn't hate you as much as you think," Thomas said. "If he did, he wouldn't have helped save you today."

George chuckled, but there was no hint of humor in the sound. "Save me? How? By abandoning me in a flooded chamber and telling you I was trapped as he scurried up the ladder like the rat he is?"

"Frederick didn't abandon you. He was the one who helped me free your leg and swim you to the ladder."

George stared at Thomas as though he were waiting for the punch line. "Wait. You're serious? Eton came back for me?"

Thomas nodded. "I told you, if you'd died, you'd have been missed, even by Frederick."

George shook his head in disbelief. "Tommy, you and I both know, whether I survive this war or not, when it's all over, everyone will go back to their lives and families and not spare another thought on me."

“That’s not true.” Thomas looked George in the eyes. “I promise.”

“Do you promise to have a memorial made for me if I don’t survive this bloody war?”

“You’re not going to die.”

“Answer the question, Tommy.”

“Yes, I promise to make a memorial for you.”

“Really? And what name will you write on it?”

“George.”

“George what?”

Thomas started to answer and then stopped. When George decided to join Norton-Griffith’s recruits, he’d told the man in the bowler hat his name was Georgie Porgie. They’d had a good laugh at the joke at the time, but Thomas no longer found it funny. The truth was, he didn’t know George’s real last name. No one did. Not even George.

TWENTY-SEVEN

"**DO YOU KNOW** your name?" a voice thick with a German accent asked. Fingers snapped inches from the young soldier's ear. "Can you hear me?"

The soldier pretended not to hear the sharp sound or the doctor's questions. The constant ringing in his ears had gradually quieted over his weeks spent in the German field hospital. Its absence had revealed other sounds.

The steady clomp of military boots on the stone floor.

The scrape of medical instruments on metal trays.

The anemic, rattling coughs of gas victims.

The terrified screams of patients in the throes of night terrors.

The soft, soothing hum of his nurse as she changed his bandages.

Voices with different accents—British, French, Canadian,

Belgian, Australian—crying out from their beds, begging for help.

The young soldier stared at the hospital bed to his right and the sheet draped over the face of the man lying there. The Australian soldier was the bed's eighth occupant since the young soldier had realized the hands that were nursing him back to health were not friendly. As the doctor continued to ask him questions and he continued to feign deafness, two medics removed the body, and a nurse changed the sheets in preparation for the bed's next occupant.

The German doctor leaned closer and asked his questions again, this time slower and louder, but the young soldier wasn't listening. His thoughts were with the dead Australian. Would his body be returned to his troops to be transported home for a proper burial? Or would it be hastily dumped in an unmarked grave on foreign soil or discarded like rubbish in a field for wild animals to find?

These thoughts had become as routine as the nurse checking his vitals and the doctor asking him questions, and just like the seven times before, his wondering about the fate of the former occupant of the bed to his right led him to ponder his own fate should he die as a prisoner of war. He knew he'd taken a risk volunteering to fight in the war, but he'd assumed that should he die in battle, his remains would be recovered by his comrades and returned to his family, who would bury him near the cliffs of Dover, where they could visit his grave.

The thought, though frightening, had given him a small sense of peace about his decision. That sense of peace no longer existed.

A primal scream ricocheted off the stone walls of the church the Germans had converted into a hospital. The young soldier's head snapped in the direction of the scream.

Four beds over, a Canadian soldier, the victim of a mustard-gas attack, had bolted upright in bed. His arms swung out wildly, striking a nurse who'd been treating the pus-yellow boils covering his arms and face. The impact of the strike threw her to the ground.

"Over the top, boys!" the patient screamed, climbing off the bed.

The young soldier had heard talk of soldiers whose bodies returned from battle, but not their minds. There was little help and even less sympathy for those suffering shell shock. Watching the Canadian belly-crawl between two beds, the young soldier was certain the other man's wide, unblinking eyes no longer saw a hospital room. He saw no-man's-land, and he was fighting for his life.

The doctor rushed forward with a syringe of morphine to sedate the Canadian. The prisoner lunged at him, and chaos erupted as they wrestled for the needle. With another guttural scream, the prisoner threw the doctor to the floor. Medical staff rushed to help their injured colleagues and calm agitated patients. The prisoner plowed through the main aisle knocking over everyone and everything in his path. A German officer stood at the church's one exit, blocking the man's escape.

"Halt!" he ordered as the prisoner barreled toward him. He pulled a revolver from the holster hugging his chest and aimed.

"No!" the young soldier screamed as the shot punctured the bedlam in the hospital.

The prisoner's head jerked back, and his body collapsed in a heap on the floor. His boil-covered face came to rest at a crooked angle. Blood pooled around his head, and his lifeless eyes stared at the young soldier, burning in his memory, joining the others.

TWENTY-EIGHT

FOLLOWING A RESTLESS six hours of sleep, riddled with nightmares of flooded galleries and nameless graves, Thomas pulled on his boots and stood to join Charlie, Max, and George for their daily search of the trenches before their next shift. They were exiting the dugout when George stopped at the doorway. "You coming, Eton?"

The men looked up from their card game. Their curious gazes traveled from George to Frederick, seated on his bunk. Charlie braced himself for the snide remark Frederick would make before returning to his writing, but Frederick closed his book and silently followed George out of the tunnels.

No more invitations were extended after the first. None were needed. Charlie drew an extra sketch of James, and Frederick joined the boys every morning on their search of the trenches. After their first outing together, he brought along his notebook and jotted down information he thought might be important.

When the boys returned to their dugout after their third outing, Frederick reviewed his notes. "From the soldiers we've questioned, we can rule out James being along this stretch of the front any time after their arrival in December."

"Of the soldiers we've talked to," George said, pulling up a chair next to Thomas at the table. He handed Thomas a cup of tea.

"We've talked to hundreds," Thomas said. He knew George was trying to help; they all were, but Thomas didn't want to talk about their failed search for his brother. He wanted to curl up on his bunk with Max and wallow in his despair. He wished Bagger and the men hadn't taken the terrier into the trenches for some friendly wagers. Petting Max always calmed his nerves when panic at the thought of never finding James overwhelmed him.

"But there are thousands we haven't talk to yet," Frederick said. "Hundreds of thousands." Frederick had only been helping them look for five days. Reality hadn't loosened his grip on hope like it had Thomas's. Miles of trenches and hundreds of discouraging answers had only served to pull James farther from Thomas's reach.

. . .

George understood Thomas's disappointment, but he also knew wallowing in despair helped nothing. If he'd given in every time life kicked him in the teeth, he would have died years ago. He slung a bony arm around Thomas's shoulders. "You know what you need?"

"To find my brother," Thomas muttered.

"Besides that." George retrieved a small leather cup and three six-sided dice from his kit bag. "You need to relax for a couple hours." He shook the dice in the cup and then tossed them onto the table. "We all do. Get down here, Mouse. We need your artistic skills."

Charlie closed the door to Poppy's cage and lowered himself from his bunk into an empty chair next to Thomas.

"You too, Eton," George said. "And bring that fancy fountain pen of yours and one of those handkerchiefs you use to polish your boots."

Frederick closed his notebook and joined them at the table. "What are we playing?"

"Crown and anchor."

"The army doesn't allow that game. What about Bagger and the others?" Frederick asked.

"If they catch us, they'll probably ask to play. Give me your pen and handkerchief."

With some hesitance, Frederick passed George both items.

George drew a long rectangle on the cloth.

Frederick groaned. "I'll never get that out."

"Settle down, Eton," George said, drawing another long line to divide the rectangle in half and then three vertical lines to separate the rectangle into six even sections. "It's not like you don't have a half dozen more in your kit bag."

"Wait. You looked through my bag?"

"That's not the point, Eton. The point is you can spare one." George then passed the handkerchief and pen to Charlie. "Mouse, I need you to draw the symbols on the dice in the squares."

Charlie picked up one of the dice. Crudely carved symbols marked each side. A heart, a club, a diamond, a spade, a crown, and an anchor. He copied one into each of the squares on the handkerchief and handed it back to George.

"Perfect," George said. "Do any of you know how to play?"

The boys shook their heads.

"Not even you, Eton?"

"No."

"What *do* they teach you in that fancy school of yours?" George asked.

"Not illegal dice games."

"Well, they should. It could save your life." He held up his left hand and wiggled his fingers. "If it weren't for crown and anchor, I'd be five fingers shy of a handshake."

"Crown and anchor saved your fingers?" Frederick asked, unable to hide the skepticism in his voice.

"Sure did. After I'd escaped my job at the factory, I wandered down to the docks and talked my way into a game one of the managers was running out of his warehouse. The first few rounds didn't go my way, and unfortunately, I'd exaggerated by a smidge how much money I had on me."

"How much did you say you had?" Charlie asked.

"Five pounds."

"Five pounds!" Thomas asked. "How much did you actually have?"

"Four pence."

Thomas laughed. "You thought you could bluff your way into a game with dockworkers with four pence?"

"I *did* bluff my way into a game with dockworkers with four pence. My plan was to win enough that they'd never discover my lie, but my first few wagers didn't go well, and when the man running the table learned I couldn't settle my bets, he threatened to take my hand to teach me a lesson."

"How'd you get out of it?" Charlie asked.

"Convinced him to let me play one more round, double or nothing."

"You bet both your hands?" Thomas asked.

George glanced over at him. "I had nothing left to lose."

"You had your hands to lose," Frederick pointed out.

"But I didn't lose, did I? Walked away with all ten fingers *and* ten crowns that night. Played so well, the owner gave me work and let me sleep in his warehouse. Crown and anchor kept me from starving for a few months. So you see, Eton, crown and anchor could save your hand or life someday, so pay attention." He then explained the rules and declared he would be the banker and toss the dice for each round of play. The boys bet on each toss by placing coins on the symbols Charlie had drawn. As they played, they talked about everything—from what they thought the older crew members' real names were to which nurses at the ADS were the prettiest.

"Confession time, boys," George said, clearing the board of the winnings and losses. "What are your real birthdays? You first, Mouse."

"October 12, 1902."

"How about you, Eton?"

"December 6, 1901."

"I've got you by five months," George said. "Mine's July 24, 1901. At least that's what Miss Wachonick at the orphanage claimed it was. For all I know, I could be older than Bagger."

"No one's older than Bagger," Charlie said.

Thomas laughed. It felt almost normal, but the moment of joy was quickly replaced by guilt. He shouldn't be playing games or laughing. He should be looking for his brother.

George collected the dice and dropped them in the leather cup while the boys placed new bets. "Bagger claiming to be under forty years old is almost as believable as Thomas claiming to be eighteen. Fess up, Tommy. What's your birthday? And don't give us that line you tried on the recruiting officer at Trafalgar Square." George stood up from his chair, squared his shoulders, and gave a crooked salute. "Timothy Bennett. March the first, 1602, sir."

Everyone but Thomas laughed. "My birthday's May 17, 1903."

"May 17?" Frederick retrieved his notebook and opened to the page he'd been writing on when George called him over. He pointed to the top right corner. "That's today!"

"Tommy! It's your birthday?"

Thomas shrugged. "I guess. It's hard to keep track of days down here."

"Happy birthday, Thomas," Charlie said.

Frederick quickly calculated the numbers in his head. "You're fourteen today."

"Not so loud," Thomas said, his eyes darting to the doorway.

"Just think, Tommy," George said with a wink. "In four short years, you'll be eligible to join the army!"

The boys laughed again.

"Shut up and roll," Thomas said, unable to hold back a smile.

With a flick of his wrist, George tossed the dice onto the table. "Now that we've established that I am the oldest of our little crew, I believe that means I outrank you all."

Frederick shook his head. "That's not how seniority in the military works."

George passed Charlie three pence for his winning bet and collected the others' losses. "Maybe not for the common soldier, but we're not common soldiers, are we?" He shook the dice with a mischievous smile that crinkled the corners of his eyes. "We're *secret* soldiers. We make our own rules, and I rule that as oldest, I deserve a promotion."

"What kind of promotion?" Charlie asked. "Officer commanding?"

"No, I was thinking higher than OC."

"How much higher?" Thomas asked. "Commanding officer?"

George drummed his fingers on the table. "CO George does have a nice ring to it, but as the oldest of our crew, I deserve the highest rank."

"Field marshal?" Frederick asked.

"I was thinking more along the lines of king."

"King George?" Frederick chuckled. "Britain already has one of those, and I don't think he'll be abdicating his throne to you."

"King George the Fifth can keep his throne and rule aboveground. I'll rule beneath it." George ran a hand through his ginger curls. "I've always thought I'd look good with a crown."

"There isn't a crown large enough to fit your big head," Thomas teased.

"Blasphemy!" George yelled, throwing one of the dice at Thomas.

Thomas dodged the first die, but the second struck him between the eyes.

George readied the last die. "You will not insult your king, peasant."

Thomas held up his hands in surrender. "My apologies, Your Majesty."

"If you're to be king, you do need a crown," Frederick said. "Mouse, is there anything left in that Maconochie tin?"

Charlie grabbed the can next to him and looked inside. "No."

"Toss it here."

Charlie passed him the can that had contained the crew's dinner, a beef stew of thin gravy, sliced turnips, carrots, and, if a soldier was lucky, a few chunks of fatty meat. Frederick held the tin above George's head. "I, Frederick Chamberlain the Third, one hundred and fifteenth in line to the throne—"

George glanced up at him. "Seriously?"

"Yes, and don't interrupt during a coronation. It's uncouth."

"I'll give you uncouth," George mumbled.

Frederick cleared his throat. "I, Frederick Chamberlain the Third, one hundred and fifteenth in line to the throne of Britain, crown you George, King of the Secret Soldiers." With an exaggerated flourish, he placed the soup can on George's head.

The small battered tin rested at an angle in George's hair, and a drop of soup dribbled down the side of George's face.

"Told you no crown would fit," Thomas said.

Ignoring Thomas's comment and the chunk of pale orange carrot sliding down his cheek, George puffed out his chest and lifted his head with an absurdly regal air. "Aren't you supposed to bow to me now?"

Thomas bent forward, nearly brushing the floor with his hands. "Long live King George!"

"Long live King George!" Frederick and Charlie echoed between laughs.

TWENTY-NINE

AS TALKATIVE AS he was after their shifts, following his near-drowning George didn't speak a word while working in the galleries. His silence crept beneath Thomas's skin. When George was calm and comfortable enough to talk about everything from the woman with eleven fingers he'd met in London to the size and smell of his last bowel movement, Thomas's anxiousness about being back in the tunnels decreased—at least a little. But George's silence left too much space in Thomas's thoughts. Space that fear, guilt, and grief eagerly filled. The unwelcome emotions dragged Thomas back to his conversation with George outside the tunnels.

As tough as it had been to hear, George had been right. In Thomas's determination to find James, he'd given little thought to how his leaving would hurt his mum and dad and even less consideration to what would happen to them if, like James,

Thomas never returned. The thought of dying beneath no-man's-land, never to be found, terrified Thomas, but knowing his parents were thinking of him, even if they didn't know where he was, gave him a small sense of peace. When fear kept him awake, he pictured his mum kneeling beside her bed, saying her rosary and praying for his safe return. But what had Thomas left behind for his mum to calm *her* fears? When she closed her eyes, she had only her imagination to fill in the many blanks he'd left, and Thomas knew how cruel imagination could be when stoked by fear.

After the flooding scare, every time the crew descended beneath no-man's-land, Thomas remembered when he and James used to compete to see who could hold their breath the longest underwater. Time slowed when you were a breath away from death. Seconds felt like minutes, and minutes like hours. The crew's eight-hour-shift felt like an eternity. By the hunch of George's shoulders, Thomas knew he wasn't alone in his dread.

To avoid another flooding, the crew was forced to dig lower to get beneath the wet-sand layer while carving out a new gallery and chamber. With their deadline looming, they doubled their efforts, muscling through the constant pain burning and twisting in their backs and shoulders.

Explosions trembled through the tunnel's walls and ceiling. Clods of dirt and clay shook loose between the timbers and pelted their helmets. Thomas tried not to think about the shells hitting above their gallery or about how his decision to come to the Western Front might cause his parents to lose both their sons. Instead, he focused on his work.

Push, pull, bag, drag, raise.

The crew fell into the rhythm of their choreographed dance.

Push, pull, bag, drag, raise.

Push.

Push.

Mole's large boots pressed against the spade, but it wouldn't slide all the way into the clay. "Must have hit a rock," Mole whispered, retracting the spade and placing it lower on the tunnel face. "I'll try to get beneath it." He motioned for Thomas to help.

Thomas moved into position.

Push.

The spade slid into the clay with ease. Mole pressed down with his heels to work the rock free. "It's a big one," he whispered, wiggling the spade up and down as he slowly extracted it from the wall.

Thomas grabbed a short slab of clay from the spade and handed it to Bagger, who placed it in a sandbag. Thomas then reached into the narrow hole with both hands. His fingers jammed against something hard.

"Do you feel it?" Bagger mouthed.

Thomas nodded.

"Can you work your fingers around it?" Mole whispered.

Thomas nodded again. The clay encasing the rock squished

beneath Thomas's fingers, so he dug them in deeper to strengthen his hold. He tried pulling the rock out, but it wouldn't budge, so Mole carefully carved around Thomas's arms and hands, widening the hole, while Bagger removed the clumps of clay holding the rock in place.

The men stepped back, and Thomas wedged his feet against the wall and pulled back on the rock. After several unsuccessful tugs, he looked at Bagger and shook his head. Bagger signaled for Charlie to bring him a light. Charlie scrambled over, lantern in hand. Thomas pulled his arms from the opening, and Bagger held the lantern up to the hole.

Thomas ducked beneath the lantern and peered into the opening. It took several impatient seconds for his eyes to adjust to the darkness after the glare of the lantern. As his vision continued to adjust, the darkness separated into varied shades of gray, and outlines took shape.

Thomas squinted, straining to make sense of the shapes, but his mind couldn't puzzle the pieces together. In all his years in the mines, he'd never seen a rock like this before. He waved the light closer.

Bagger adjusted the lantern. Light and shadow swept through the opening, casting movement over the wide curves, sharp corners, and flat holes of the rock. When the swing of the lantern settled, a shaft of light cut above Thomas's head into the opening, sending the shadows on the rock scattering, and the pieces fell into place.

Thomas scrambled back from the wall, knocking Bagger over. Mole reached down to help Bagger up, and the others gathered around.

"What's wrong, Tommy?" George whispered.

Thomas couldn't speak. He couldn't breathe. He needed air. Pushing past George, he sprinted to the shaft and upper galleries. Dan's words echoed in his mind with each panicked step.

If we don't bury our dead, the war will, and us with them.

Thomas stumbled out of the tunnels and into the support trench. And then he vomited.

Back in the gallery, George grabbed the lantern and peered into the opening. "Oh, no," he whispered as the light fell upon the object they'd mistaken for a rock.

A dented helmet.

Cracked goggles.

A gas mask.

And tufts of blond hair. The same shade as Thomas's.

THIRTY

TIME, FOR THE young soldier, dissolved in a haze of drug-induced sleep and paralyzing flashbacks. He could no longer measure its passing in minutes, days, weeks, and months. He marked it by the only constants in his life: morphine injections, recurring nightmares, nurses' shifts, and the changing faces of the occupants in the beds surrounding him. A few of the occupants recovered enough to be transferred to prisoner of war camps, but most lay behind the field hospital, in shallow unmarked graves.

The young soldier had been in the German field hospital for nineteen new faces when he woke from another nightmare about his first night in the trenches and found himself staring into the terrified eyes of the twentieth new face. Bandages hid most of twenty's features, as well as his small body, but his messy black hair and dark eyes, swimming with tears, sparked memories of the last time the soldier had seen another young boy with a headful of cowlicks, crying and waving goodbye from the platform of a train station.

Twenty, noticing the soldier staring at him, reached out a bandaged hand and spoke in a hoarse, hurried whisper. The young soldier did not know the French words spilling from the prisoner of war's trembling lips, but he had no trouble interpreting their shaky, hitched delivery. The boy was in terrible pain and very scared. The faster he spoke, the more his tears flowed, until they choked off his voice completely. His wide eyes locked on the young soldier's face. The boy's chest heaved in panicked breaths.

The young soldier stretched out his hand and took hold of the boy's exposed fingers.

THIRTY-ONE

AN HOUR LATER, the crew had removed the body from the tunnel, and the boys went looking for Thomas. When they didn't find him in the dugout, George asked Bagger if they could take Max for walk.

"Find Tommy, Max!" George said when they exited the tunnels. The terrier raced through the communication trench past the reserve trenches toward the fields behind the Allied lines. When the boys caught up to Max, he was curled up in Thomas's lap beneath the elm tree where they'd buried Feathers. The month of May had ushered in warmer temperatures and sunny skies that coaxed thousands of poppies from the fertile ground. The small red flowers carpeted the field. Thomas petted the dog's head in distracted, halfhearted strokes. His hand paused between the terrier's ears when he heard the boys approaching.

"It's not James," Charlie said, sitting down next to him.

Thomas picked at the clumps of blue clay clinging to the worn knit of his soiled socks. "I know. But for a moment I thought—"

Frederick sat to his other side. "Bagger notified the Fiftieth that we'd found one of their men. They helped remove the body, and their corporals identified the soldier."

"It was a bloke from Alnwick," George added.

Thomas's shoulders sagged with relief. "But it could have been James. He could be buried under that battlefield, and if he is, I'll never find him." Tears slid down his cheeks. Embarrassed that the others were seeing him cry, he tried to wipe them away, but they only came faster, so he gave up and let Max lick them from his face. "James never should have joined this stupid war. He should have stayed home. Our parents and sisters needed him. I needed him. And now I'll never see him again."

Charlie reached up and rubbed his brow to shield his own tears from the others. He was no better than Thomas's brother. No, he was worse. James had left his family to earn enough to build them a better life. Charlie had left for no one but himself.

"We'll find him, Tommy," George said.

"But you said the chances of him surviving this war—"

"I know what I said, and I shouldn't have." George dug the toe of his boot into the soft soil.

"But you were right," Thomas said. "That could have been James. Next time, it could be me. What if I don't make it home? For the rest of their lives, my parents will be wondering where

I am and what happened to me. It's been torture for them not knowing what happened to James. How can I do that to them again?"

"Are you thinking of leaving?" George asked.

"I can't, can I? Not without admitting I lied. Besides, we have a mission to finish." He turned to Frederick. "But before I go back in those tunnels, I need you to write a letter for me."

Frederick stood. "I'll be right back." He returned minutes later, notebook and pen in hand, and sat down next to Thomas. "What do you want me to write?"

Thomas picked a poppy. Max woke, sniffed the small flower, and then closed his eyes again. Thomas stared out at the horizon, where the promise of morning warmed the night sky in fiery reds and burnt oranges. He pictured his parents receiving his letter. His chest ached with the pain they would feel because of him, and then he knew what he needed to say: *Dear Mum and Dad, I'm sorry.*

Twenty minutes and three pages later, Thomas had explained why he'd left home and why he could not leave the war now. He'd told them of his search for James and the importance of their crew's mission. He spoke of the things he'd seen and the friends he'd made. But mostly, he told them how much he missed and loved them.

When Thomas had said all he had to say, Frederick folded the pages and handed them to him. "You know when they receive that letter, they'll tell the army your real name and age, and you'll be sent home."

"That's why I'm not sending it."

"What are you going to do with it?" George asked.

"I want you to take it." Thomas held out the folded pages to George.

"Me?"

"Yes. I need you to promise that if I don't make it home, you will deliver this for me."

George backed away from the letter and request. "Come on, Tommy. You're going to make it home. And when you do, you can give your family the letter."

"Please," Thomas said. "I need to know if something happens my family won't be left waiting for me to come home. Promise me you'll take it to them."

"You do not want to entrust me with that. Remember, I'm a lyin' thief. Give it to Eton or Mouse."

"It needs to be you," Thomas said.

"Why?"

The boom of cannons thundered over no-man's-land.

"Because chances are, if any of us survives this war, it'll be you. And like you said, you may be a lyin' thief, but you're a lyin' thief who keeps his promises."

George snatched the letter from Thomas's hand. "Pretty low using my own words against me, Tommy."

"Promise you'll give it to them."

George shoved the letter in his coat pocket. "I promise."

"And my pay book too," Thomas took out a small,

brown-covered book he'd been issued when he'd joined the army to keep a record of all his active-duty earnings. "Make sure they get this, so they can claim what I've earned here. It's always in this pocket." He tucked the worn ledger back in his trouser pocket.

"What am I, the British Army Postal Service?"

"Promise," Thomas pressed.

"Fine. You have my word." George flopped down on the ground and lit a cigarette. "But nothing's going to happen to you, so can we please stop talking about this?"

"It's not a bad idea," Frederick said, turning to a new page.

"See, even Eton agrees."

"No," Frederick said. "Thomas is right. I should write a letter for each of our families. We could hold on to them for one another in case something should happen."

"Well, I don't have a family, so that'll save you some ink and paper." George placed his hand on the wad of bills bulging his pocket. "And I plan to spend every shilling of my wages and winnings."

"What about you, Charlie?" Frederick asked. "Do you want me to write to your brother?"

Charlie nodded. He had far less to say, so his letter barely filled a page. The boys then lay back in the field and watched the sun creep higher in the morning sky while Frederick wrote a letter to his own parents. When he had finished, he folded his pages, and he and Charlie traded letters, both promising to deliver the other's should one of them be killed.

"Everyone feeling better now?" George asked, stretching from his rest. "Because we have a brother to find, right, Tommy?"

"Right," Thomas said. "Thanks, George."

"Don't mention it. Seriously. It makes me uncomfortable. Besides, nothing is going to happen to us. And when our mission is over and we get out of here, I'm giving this back." He patted his jacket pocket. "And you can deliver it to your family yourself. Deal?"

"Deal. And if we do get out of here—"

"*When*," George corrected.

"*When* we get out of here," Thomas said. "I think you should come to Dover with me."

George sat up. "Dover? What would *I* do in Dover?"

"After your experience in the tunnels, you'd easily get a job in the coal mines, or if you want, you could help James and me start our shipping business."

"It's going to be your family business. You don't need me mucking it up."

"You said you had experience working the London docks. You probably have more knowledge of boats than James and I combined."

"That's true." George reached up and rubbed the back of his neck. "Still. Dover?"

Max rolled over in Thomas's lap, and Thomas scratched the dog's belly. "You said it yourself, there's no one waiting for you in London except that bobby who chased us to the train station."

"Fair point," George said. "And his anger won't have calmed while I was gone."

Frederick closed his notebook and tucked his pen behind his ear. "All the more reason not to return to London after the war."

"But where would I stay in Dover?"

"With my family," Thomas said, "you know, until you've saved enough to get your own place."

"Your parents wouldn't want me around."

"Sure they would. My sisters would love you, and Mum's always happy to have company, especially company that helps around the house and compliments her cooking. And Dad's happy as long as Mum's happy." Thomas moved Max off his lap and stood. "Think about it."

George smiled. "I will." But his smile faltered as they walked back to the tunnels. As much as he wanted to believe that Thomas's family would welcome him into their home, he knew the truth. Every person he'd ever met had made sure he knew it: No family would ever want George.

THIRTY-TWO

WITH THEIR LETTERS written and pacts made, the boys headed back to the tunnels to complete their mission, but time was not their ally. Their deadline was less than three weeks away, and the command center demanded daily progress reports and responded with the same directive: Work faster.

Tension in the tunnels and trenches swelled with the news that the Germans had increased their daylight raids on London and the surrounding towns. Charlie became so concerned about his brother, he asked Frederick to write another letter, which he sent to his family's pastor, inquiring about Henry's safety and imploring that he tell no one he had heard from Charlie, especially his father.

One morning, as the crew neared the end of another long shift in the tunnels, Boomer, Thomas, and George carried the last bags of spoil to the PBIs waiting at the entrance. The remaining crew members had started to gather their tools when Bats, who was listening at the wall, held up his hand.

Careful not to make a sound, he placed the geophone to the right and lower on the wall. His brow furrowed, and his glasses slid down his nose, but he made no move to fix them. With slow, silent steps, he inched his way toward the tunnel face. Charlie stepped back to make room as the listener inched closer to where Bagger waited. Poppy flapped on her perch and let out a high-pitched trill. Bagger signaled to Charlie, who crept over to the cage and stroked Poppy's head, quieting the canary. Sweat trickled down the sides of Charlie's face. He didn't dare move to wipe it away, fearful that any motion might be heard by the enemy.

Everyone strained to hear what Bats heard, but the tunnel was silent. Still holding an empty sandbag, Frederick swallowed hard. Their enemies were unaware of the stealthy techniques of the clay kickers. The German tunnelers were miners, like Boomer and Thomas. The Germans dug faster than the Brits, chopping at the clay with picks and shovels, but their speed came at a price. Bats had been tracking their noisy digging and conversations for days. He could hear the scrape of their shovels up to seventy feet away. Their voices he could detect from up to fifty feet. Over the last two days, both had grown louder. The news had made the crew nervous, but Bats assured them that as long as he could hear the enemy, they were safe. Noise followed by silence meant one of two things: Either the enemy had succumbed to carbon monoxide or they were preparing to fire a charge.

Bats pulled his glasses from his face with a quick jerk and closed his eyes. He moved the geophone lower on the wall, and his forehead wrinkled in concentration. After a taut minute, Bagger tapped Bats on the shoulder and raised his eyebrows in question. Bats shook his head, and Bagger mouthed a few vulgarities that would have made Charlie's dad blush and then he signaled for everyone to exit that section of the tunnel.

Frederick, who was positioned closest to the exit, turned and ran. Charlie, still holding Poppy's cage, and Mole had just moved to follow when an explosion tore through the clay wall where Bats and Bagger stood. The blast threw the crew to the ground as clots of clay and splintered wood rained down on them.

A high-pitched ringing filled Charlie's ears, and smoke filled the gallery. Charlie fumbled around blindly for Poppy's cage, which he'd dropped in the explosion. His fingers found the metal cage, and he pulled it into his lap. He coughed and wheezed, fighting for a clean breath, but Poppy's muted chirps and fluttering assured him that despite everything polluting the tunnel's air, at least carbon monoxide wasn't present—for now. He pulled on his gas mask, just in case.

A trickle of warmth crept down the side of his face. He touched his head, and when he pulled back his fingers, they were wet and sticky. Holding Poppy's cage close to his chest, he peered in the direction where Mole, Bats, and Bagger had stood seconds before, but smoke and dust obscured his view.

Screams echoed in the darkness. "Geh! Geh! Geh!"

Charlie did not recognize the voices or words. Pulling off his mask to see better, he pressed to his feet and stared at the gaping hole in the clay wall. A stocky man holding a shovel peered through the opening. Charlie's panicked gaze swept the area, searching for anything he could use as a weapon, but all he had was Poppy's birdcage, which the canary still occupied.

The man with the shovel noticed the cage and smiled at Charlie. The smile held no warmth or mercy. Charlie had witnessed many such cruel smiles throughout his short life. They lived in the night and reeked of barley and hops. They slurred their words and proclaimed harsh punishments for crimes Charlie never committed. They tasted of blood and tears.

The man stepped through the opening, and Charlie set down the cage. He would not cower before this man or his taunting smile. He was a soldier. He would never cower before any man again. He brought his trembling hands out in front of him, like Bagger had taught him in their short boxing lesson. He was preparing to throw a punch when Mole charged out of the rubble and crashed into the German miner. As the two men grappled atop broken timbers and chunks of clay, fighting for control of the shovel, a second enemy stepped through the blast opening.

He was smaller than the first. His German uniform draped loosely over his narrow shoulders, and his freckles and rounded cheeks reminded Charlie of Henry. Charlie lowered his fists, a move he reversed the second the boy pulled a knife from his belt and lunged at him.

With little space to move in the narrow tunnel, Charlie pivoted, pressing his back against the wall and sucking in his stomach. The knife sliced across the front of his uniform, tearing fabric and severing a button. Both boys froze and stared at the front of Charlie's shirt. A faint line of crimson appeared across the fabric, but Charlie felt no pain, only adrenaline and anger. He grabbed his attacker's wrist and twisted his arm until the boy cried out and dropped the knife.

"Never again," Charlie snarled. Then he hit the boy. Closed fist. Hard.

One.

Two.

With every ounce of the fear and rage his father had beaten into him for fourteen years, Charlie struck his attacker. Every word he'd ever wished to scream burst from his mouth at once, in a primal cry that buried the sound of Mole's fight raging yards away.

Three.

Four.

Charlie's attacker held up his hands. Words, foreign to Charlie, rushed from the boy's lips. Charlie didn't understand or care. The German had tried to kill him.

Five.

Six.

His enemy fell to the ground. Charlie and his fists followed.

Seven.

Eight.

Nine.

Ten.

Over and over.

Until he lost count.

Until he lost control.

Until one word paralyzed his fists.

"Mama."

His attacker mumbled the word through bloodied lips.

Charlie blinked rapidly to clear his vison and to remember where he was. To remember *who* he was. "I'm sorry," he whispered, leaning down to help the boy.

The boy recoiled.

"I'm so sorry."

Charlie looked down at his hands, still balled into fists. His knuckles were swollen and smeared with blood. He couldn't tell if it belonged to him or the boy.

"Never again," he said. He unclenched his fists, wincing at the pain throbbing through his knuckles. He stared at the boy cowering on the floor and pointed to the hole in the wall. "Go."

The boy didn't move.

"Go," Charlie repeated.

Mole had subdued the larger German and was digging in the rubble for Bats and Bagger.

"Go!" Charlie yelled.

The boy scrambled to his feet.

Charlie had bent down to fetch his gas mask so he could help Mole dig when he heard his name.

"Mouse!"

Charlie turned to see Frederick rushing toward him with a spade raised in his hand.

"Duck!" Frederick yelled.

Charlie fell to the ground, and Frederick swung the spade. There was a sharp smack of metal striking flesh, followed by the thud of a body collapsing behind him. Charlie looked over his shoulder at the German boy, lying on the floor inches from him. Blood spilled from a gash on the boy's forehead.

"What did you do?" Charlie screamed as Thomas and George skidded to a halt behind Frederick, followed by a winded Boomer. "He was retreating!"

Frederick, his face pale and his eyes wide with shock, pointed to the dead boy's outstretched arm and the knife gripped in his hand.

THIRTY-THREE

AFTER THE CAPTURED German miner was treated and taken into custody and Charlie's cuts were bandaged, Boomer detonated a second explosion to seal off the opening, and the surviving clay kickers buried the dead a mile behind the Allied reserve trenches, in a field crowded with row upon row of fresh graves.

Bats.

Bagger.

Even the German boy.

Mole, Boomer, and the boys were joined by several infantrymen, including Johnny and Dan, who shared memories, recited prayers, and sang Bagger's favorite song, "Danny Boy." Standing before the graves, Thomas remembered his brother singing the song while their dad played the tin whistle and his mum, sisters, and he sat around the fireplace after Sunday dinner. His mum used to say James had vocal cords plucked straight from an angel's heavenly harp. What Thomas wouldn't give to hear his brother's voice lifted in song again. Grief, hard and unmoving, ached in his throat, choking off the lyrics. George reached over and put a hand on his shoulder. He gave Thomas an understanding nod and then raised his voice louder for both of them.

When the boys and men finished the song and had said all they could manage to say, Thomas picked up Max, who lay whimpering on Bagger's grave, and carried the small dog back to the dugout.

Boomer accompanied Mole to the Regimental Aid Post to have his ears examined for hearing damage from being so close to the blast. Though the boys were alone, they did not venture into the trenches that day. They stayed in the dugout, where Charlie drew sketches of Bagger and Bats while George constructed wooden frames for the pictures from scrap wood he'd scrounged up in the trenches. Thomas consoled Max, who paced the dugout and jumped onto Bagger's bunk, searching for his master, and Frederick spent hours writing and rewriting condolence letters to the men's families, telling their wives and children how nobly both men had served their country.

Thomas's chest ached with renewed grief when Frederick asked Mole the men's real names to use in the letters. Their nicknames had confined Bagger and Bats to the tunnels and the war, in Thomas's mind. Before their deaths, he'd given little thought to the lives they'd lived prior to the war or hoped to reclaim after. Now suddenly they weren't just tunnelers. They were husbands and fathers with families praying for their safe return. Was Bagger's wife saying the rosary beside a photo of her husband before bed? Were Bats's children struggling to get by in their father's absence?

While the others slept that night, Thomas lay awake in his bunk with Max curled up next to him on one of Bagger's shirts. Thinking of all Bagger and Bats had sacrificed for their crew and all their families had lost, Thomas couldn't help but wonder if his decision to follow James into the war would cost him and his family more.

. . .

A somberness filled the tunnels and dugout in the week following their crew members' deaths. The medics assured Mole that his hearing loss was most likely temporary, but his annoyance over the constant ringing in his ears and having to ask everyone to repeat themselves, coupled with his grief over the loss of his closest friend on the Western Front, soured the kicker's normally cheerful disposition. Listeners and baggers from other crews that had completed their mines helped Mole, Boomer, and the boys with their gallery. Each shift brought two new temporary members to their crew. Recalling Mole's advice to Charlie after Feathers died, Thomas didn't bother to learn their names.

In the dugout, Bagger's and Bats's empty bunks served as constant reminders that death had found their crew under no-man's-land, and the boys feared, as they continued to dig beneath the battlefield, that it would hunt them down again. Even George, who'd faced death all his life and laughed at its attempts to claim him in London, counted down the minutes to the end of each shift in the tunnels. He hadn't lied to Thomas when he claimed he'd never feared death because he had nothing to lose, but that was before.

The moment Thomas had invited George to come home with him after the war, he'd given George hope for a future George had never dared imagine before, and with that gift of hope came the burden of fear. Fear that death would steal it all away.

Early one morning, a week after the breach in the tunnel, George went looking for Thomas to tell him he'd decided to accept his invitation to join him and his family in Dover after the war. He checked Bagger's and Bats's graves first, as Thomas often visited there after their shifts to say a prayer and tell them about the progress the crew had made, but he didn't find Thomas there that morning. George had turned back to look for him in the trenches when he spotted Thomas sitting in the poppy field under Feathers's elm tree.

His head bowed and his back to the battlefield, Thomas did not see George approaching. Max slept curled up on his lap, and as George got closer, he overheard Thomas talking.

"We finished the Maedelstede Farm mine today. Other crews sent men to help, so we'd finish on time."

Not wanting to intrude on a private moment, George

stopped and waited as Thomas continued the one-sided conversation.

"All that's left is to charge the chamber. Boomer said they'll blow twenty-three mines on the seventh." His voice trailed off. "Only three more days."

Three more days, George thought, *and our mission will be over.* But what would that mean? Would the remnants of their crew be sent home? Not likely. George knew how to play the odds, and the odds were that if the mission succeeded, they'd be sent to another stretch of the Western Front, where they'd be ordered to again burrow beneath a battlefield and undermine the enemy's position. If the mission failed, they'd be handed a weapon and put in the front-line trenches. Either way, the odds of the rest of the crew surviving the war were dwindling with every day they remained on or under its battlefields.

Thomas reached up and gripped the medals hanging from his neck and said something George didn't expect.

"I'm sorry, Grandad. I've tried to find James, but I've failed. If I don't make it home, my friend George has promised to give Mum and Dad a letter from me, so they'll know what happened and hopefully someday find some peace." His voice cracked. "But they'll never be at peace if we don't find James, so please, if James is with you"—Thomas sniffled back tears—"send me a sign. Please, Grandad. I can't do this alone." Max stirred from his slumber and licked the tears sliding down Thomas's face.

George left before Thomas spotted him. He walked to the

dugout, where he found Charlie asleep on his bunk and Frederick writing in his notebook.

"Where are Mole and Boomer?" he asked.

Frederick did not look up from his writing. "In the trenches, scrounging up some food."

George checked Charlie's bunk to make sure he was really sleeping, then he pulled a chair close to Frederick and straddled it backward. "We need to talk," he whispered.

Frederick closed his notebook. "Is something wrong?"

"Yes . . . No . . . I don't know. I just need you to do me a favor."

"What kind of favor?"

"I need you to write me two letters."

His curiosity piqued, Frederick opened his notebook to a clean page. "To whom?"

"You're not going to like the first."

"Why not?"

"Because I need you to write to your father."

Frederick snapped the notebook closed again. "You're right. I don't like it."

"But he's the only one who can help."

"Help what? Send me home?"

"No. Find James." George ran a hand through his hair. "We'll never find out what happened to him searching the trenches, and with the end of the mission less than three days away, we're running out of time. Your dad is our best hope. He could ask around. Someone higher up has to know what happened to Thomas's brother."

"He'll send for me the minute he gets the letter," Frederick said.

"Who cares if he drags you home? Get out of these tunnels before you end up under the poppy field with Bagger and Bats."

"I can't go home." Frederick grabbed his notebook and pen and stood. "Not yet." Then he left the dugout.

George followed him into the tunnels. "Why not?"

"I don't want to talk about it, George."

"Because of your father?"

"No." Frederick kept walking, determined to get out of the tunnels and away from George, but George ran ahead of him and blocked the exit.

"Let me pass," Frederick said.

"Not until you tell me why you can't go home."

"Why do you care?" Frederick asked.

"Because whatever the reason, it's stopping you from helping Thomas find his brother."

Frederick's shoulders slumped.

"Why can't you go home, Eton?" George repeated.

"You wouldn't understand."

"Try me."

"Because I haven't done what I came here to do."

"And what's that?"

Frederick's head dipped. He exited the tunnel and sat down

in a small dugout in the support trench wall. "Prove I'm not a coward."

George followed him outside. "To who?" he asked, his voice rising with frustration. "Your father?"

"No." Frederick pulled the broken white feather from his pocket. "To myself."

George stared at the feather. He'd seen men on the streets of London receive white feathers for not joining the army. He didn't know who had given Frederick the feather, but he knew what it meant. "Eton, you're not a coward. Look at all you've done. Charlie and I would be buried beside Bagger and Bats if it weren't for you. You're as real a soldier as any man on the front line, and I'll fight anyone who dares say otherwise."

Machine-gun fire ripped across no-man's-land, shattering the silent stalemate between the trenches. Frederick crouched down behind the sandbags. When he realized he wasn't in danger, he looked up at George. "Real soldiers don't run away from a fight or hesitate in the heat of battle. They don't tremble in fear in their bunks or cry over the enemies they've killed."

Pressure built in Frederick's throat and behind his eyes, but he would not cry. Chamberlains did *not* cry. "I came here a coward, George. I can't leave here as one."

George took the feather from Frederick and ran it between his fingers, straightening out the bent spine. "You think being scared makes you a coward? What kind of rubbish do they teach you at Eton? That soldiers aren't scared? We're living beneath the front line of a war. Only a fool wouldn't be scared. What matters is you came here anyway, and when your crew needed you, you were there for them, despite being scared. That's real courage, Eton. And if that doesn't make your father proud or get your name engraved on the wall of that fancy school of yours, you let me know." He lifted the feather. "I'll carve your name on the bloody wall myself."

Sniffing back unshed tears, Frederick smiled. "You don't know how to write."

"I have no doubt you'll make sure I spell your name correctly."

Frederick laughed. "You're probably right."

"Of course I am." George tucked the feather in his unruly hair, so it stuck up like the plume of a hat. "You should wear this with pride."

"You're crazy."

"Probably, but that doesn't mean I'm not right." He handed the feather back to Frederick. "That feather may have brought you to the front, Eton, but your courage has kept you here."

Frederick tucked the feather behind his ear. "Who knows? Maybe it's a new style that will catch on here in the trenches."

"Absolutely. Especially after we blow the ridge and become war heroes. Everyone will want a white feather just like yours." George lit a cigarette and sat beside Frederick.

"Do you really think the army will reveal what we're doing?" Frederick asked. "If we fail, they'll cover up the work we did. If we succeed, they'll want to keep our work secret to maintain the element of surprise over our enemies, so they can reuse the method under other battlefields. No one will know what we've sacrificed for crown and country." He stared off in the direction of Bats's and Bagger's graves. "Or what we've lost."

"We'll know," George said.

Frederick nodded.

"So," George asked, "will you write to your dad about James?"

Frederick nodded again and then opened his notebook and wrote a brief letter to his dad explaining where he was and the situation with Thomas's brother. When he finished, he pushed up his glasses to rub his eyes and turned to a fresh page. "What about the second letter?"

"I need you to write me one, like you did for Tommy and Mouse, and if things go wrong, I need you to deliver it to someone for me. And you have to promise not to tell anyone about this." He held out his hand. "Do I have your word, Eton, as a *real* soldier?"

Frederick took hold of George's hand and gave it a firm shake. "No, you have my word as a *secret* soldier."

THIRTY-FOUR

THE SUN HURT the young soldier's eyes when he and twelve Allied prisoners were escorted from the German field hospital. Under the medical staff's care, his wounds had scarred over without infection, and his broken leg had healed. His eyes watered when exposed to bright light, and though he could hear again, the low ringing in his ears remained. The nurses had fed him and the other injured prisoners, but food was scarce even for the German troops, leaving few scraps for their captives. During his recovery, the soldier had lost what little extra weight he'd carried with him when he'd charged into battle months earlier.

But he was alive. Through every aching step, twist of hunger, and nightmarish flashback, he reminded himself that he was alive. The young soldier tried not to dwell on what awaited him in the prison camp in Germany as he boarded a train with the other prisoners and their guards.

When the train stopped an hour later, the prisoners were marched for over two hours. In the distance, the young soldier heard the rumble of artillery and the staccato rhythm of machine-gun fire. With every dozen steps, the sounds of battle grew louder. As they crested a small rise of land, the young soldier's steps faltered, and his heart sank at what lay before them. Crooked lines of trenches framed two sides of a pockmarked battlefield. His mouth went dry, and a sharp pain radiated from the center of his chest. They were not being taken to a prison camp to be used as laborers at German farms, factories, or mines. They were being marched back to the Western Front to work on the German front line.

THIRTY-FIVE

THE CREW SPENT their last few shifts hauling explosives down the tunnels to pack in the Maedelstede Farm mine, one of twenty-three hidden beneath a stretch of seven miles of enemy trenches. The beams above their heads groaned, and clots of clay shook free from between the boards under the constant bombardment of gunfire and howitzers raining down on no-man's-land as the crew stacked the waterproof tins of ammonal from floor to ceiling in the chamber. Not an inch of space remained. Thomas helped Boomer embed an electric detonator, connected to the lead, into the powder of one of the tins before inserting loose detonators into every third tin crowding the chamber. They then ran the leads and fuse up to the top of the main shaft while the rest of the crew set to work tamping the mine.

"We spent months taking all of this clay out of here," George complained as he lifted another heavy sandbag from the shaft onto the tram to be dragged down the gallery toward the Maedelstede Farm mine, where it would be stacked on the hundreds of bags already packed tightly in the gallery. The bag left a blue streak on the front of his shirt and trousers, which were already caked with wet clay. When it dried, the blue clay ground into the crew's clothes and skin faded to a ghastly white, leaving the tunnelers looking like walking corpses. "Why are we hauling it all back down?"

"The charge chamber needs a solid back when it's fired," Boomer said, tossing another bag on the pile. "Explosions seek the path of least resistance. We want that path to be straight up under the German trenches, not back down these galleries toward ours. We're trying to break the German lines, not our own."

Frederick rolled his sore shoulders. "Fine, but how many more rows of bags do we need?

"To be safe, we need the tamping to be one and a half times the distance of the solid ground we're setting to break through, so keep hauling, boys."

The crew finished tamping the mine the day before the attack. That evening, Mole returned to the dugout from a meeting with the other crews' leaders at the command center.

"Is the mission still on?" Boomer asked.

With a frustrated groan, Mole rubbed his ears. "What?"

"Is the mission still on?" Boomer repeated louder.

"Yes," Mole said, pouring himself a cup of lukewarm tea from the crew's kettle. "British planes will bombard the German lines to camouflage the noise of the Allied tanks moving into position on our lines over the next two hours, and our infantry has been notified about the mission and will storm no-man's-land and take the German trenches after the mines are fired. If all goes as planned, they should meet little resistance."

"So our mission's not so secret anymore?" George asked.

"Not to anyone except hopefully the Germans." Mole drained the last drops of tea from his tin cup. "Though it won't be a secret from them for much longer."

"Are the other mines ready?" Boomer asked.

"General Plumer said the Germans withdrew from the area above the Birdcage mines. He ordered all four mines in that area be held in reserve and not fired, but the nineteen other mines are set to detonate. Zero hour is 3:10 A.M."

"That's going to be one hell of an explosion," Boomer said.

"The largest the world has ever seen," Mole said. "Before he dismissed us, Major-General Harington told us we may not make history tomorrow, but we'll certainly change the geography."

George glanced over at the empty bunks of their lost crew members. "Just wish Bagger and Bats were here to see it."

Thomas nodded. "We have to make sure those mines blow, in their honor."

Before Mole and Boomer left the boys to recheck the leads and fuses running from the Maedelstede Farm mine to the top of the gallery shaft, Mole pulled an envelope from his pocket. "I almost forgot, Mouse. This came for you." He handed the envelope to Charlie. "Last day in the tunnels and one of you lads finally gets some mail from home. Better late than never, I guess."

Charlie stared at the envelope for several minutes after the men left.

"Aren't you going to open it?" George finally asked.

Charlie swallowed hard. "What if it's bad news?"

"What if it's good news?" Thomas replied. "Only one way to find out."

Charlie tore open the envelope and pulled out a single sheet of folded paper, which he handed to Frederick. "Would you read it for me, please?"

Frederick read the signature first. "It's from Pastor Miller."

"What's it say?" Charlie asked.

Frederick skimmed the letter. "Your home wasn't hit. A zeppelin did drop a bomb on a warehouse nearby, but it happened at night when the building was empty."

Charlie sank down onto his bunk. George sat down next to him. "See there, Mouse. Nothing to worry about. Everything's fine."

"Not everything," Frederick said, continuing to read down the letter.

"What's wrong?" Charlie asked. "Is it my brother?"

Frederick handed him the letter. "It's not serious. Henry just broke his arm."

"How?"

"Your father told Pastor Miller it was an accident. Henry fell running through the house."

Charlie felt the anger he'd fought to bury after the fight in the tunnels clawing its way back to the surface. "He always says it's an accident." His hand squeezed into a fist, crushing the letter. "It never is."

. . .

While they waited for Mole and Boomer to return, George tried to distract Charlie from the news about his brother.

"Come on, Mouse. How about one last game of poker in the dugout?"

Charlie pocketed his letter and reluctantly joined George, Thomas, and Frederick at the table.

"Just think, if this mission goes well tonight," George said, dealing out the cards, "it will definitely end this bloody stalemate."

Thomas fanned out his cards, careful to keep them close to his chest. George claimed it wasn't cheating to look at an opponent's hand if the chap was careless enough to show them to you.

Frederick placed two of his cards facedown. "If we can

take Messines Ridge, we might be able to drive Fritz back to Germany."

"If all the mines blow, we'll drive them back farther than Germany," George said, dealing him two new cards.

"They'll all blow," Frederick said.

Charlie tossed down one of his own cards. "I don't know. Boomer's concerned the tunnel the Germans broke through will collapse if artillery hits within yards of it."

"It doesn't help that our troops have been shelling the German trenches for weeks," George complained.

"It's a good strategy," Frederick said. "With the increase in guns and infantry gathering on our front, the Germans have to know a ground assault is imminent. The constant shelling will keep them focused on what's happening in our trenches and not what we might have been doing beneath theirs. It should gain us the element of surprise at zero hour."

"That's if our shells don't trigger the mines before then," George said. "The sooner we detonate those mines, the better."

"And the sooner this war will be over, and we can get back to our lives," Frederick said.

George dealt Charlie three new cards. "You headed back to London after the war, Mouse?"

Charlie did not hesitate in his response. "Yes."

"What about your father?" Thomas asked.

"If Mouse can face Germans in the tunnels, he can face his father," George said. "Right, Mouse?"

"I have to get my brother away from him." He looked over at Thomas. "I never should have left. He needs me."

Thomas nodded.

"Good for you, Mouse," George said. "What about you, Thomas? You still going back to Dover?"

"As soon as they will let me." Thomas dreaded the thought of going home without James, but once the war ended, he couldn't leave his parents and sisters faring for themselves any longer.

"And I suppose you'll be heading back to that fancy school of yours," George said, dealing Frederick new cards.

"If my father doesn't lock me in my room for the rest of my life," Frederick replied.

"What about you, George?" Charlie asked. "Will you go back to London?"

"No. I've seen enough of London. Think it's about time I check out some of the rest of the country." He smiled at Thomas. "I hear there might be work for someone with my skills in Dover."

"Absolutely," Thomas said, returning George's smile.

"Wherever we go," Charlie said, "we should make a pact to meet up again."

"That is a fine idea, Mouse!"

"When should we plan to meet?" Thomas asked.

"How about a year after the war ends?" George said.

"Better make it two," Frederick said. "Hopefully by then I'll be done with whatever punishment my father doles out."

"Two years from the day the war ends it is," George said.

"We'll meet and celebrate the Great War being over and having survived it."

"Where should we meet?" Charlie asked.

George waved away his question. "Details. We'll figure that out after the war."

"So we'll meet up two years to the day after this war ends, which, if our mission succeeds, could be tonight." Frederick extended his arm over the middle of the table. He leaned in and whispered, "It will be a secret soldier reunion."

Charlie placed his hand atop Frederick's. "Count me in."

"Me too," Thomas said, putting his hand on Charlie's.

George added his hand on top of the pile. "I wouldn't miss it."

. . .

Mole and Boomer returned to the dugout as George finished collecting his winnings from the others.

"Time to pack up, chaps," Mole announced. "Command wants all tunneled dugouts in a four-hundred-yard radius of the mines evacuated before zero hour. Grab your things and head up top to wait for the show, but stay away from the front-line trenches. They've ordered all men out of the trench dugouts within a two-hundred-yard radius until after the mines fire."

"Why?" Frederick asked. "Do they expect the blasts to collapse our trenches?"

"No one really knows what to expect," Boomer said, shoving his army blanket into his kit bag. "Nothing like this has ever been attempted before, so they're being extra cautious. Stay out of the infantry's way. As soon as these mines blow, they'll be going over the top. It's best you find a spot in the support or reserve trenches to watch. Understand?"

The boys nodded.

"What about you and Mole?" Thomas asked. "Won't you be in danger at the top of the shaft?"

"I have faith in our tamping," Boomer said, jamming his feet inside his boots. "We packed an additional three yards of sandbags in the gallery. It'll hold."

Mole checked his watch. "I guess we'll find out one way or another in three hours."

After the boys had gathered their meager belongings, Boomer left to speak with two of the other crew leaders who, like him, had been tasked with pushing the plungers that would detonate the mines.

"How can he be so calm about all this?" Charlie asked Thomas.

"He knows we've done all we can to make sure this mission is successful. All we can do now is wait."

The dugout trembled beneath another wave of shelling.

"Well, I, for one, am not waiting down here," George said, slinging his kit bag over his shoulder. "Think I'll go scrounge up some food in the reserve trenches."

Max jumped off Thomas's lap at the word *food* and followed him to the doorway.

"I'll join you," Frederick said, packing up the last of his books. "All this sitting around and waiting is making me nervous."

"You chaps coming?" George asked Charlie and Thomas.

"I have a few things left to pack," Thomas said.

"Me too," Charlie said, taking down the framed sketches of Bagger and Bats and placing them carefully in his bag.

"If we can't find you in the reserve trenches," Thomas said, "we'll meet you at the corner of the support and communication trenches. That should be a safe enough distance from the mine blasts to watch the assault."

"Sounds like a plan," George said. "How about you, Mole?"

"What?" Mole said, angling his right ear to better hear.

"Are you coming with us?" George yelled.

Mole shook his head. "I'll grab some food after the dugout's cleared and then join Boomer at the top of the shaft to count down until zero hour. We'll see you boys in the reserve trenches after the show."

"Good luck, sir," Frederick said.

Mole smiled. "You too, Eton."

Thomas watched as Frederick and George exited the dugout with Max trotting along at George's heels.

Five minutes later, Charlie and Thomas finished packing their belongings and told Mole they'd see him up top after the mines fired.

. . .

As they made their way through the gallery to the tunnel entrance, Thomas imagined the thousands of unsuspecting German soldiers across no-man's-land, sleeping in their dugouts and trenches, yards above one million pounds of explosives. The more he thought about the surprise attack they would soon unleash on the enemy, the more he wondered if the German miners hadn't executed a similar plan. Staring down at the worn boards lining the gallery floor, Thomas quickened his pace, suddenly worried that at any moment the earth beneath him might explode. Anxious paranoia hummed through his body. He pushed thoughts of the impending explosions and the battle that would follow from his mind and thought about Charlie's decision to return home after the war to help his brother. He knew James had planned to return home after the war to help Thomas start their shipping business. They'd had so many dreams for their future, but then James went missing, leaving Thomas with only a battered family picture and a Saint Joseph medal to remember him by.

Thomas reached up to touch his medals, but found only fabric and flesh. He felt all around his neck, but the necklace was gone. He stopped at the tunnel entrance.

"What's wrong?" Charlie asked.

"I left something in the dugout," Thomas said. "You go on ahead."

"You sure? I can wait."

"It'll only take a minute. I'll meet you and the others in the support trenches."

Before Charlie could argue, Thomas turned and hurried back toward the crew's dugout.

On the way, he mentally retraced his steps, thinking back to the last time he'd touched the medals. The memory surfaced cold and sweaty.

Before Thomas had embedded his first loose fuse in the mine, he'd gripped his medals and said a prayer, asking his grandad and James to watch over them. When the crew built the final wall of sandbags to seal off the gallery, Thomas's gas mask came loose for the sixth time that shift. He'd pulled it down from his face and let it hang beneath his chin. When Boomer noticed, he'd signaled for Thomas to put it back on. With a frustrated jerk, Thomas had yanked the mask back onto his face.

Standing outside the dugout, Thomas squeezed his eyes shut. "No, no, no, no . . ." He stared down the dark tunnel that led to the shaft and gallery where he knew his necklace must be. He had to hurry and find it before it was lost forever. Grabbing the door frame, he leaned inside the dugout. Mole stood with his back to him, folding up his Tommy's Cooker and placing it with the crew's tin cups in the crate they'd used as their table.

"Mole, I lost something in the gallery," he said, grabbing a lantern from the wall. "I'll meet you up top."

"What?" Mole said, turning to face the doorway, but Thomas was already gone.

Mole rubbed his ears and grumbled to himself, "Blimey, now I'm bloody hearing voices." He then finished packing the crew's belongings and took the box topside to meet up with Boomer.

THIRTY-SIX

FOR OVER A MONTH, the young soldier spent sixteen hours a day toiling alongside his fellow prisoners of war in the German trenches. He dug and hauled spoil, loaded artillery shells into howitzer cannons, and scurried onto no-man's-land during ceasefires to retrieve injured and dead German soldiers. He regretted every shovelful of earth he removed that helped fortify the enemy's position, he begged God for forgiveness with every shell he loaded into a howitzer aimed at the Allied trenches, and he said silent prayers for the fallen comrades he left behind every time he carried the body of a fallen enemy off the battlefield. But the young soldier never questioned or refused an order. To do so would have earned him a bullet to the head and an unmarked grave.

At night, when he lay awake, too hungry and afraid to sleep, he stared across no-man's-land. When the guns fell silent, he could hear the voices of Allied soldiers drifting over the battlefield. He dreamed of running across the stretch of desolate land to join them. It would only take him a few minutes to reach the other side if a German or British sniper didn't stop him first. With a heavy sigh, he pushed the fantasy of escaping from his mind and curled up next to the French boy in their dugout. Trying to escape would be too great a risk. If he hoped to ever get home to his family again, he had to stay alive, and, burrowed deep into the higher ground bordering no-man's-land, there was no place safer on the Western Front than the German trenches.

THIRTY-SEVEN

IN THE RESERVE trenches, George and Frederick managed to scrounge up two tins of Maconochie beef stew and a small package of bread. As they made their way back to the support trenches, Max trotted behind them, his attention focused on the food in their hands.

"This is *not* the three meals a day I was promised." George tore open the K-Brot package and handed Frederick a piece of the tasteless bread. "When this war is over, the first thing I'm going to do is eat real stew and dumplings until I get sick."

"And a whole roast," Frederick said.

"And meat pudding." George sighed.

They continued listing off foods as they rounded the corner to find Charlie sitting alone in their designated meeting place.

George tossed him a tin of beef stew. "Here you go, Mouse."

Max sat before Charlie and licked his chops as Charlie opened the tin. "Where's Thomas?" he asked.

“He’s not with you?” Frederick asked.

“No. I thought he was with you two getting food.”

George sat on the bench beside Charlie. “Last we saw him was with you and Mole in the dugout. When was the last time you saw him?”

“Over an hour ago,” Charlie said.

“Where?” Frederick asked.

“He was headed back to the dugout.”

George set down his open tin, and Max jumped onto the bench to lap up the cold stew. “Why?”

“He said he forgot something and he’d meet me here. When he didn’t show up after a few minutes, I assumed he’d found you two in the reserve trenches and was getting food.”

“We never saw him,” Frederick said. “Do you think he’s with Mole and Boomer checking the leads again?”

George stood. “Only one way to find out.” He grabbed his gas mask and hurried down the support trench to the tunnel entrance. Charlie, Frederick, and Max followed him past their empty crew dugout to the shaft that connected the upper galleries to the lower galleries.

Boomer and Mole sat near the lip of the shaft. They were focused on checking the wiring of the leads to a pair of raised metal screws on the lid of a wooden box situated between them and didn’t hear the boys approaching. Black capital letters spelling out EXPLODER were stenciled on the side of the box, and a long wooden dowel capped with a wooden handle extended from the top.

"It passed the resistance test," Boomer reassured Mole. "Even if the aerial bombardment collapses part of the gallery, the leads should remain intact, and the mines should fire."

"Good." Mole checked the time and smiled. "Barring any unforeseen problems, Maedelstede Farm is ready to fire."

He looked up from his watch as George skidded to a halt before them. "Shillings? What are you doing in here?"

Charlie and Frederick joined George beside the men. Max paced back and forth in front of the shaft and whined.

"What are all of you doing in here?" Mole asked. "I told you boys to watch from the support trenches."

"I know," George said, "but we can't find Thomas. Have you seen him?"

"Not since I left you boys packing up the dugout," Boomer said.

"What about you, Mole?" Frederick asked. "Where did Thomas say he was going after he came back to the dugout?"

"Thomas didn't come back to the dugout."

"Yes, he did," Charlie said. "After he and I left you, Thomas said he forgot something in the dugout and headed back into the tunnels."

Mole shook his head. "I'm telling you, the last time I saw Dover was when he left with you, Mouse. If he'd come back, I would have seen or . . ." Mole's voice trailed off.

"What is it?" George asked.

"When I was packing up the last crate, I thought I heard a voice, but when I looked, no one was there."

"Maybe he found what he was looking for and left," Frederick said.

Boomer shook his head. "I was waiting for Mole at the entrance. No one but Mole came out, and one of us has been here ever since."

"Then where is he?" Frederick asked.

George inched closer to the lip of the shaft, where Max continued to pace and whine. He peered down into the darkness.

"You don't think he went back down into the galleries, do you?" Charlie asked.

"There's nowhere else he could be," George said.

"It doesn't make any sense." Frederick looked at the men. "Why would he go back down there this close to zero hour?"

But George did not wait for an explanation. Picking up Max with one arm, he grabbed hold of the ladder and began climbing down the shaft, ignoring Mole's order for him to wait.

He skipped several rungs in his descent. When he reached the bottom of the shaft, he found Thomas's kit bag and boots abandoned beneath the last rung. He put Max down and lit one of the extinguished lanterns embedded in the clay walls. It cast a weak light down the narrow corridor. "Find Thomas, Max!"

The terrier sniffed twice and then took off down the gallery toward the Maedelstede Farm mine.

The voices of the others, echoing off the shaft walls, grew closer, but George couldn't wait for them. Heart pounding, he chased after Max and calculated how much time was left before the mines were detonated.

Two hours.

Two hours to find Thomas, climb back up the shaft, get out of the tunnels, and get back to the safety of the support trenches before the mines exploded, taking anyone on or under no-man's-land with them.

Plenty of time, he thought, but he still kicked up his pace.

. . .

As Frederick and Charlie chased the shrinking light of George's lantern, Charlie tried not to jostle Poppy too much in her cage or think about the last words Boomer had shouted to them as they'd descended the shaft ladder in pursuit of their friend.

The mines are firing at 3:10 whether you're out of there or not.

A string of mumbled vulgarities and the heavy footfalls of Mole trailed them through the gallery.

"I'm gonna kill Shillings when I get my hands on him," the kicker wheezed as he lumbered behind the boys.

. . .

As George neared the tamped portion of the gallery, he came upon an overturned lantern and Max whining and pawing at broken beams on the floor. Beneath them, George spotted a stockinged foot.

"Tommy!" He lifted the beams off his friend's motionless body.

Thomas didn't answer. Blood from a gash on his forehead ran down his face and stained his blond hair a dark red.

"Tommy," George whispered, wiping Thomas's face with his sleeve, "please wake up."

A pained groan grumbled in Thomas's throat as he struggled to open his eyes. "Ouch."

Max placed his front paws on Thomas's chest and licked his chin and cheeks.

"It's all right, boy," Thomas said, patting the dog's head. "I'm all right."

The remaining beams above them creaked, and clots of clay broke free under another barrage of shelling.

"You will be as soon as we get you out of here." George took Thomas's hand and started to help him up, but Thomas cried out.

"What's wrong?" George asked, lowering him back to the ground.

"My leg. I think it's broken."

"Then I'll have to carry you." George looked around Thomas. "Where's your gas mask?"

"I couldn't see with it on to find my necklace. I threw it to the ground just before the beams fell."

George searched under the broken beams and pulled Thomas's mask from the rubble. The material was torn, and the lens shattered. "It'll have to do." He pulled the mask over Thomas's head.

Thomas winced when the coarse material dragged across his cut.

"Sorry," George said, adjusting the mask, so Thomas could see through the cracked lens.

"I'm the one who should be apologizing. I just wanted to find my necklace. I didn't mean to get us in this mess."

"Did you find it?" George asked.

Thomas pulled the broken chain and saints medals from his pocket.

"Good."

The earth around them shook as another explosion echoed on no-man's-land. George covered his and Thomas's heads as more chunks of clay fell from the ceiling.

"I'm really sorry, George."

"Let's save the apologies for when we're aboveground." Trying not to jostle Thomas's injured leg, George started to pick him up when he spotted Frederick, Charlie, and Mole running toward them.

"Don't come any closer!" he hissed. "This section's not stable!"

Mole and the boys stopped and watched George carefully lift Thomas into his arms. He took a step forward, but Max paced circles around his feet and pawed at his legs, trying to get to Thomas. Afraid he was going to trip over the dog, George ordered the terrier to go to Mole. Ears and tail low, Max reluctantly obeyed. As soon as the dog was within reach, Frederick scooped him into his arms before he could scoot back to George and Thomas.

Another distant explosion rumbled, shaking more clots from the exposed clay ceiling. No one moved until the ground around them settled again.

"Have they started blowing the mines?" Thomas whispered to George.

"They're not supposed to for another couple hours. That must have been an artillery shell or a bomb from one of our planes."

George secured his grip on Thomas and started to walk again. At the other end of the gallery, Charlie gnawed on his fingers while Frederick held a squirming Max in his arms and Mole motioned for George to hurry.

Another tremor shook the ground surrounding them as explosions rocked the battlefield. "Come on, Shillings!" Mole ordered.

Keeping an eye on the creaking beams straining to hold back the tons of earth, sand, water, and clay above their heads, George walked faster. "Just another one of our wild adventures, eh, Timothy Bennett?" He chuckled, but his smile was strained, and Thomas could tell from how fast his friend kept talking that the London street urchin who'd scaled the chimneys of lit fireplaces and bet his hands in games with dockworkers was scared. "I'll be honest with you, Tommy. I was hoping for a front-row seat to the fireworks tonight, but this is a bit too close for my liking. I mean, don't get me wrong, I've enjoyed our time working the tunnels together, but I have no desire to spend eternity with you down here."

Thomas managed a weak smile. "The feeling's mutual."

George stopped as another series of explosions fell on no-man's-land. He and Thomas looked up as the beams lining the stretch of ceiling between them and the others started to snap.

"Watch out!" Mole yelled.

"It's gonna fall!" Frederick screamed.

Losing his grip on Thomas, George stumbled backward as the ceiling above them collapsed in an avalanche of wood and clay.

THIRTY-EIGHT

SHARP PAIN LANCED through Thomas's injured leg as he dragged himself away from the collapsed portion of the gallery.

"George!" he yelled, grabbing the overturned lantern.

"Over here," a weak voice answered.

Thomas swung the lantern in the direction of the voice. George sat on the ground, his back pressed up against the tunnel wall. A broken beam lay beside him. The lantern cast George's face in a jaundiced yellow, and as he bent forward to press up to his feet, he groaned in pain.

"Are you hurt?" Thomas asked.

George held his side. "Probably just a bruised rib. Nothing I can't handle. How about you?"

"Nothing new."

"Good." George hobbled over to the wall of clay and timber.

"Do you think the others are all right?" Thomas asked.

"I hope so. We're going to need them digging on the other side if we're to get out of here before these mines blow."

Thomas glanced down the stretch of gallery behind them to the wall of sandbags separating them from the charged mine.

George cupped his hands around his mouth. "Mole! Mouse! Eton!"

Thomas and he listened for a response.

"They're not answering," Thomas said.

"Either they can't, or this wall's too thick for us to hear them." George put on his gas mask. "Either way, we need to start digging."

Gritting his teeth against the pain in his leg, Thomas hobbled over to the collapsed wall and helped George pull large clumps of clay and pieces of timber from the pile. Sweat ran down their faces, necks, and backs as they worked. Pain accompanied their every movement, but they kept digging. The alternative was to sit and wait for the Allied commanders to detonate the mines, a thought that made them work faster.

"Hey, Tommy," George said, thrusting his fingers into the clay. "About this plan of yours for after the war."

"What about it?" Thomas asked, pulling another clump of clay free from the pile.

"Were you serious about me coming to Dover and helping your brother and you start up your shipping company?"

"Absolutely."

"Then we should probably work out the terms of my contract."

"Now?" Thomas asked as he pushed and pulled against a broken beam to work it free.

"Can you think of a better time?" George asked.

"Yes. Several, actually."

"Well, I'm not comfortable accepting your offer of employment until we've agreed to the wages and terms of my position in your company."

Despite the pain in his leg and the fear that at any second the mines could detonate, Thomas chuckled. "Okay, but we won't be able to pay you until we get some steady business."

George grabbed another handful of clay. "That's not an ideal proposition, Tommy, but I guess I'd be willing to work for a place to sleep and two home-cooked meals a day."

"We can do that."

"Until you turn a profit. After that I expect my fair share."

The chunk of timber broke free, and Thomas tossed it aside. "Of course."

"And," George added, heaving another handful of clay over his shoulder, "I want one of the boats named after me. Every king has boats named after him. And I am the King of the Secret Soldiers."

"This is true. Is that all?"

"Yes, well, except for one small problem."

"What's that?" Thomas asked.

"If I'm to be spending most of my time on a boat, it would probably be good if I knew how to swim. Almost drowning once was one too many times for me."

"James and I can teach you how to swim. We Sullivan brothers take care of our own, you know? So do we have a deal?"

"We have a deal."

After that, the boys dug in silence, focusing every ounce of their waning energy on escaping. Fear of dying underground had been Thomas's constant companion since his first day as a miner at age ten. It had taunted him with whispers of danger in the coal mines of Dover and stalked him to the tunnels of the Western Front. It had clung to him, cold and damp, during fitful sleep in the dugout and prickled across his skin like a low current of electricity as he'd descended beneath no-man's-land night after night.

Yet now, as he stood on a broken leg, yards away from a chamber stacked with explosives, clawing at the cold blue clay with bare hands until his fingers ached, an unsettling calm swirled through Thomas's mind. He burrowed his fingers into the clay and ripped two handfuls from the wall, and as he did, laughter, abrupt and deranged, burst from his throat.

"What's so funny?" George asked.

Thomas threw the fistfuls of clay behind him. "Nothing really. I just can't believe, after everything, we're stuck down here."

"Well, I don't intend to *stay* stuck down here, so keep digging."

Thomas lifted a clay-covered hand to his forehead in a crooked salute. "Yes, sir!"

George shot him a strange look that made Thomas laugh louder.

As Thomas pulled another clump of clay from the pile, the memory of finding the dead British soldier in the tunnel walls shuddered through his body. His fingers chilled at the thought of the soldier's flesh beneath them, but he drove them deeper. James could be trapped in the clay, waiting for Thomas to join him. The grief and guilt that had consumed his every thought of James for months morphed into overwhelming relief and a strange euphoria as he felt the seconds of his own life ticking down. If he died in the tunnel, he would finally see his brother again. Maybe it was the fate of every Sullivan to dig his own grave.

He chuckled to himself and started humming "It's a Long Long Way to Tipperary." "Hey, George, do you remember the day we met?"

"How could I forget?"

"Remember when I told you I didn't need help from the likes of you?"

"Yes. What about it?"

"Look at me now!" He threw out his arms. "I'm trapped under no-man's-land, yards away from a mine packed with almost one hundred thousand pounds of explosives that could detonate at any moment and look who's here to help me." He pointed a clay-covered finger at George. "You! The lying, thieving street urchin from London."

"What's your point?" George answered. "Aside from insulting me."

"My point is I was wrong. About you. About everything. And I'm sorry. I'm glad you're here to help me and I'm glad you're coming home to Dover with me after the war. It's like you said when we met. You're my guardian angel."

"Yeah, well, don't go nominating me for sainthood yet. Who says I'm trying to save you? Maybe I'm just trying to save my own hide."

Thomas laughed. "Yeah, well, you wouldn't be stuck down here if it wasn't for me."

"Then we're even," George said, "because you wouldn't be on the Western Front if it wasn't for me."

Thomas laughed again. "That's true. Tell you what, if we get out of here—"

"*When* we get out of here," George corrected.

"*When* we get out of here, let's make a pact to never lie about our ages to join a war again."

"Deal. *And* let's get that clasp on your necklace fixed."

"Deal."

The boys continued digging, and Thomas resumed his humming. After a few bars, his humming morphed into singing, but then he stumbled over the words, pausing between and slurring the well-known lyrics. George stopped digging when Thomas started repeating the same four lyrics over and over.

"Tommy?"

"It's a long way . . . it's a long . . . it's a—" Thomas swayed on his uninjured leg.

"Tommy!" George yelled, grabbing Thomas as his eyes rolled back and he collapsed.

George eased him to the ground. "Did you get hurt somewhere else?"

Thomas moaned, and his eyes fluttered open. He tried to focus on George's face, but his vision wouldn't adjust. "I don't think so."

"How do you feel?"

"I feel . . . I feel . . ." Thomas failed to find the words he needed to explain the dizzying, throbbing pain pounding in his skull.

"You feel what?" George asked.

"Like I'm going to be sick." Thomas yanked off his mask, lurched forward, and vomited all over the front of George's uniform. When the retching stopped, he collapsed back on the ground, too weak to lift his arms to wipe off the vomit. George cleaned Thomas's mouth with his sleeve and eased his mask back onto his face.

"Thank you, James," Thomas slurred as his eyes fluttered closed again.

"Thomas, it's me. George."

"I tried to find you," Thomas mumbled. "I tried so hard."

"I know you did," George said.

Thomas's unfocused eyes fluttered open behind his gas mask. He looked up at George. "But I failed." His voice hitched. "I'm so sorry."

George swallowed back tears. "It's okay, Tommy. I'm here now."

Thomas's eyes slid closed again, pushing tears down his cheeks. "James?" he whispered. "I'm scared."

"Me too, Tommy," George whispered. "Me too." He helped Thomas sit up when he noticed crooked cracks in the clay wall, branching from across the ceiling down to the floor like a tattered spiderweb. He glanced back to Thomas and the cracks lining the lenses of his gas mask. Looking closer, he noticed a gash torn in the fabric of the face piece near the outlet valve. He fell to his knees and pulled the broken gas mask off Thomas's head. Dropping the useless mask on the ground, he took off his own mask and placed it over Thomas's face.

"What are you doing?" Thomas mumbled.

"Saving your life," George said, tightening the straps.

Thomas's eyes flew open, and he tried to push George's hands away. "No, James. That's yours. You need it."

"What I need is for you to stay still," George said, cinching the last strap. "That's a royal order."

"Why are you doing this?" Thomas asked. He reached up to pull off the mask, but his arm felt like it was filled with clay, heavy and wet. It fell limp beside him, and his head lolled to the side.

George leaned over and placed an ear to Thomas's chest. It rose and fell with his shallow breaths and pulsed with a slow but steady heartbeat. Wincing against the pain in his side, George pulled on Thomas's broken gas mask. "It's what brothers do."

THIRTY-NINE

THOMAS WOKE TO silence. He tried to open his eyes, but they rolled back in his head again and his eyelids drooped closed. He took a deep breath. The air was hot and stale. He drew in a second breath and forced his eyes open. His vision was cloudy and dim. The memory of the cave-in came flooding back in a rush of terror. He scrambled back, but a sharp pain radiated through his leg at the sudden movement. Thomas cried out, but his voice sounded muffled. He lifted his hands to his face and felt the rough fabric, cold metal, and round glass eyepieces of a gas mask.

"George!" Through the fogged-up lenses, he scanned the tunnel for his friend. He spotted him seated on the floor, leaning against the collapsed wall, mere feet away, wearing Thomas's cracked mask.

Thomas grabbed hold of the lantern and crawled over to

him. "George." He nudged his shoulder, but George didn't respond. "George!" He shook him harder, and George slumped forward.

"No, no, no, no." Thomas pulled his broken mask from his friend's head. The shadows of the tunnel leached the color from George's freckled face.

"What did you do?" Thomas screamed. He yanked George's mask from his own head and pressed it to George's face. Ignoring the heavy dizziness swirling through his head, Thomas held the mask firmly over George's nose and mouth and pounded on his chest. He leaned his forehead against George's. "Please! Don't do this to me!"

Pain, grief, anger, and fear clawed up his throat in ragged cries.

His screams filled the small cavern, echoing off the clay walls and trembling through the beams. He no longer cared who heard. Pain erupted from him with the fury of grief. He raged against God and fate and unanswered prayers. He raged until his voice broke and his vision blurred. He collapsed next to George. And then, taking his friend's cold hand in his, he waited to die.

"You won't go alone," he whispered. "I'm here. You're not forgotten." His breathing shallowed, and his vision dimmed as the carbon monoxide seeped into his blood. Numbness crept from his fingers and toes through his hands and feet, up his arms and legs. After years of tormenting him, death was finally showing mercy.

No fear. No pain. A peaceful numbness.

"We'll face it together," he whispered to George. "As soldiers. As brothers." Then he rested his head against George's shoulder, closed his eyes, and waited for death to claim him. He didn't know if it would ride in on a thunderous explosion or slip in on the whisper of a final sigh.

But death did neither. It scraped and groaned, creaked and clanged, mumbled and barked.

Barked? Thomas shook his head to free himself of the hallucinations gripping his mind, but the noises grew louder. Someone called his name. Large hands grabbed him. Pain seared through his leg as his body was jerked up, but he'd screamed his throat raw and could only release a weak whimper. Strong arms held him tight against a barrel chest. A voice screamed.

"Go! Go! Go!"

His limp body was jostled with every pounding step.

"What about Shillings?" another voice asked.

"He's there, but I'm not sure he's alive."

Thomas tried to tell them they couldn't leave George behind, but his head spun with dizziness, and the words he needed swirled past too fast for him to grasp. The only word he could find was "No."

They couldn't leave George to face death alone. He'd promised.

His rescuers ignored his plea. At the base of the shaft, he was passed up the ladder from one set of hands to another.

"Get to the support trenches! Now!" a gruff voice ordered.

And then they were running again. Timber beams and clay walls blurred past. Night air chilled Thomas's damp hair and clammy skin as they broke free from the tunnels and pressed through the trenches. Thomas's head fell back. His unfocused eyes trailed the full moon glowing against the darkness of the early morning sky.

The arms eased him gently onto a bench. "Take deep breaths, Thomas." Frederick's face came into focus. He held a canteen up to Thomas's lips. "Drink."

Thomas took one small sip and then another. His throat burned with each swallow.

"As soon as we can get a medic, we will," Charlie said. "Stay awake until then."

Max jumped into Thomas's lap. Thomas winced at the pain in his leg but wrapped the dog up in a tight embrace while Max licked his face. Frederick and Charlie sat on either side of him.

"Are you all right?" Charlie asked.

Thomas didn't answer.

"We didn't think we'd get you out of there in time," Frederick said.

"George." Thomas forced the name through his aching throat.

Charlie's head dipped forward.

"Mole said they were able to break through faster because George had dug out a lot of clay on your side," Frederick said. "We would never have gotten you out in time if he hadn't."

"Did Mole go back for him?" Thomas asked.

"He wanted to," Frederick said, "but Boomer stopped him. He said they couldn't risk more men getting caught in a collapse this close to zero hour."

"They were still arguing when Mole ordered that we carry you to the support trenches," Charlie said.

Fresh tears welled in Thomas's eyes. "It's all my fault."

Frederick placed a hand on Thomas's shoulder. "You couldn't have known the gallery would collapse."

Shifting his leg to try to find a less painful position, Thomas heard something crinkle. He reached into his pocket and pulled out a thick envelope.

"What's that?" Charlie asked.

Thomas opened the envelope and pulled out a stack of British pounds and a small brown ledger. "George's winnings and pay book." His fingers went numb holding the money his friend had worked so hard to win and earn.

"There's more," Frederick said, pointing to a folded piece of paper that had fallen into Thomas's lap.

Thomas opened it.

"That's the letter I wrote for you," Frederick said. "The one you asked me to write to your family in case—" He didn't finish his thought.

The letter shook in Thomas's trembling hands. "I gave this to George to deliver to my parents. He must have put it and the money in my pocket when he realized—" Unbearable grief bowed Thomas's head and strangled his words. "He shouldn't have been down there. None of you should have. This is all my fault." Sobs shook his shoulders. "George gave me his mask. Why did he do that?"

"You tried to do the same for him," Frederick said.

"But I was too late."

"We all were," Charlie said.

Frederick reached into his coat. "George made me promise to give you this if anything happened." He took out a folded sheet of paper, wrinkled from the days in his pocket.

"What is it?" Thomas asked.

Frederick unfolded the paper. "After I wrote letters for our families, George asked me to write one for him."

Thomas's throat ached, and his bottom lip quivered with barely contained sobs. "Will you read it for me?"

Choking back tears of his own, Frederick nodded and cleared his throat.

Thomas,

I'm not one for words, and I'm really hoping you never see this letter because if you do that means I'm dead. You're the closest thing to family I've got out here, or anywhere, and if I'm to die in this war, there are a few things I need to say.

First, I owe you an apology. I shouldn't have conned you into coming to the Western Front. I've never met your brother, but I know James would agree that you don't belong here. You should be home with your family.

Second, I want to thank you for asking me to come to Dover with you after the war. I don't know if you meant it or if your family would really ever have taken me in, but thank you for asking.

And lastly, I hope you find your brother. You've refused to give up or forget him. If only all of us were so lucky to have a brother like you.

So, Tommy, I guess this is goodbye. May you have a long, good life, sailing the Channel with your brother. If you can, every once in a while, spare a thought for a lying thief from London. You'll be the only one who does.

George

Charlie bowed his head to hide his tears, and Frederick folded the letter and handed it to Thomas, who tucked it in his pocket.

The boys sat in silence as artillery fire continued to rain down across no-man's-land. On the other side of the battlefield, tens of thousands of German soldiers slept, unaware of the nineteen mines, packed with nearly one million pounds of ammonal and gun cotton, beneath their feet. Nineteen charge chambers, at the ends of tunnels carved from the earth by thousands of tunnelers, who'd worked tirelessly, day and night, beneath no-man's-land. Secret soldiers, who'd labored and fought on a battlefield most didn't know existed. For months and years, they'd lived, worked, eaten, and slept in those tunnels. And some, like George, had died in them.

Thomas took the necklace from his pocket and clutched his medals in prayer that George and all the tunnelers who'd sacrificed their lives under the Western Front would someday rest in peace. Suddenly, the Allied guns fell silent, and an eerie quiet settled over the battlefield. The absence of noise seized Thomas's breath. If they'd succeeded in their mission, he knew what would follow. Holding Max, Thomas struggled to his feet. "I have to see."

Frederick and Charlie helped him across the duckboards and onto a fire step, where they peered through holes in the parapet. The silence stretched on, taut and tenuous until it snapped with mute explosions that rumbled, deep and low, beneath Messines Ridge. The ground bucked and tremored, knocking soldiers on both sides of no-man's-land off their feet, but the battlefield held firm against nearly one million pounds of explosives.

Thomas closed his eyes. They'd failed in their mission. Fresh tears ran down his cheeks at the realization that Bagger, Bats, and George had died for nothing. Scrubbing away his tears, he was starting down the fire step when no-man's-land erupted.

The boys watched in horror as towers of fire punched from the bowels of the battlefield, tearing through the German trenches. The force of the blasts lifted concrete bunkers from the ground and tossed clods of earth the size of houses into the air. A wall of flame, blazing a blinding ember red, ignited the sky along Messines. The boys ducked below the parapet, shielding their faces from the intense light and blistering heat. Charlie wrapped his arms around Poppy's cage, and Thomas huddled over Max, who whimpered in his arms.

The explosions signaled the Allied troops waiting in the front-line trenches. Their rifles and artillery aimed across the battlefield, they unleashed the full fury of over two thousand guns on what remained of the German line in a creeping barrage so loud it was heard as far as London. The boys covered their ears against the gunfire, but their hands did little to lessen the deafening noise. Below the noise, a command shot through the trenches.

"Attack!"

Thomas, Frederick, and Charlie peered back through the holes in the parapet and watched in awe as eighty thousand soldiers climbed over the top of the trenches. Guns raised and firing, they rushed across the battlefield, stepping over fallen comrades and dodging falling debris, burning trees, and tangled lines of "devil's rope." Thick smoke and anguished screams rose from giant craters pocking the ridge.

Voices, wailing in pain and fear, crowded the tight spaces between artillery blasts and gunfire. Their pleas, spoken in different languages and varying accents, collided and combined into a universal cry for help.

Thomas could no longer bear to watch or listen. He turned to ask Frederick and Charlie to help him to the Regimental Aid Post when he heard another voice cry out, but this one sounded familiar. Thomas closed his eyes and strained to hear it over the battle raging in front of him. After several seconds, the voice cried out again.

"Help! I need a stretcher bearer! Hurry!"

Thomas turned to see a man rushing through the support trench toward them. Thick layers of dirt and clay encrusted the man's face and uniform, but Thomas knew him immediately by his stout build and lumbering gait.

"Eton!" Boomer yelled. "Get over here!"

"What's wrong?" Frederick asked as he ran to meet the miner. "Is Mole hurt?"

"I'm fine," a gravelly voice behind Boomer answered. "But *he* won't be if we don't get him to a medic now!"

The world tipped, and Charlie grabbed hold of Thomas as Thomas's uninjured leg gave way at the sight of the crew's kicker rounding a corner of the trench with George cradled in his arms.

FORTY

THE FIRST EXPLOSION ripped the prisoners of war from their sleep and yanked the young soldier to his feet. Panicked German soldiers ran through the trenches, grabbing any helmets and weapons they could find and screaming orders in their chaotic rush toward the explosion. When the trench was clear, the young soldier scrambled onto a ladder and carefully raised his helmeted head above the parapet. He looked north to Messines, the direction of the earth-shaking blast. Eighteen more explosions followed, each as powerful and devastating as the first. The distant ridge was a hellscape. Volcanic eruptions punched through the earth like fiery fingers, reaching up to claim the thousands of German troops positioned along the seven-mile stretch of trenches.

Those not pulverized in the explosions or swallowed by the opening earth stumbled onto the battlefield in disoriented shock and surrendered to the approaching Allied forces. The young soldier didn't know how, but after years of bloody stalemate, the Allies had succeeded in breaking the German line. He glanced down the trenches. The German troops were in disarray. Now was his chance to escape. Smoke, dirt, and debris thickened the night sky above, but the young soldier knew the Allied trenches waited just beyond in the darkness.

Fear and hope pounded through his heart in frantic beats as he scaled the last rungs of the ladder. Since his capture, home and his family had never seemed closer. He paused before climbing over the parapet and looked back to the dugout. The prisoners whom he'd worked alongside for the last month remained huddled together in the earthen shelter. Their eyes wide with confusion and terror, they watched the young soldier. With frantic gestures, he motioned for them to join him.

"Come on!" he screamed. "We must go! Now!"

When they didn't move, he jumped into the trench and pushed them toward the ladder.

"Go! Now! Hurry!"

The British, Australians, and Canadians obeyed, and after a moment's hesitation, an older Belgian followed them over the parapet and onto no-man's-land. Only the French boy remained. With his eyes squeezed shut and his ears covered, he cradled his head and rocked back and forth.

No more explosions ripped through Messines or quaked the earth, but the gunfire from the Allied lines continued, and the young soldier knew the Germans would soon regroup. Their chance of escaping lessened with every second they remained in the trench.

"Come on!" he yelled.

The boy's eyes sprang open, and the young soldier pointed to the ladder, but the boy shook his head. The Allied gunfire grew closer, and the young soldier flinched at the sound of return fire from the Central Powers, just south of their position.

He grabbed the boy's arm. "We have to go now!"

The boy yanked free of the soldier's grip and rocked faster. "*Non, non, non,*" he muttered with every sway forward. He squeezed his eyes closed again, sending fresh tears spilling down his round cheeks.

The young soldier knelt before the boy. "Please," he begged. "I have to get home to my family."

The boy stopped rocking and looked up at him. "*Famille?*"

The young soldier nodded. "*Famille.*" He pictured each of their faces.

Dad. Mum. Letitia. Charlotte. Tommy.

Taking the frightened boy's hand, the young soldier helped him to his feet. Farther down the German line, a howitzer cannon fired, and the French boy froze. His hands flew to his bare head as his wide eyes frantically searched the trench for a helmet.

The young soldier rubbed a shaky hand over the boy's messy hair. "Everything's going to be all right," he said, taking off his helmet and securing it on the boy's head. "I promise."

Then the two climbed the ladder.

EPILOGUE

THOMAS'S INJURIES EARNED him a one-way ticket to Dover—and an honorable discharge. Two months after the detonation of the mines beneath Messines Ridge, he hobbled down the dirt road to his family home and prayed to find that his brother had returned during his absence. But James never returned home.

The Great War raged on for seventeen months after the Battle of Messines, and though the British military commended the tunnelers for the successful execution of their mission, they were not asked to repeat it. Tanks and planes were mobilized for the rest of the war, breaking up years of entrenched fighting and making the tunnelers obsolete. Some were sent home. Most were sent to the front lines.

Weeks after the Allies and Central Powers signed the Treaty of Versailles, the Sullivans received an official letter stating that

James's status had been changed from missing in action to killed in action. No details were provided, and no remains were recovered. Despite Thomas having escaped the tunnels of the Western Front, his mind remained trapped beneath no-man's-land. At night, he could still hear the enemy clawing at the clay walls and feel the tremble of explosions quaking through the earth. When summer storms swept in from the North Sea and thunder cracked across the sky, Thomas scrambled for cover. His mum would find him huddled beneath the kitchen table, cradling his head and crying.

He never returned to the coal mines. The mine supervisor promised a job would be waiting for him when he was ready, but Thomas knew he'd never be ready, so when his leg healed, he walked to the docks of Admiralty Harbour to look for work. The owners of the various shipping companies were eager to hire war veterans, so Thomas spent the next two years working the docks, learning as much as he could about boats and the shipping business. Every morning, when his head and body ached with fatigue and his leg throbbed with pain, he remembered James and the dream they'd shared, and forced himself to get out of bed.

On Thomas's seventeenth birthday, he pooled his dockworker's earnings with his and James's army wages and purchased his own boat. It was a small, battered vessel, but it was sturdy and had weathered many seasons on the Channel. Thomas hoped with some repairs it would weather several more.

It took months to ready the boat, but two years after the

armistice was signed, Sullivan Brothers Shipping was ready to launch.

"That should do it," Charlie said, putting a last stroke of red paint on the stern of the boat. "What do you think?"

The lettering matched perfectly with the company name painted in blue on the starboard side. "It looks great," Thomas said, smiling at Charlie's work.

A pleased blush tinted Charlie's cheeks. "You like it?"

"You did a fine job, son," Mr. Sullivan said, resting a reassuring hand on Charlie's shoulder.

Charlie's blush deepened. "Thank you, sir."

A gust of November wind swept across the Channel. Mr. Sullivan blew into his cupped hands for warmth and then rubbed them together. "You boys couldn't have planned to christen this boat in July?"

Ignoring the aching cold in his own hands, Thomas tightened the ropes mooring his boat to the dock. "If the Germans had surrendered earlier, we might have, but they didn't, so it had to be today." He glanced up at Charlie. "Two years from the day the war ended."

Charlie smiled.

As they waited for the paint to dry, Charlie's little brother, Henry, ran up the dock with Letitia, Charlotte, and Max trailing behind him. "We did it!" he exclaimed, pride spreading in a wide smile across his freckled face. "We passed out every flyer."

"Well done," Mr. Sullivan said, patting the boy's head.

Thomas smiled. He'd been shocked to find Charlie and Henry on his doorstep a month after Frederick and Charlie had been discharged from the army. After Charlie explained that their father had been killed in a bar fight, the Sullivans had welcomed the brothers into their home without hesitation. Charlie found a job at St. Paul's, where Father Clark taught him to read and write in exchange for help around the church, including painting, which Charlie loved. Two years later, it was as though Charlie and Henry had always been part of their family.

"Look who I found," Mrs. Sullivan yelled from the end of the dock. Max let out an excited bark, scurried down the dock, and leaped into the waiting arms of a soldier with glasses and tidy black hair. A distinguished looking gentleman with a receding hairline and neatly trimmed gray mustache stood beside him.

"Max!" Frederick exclaimed, petting the terrier. Max licked his face, jumped down, ran two circles around his legs, and then sprinted back to Thomas.

"You made it!" Thomas said, striding forward to shake Frederick's hand.

"Thomas, may I introduce my father, General Theodore Chamberlain?"

Thomas saluted General Chamberlain. "It is an honor to meet you, sir."

"It's a pleasure to meet you, Thomas," Frederick's father

said. "My son has told me a great deal about you and your family."

"I apologize for our tardiness," Frederick said. "But as you well know, I've never had good luck with trains running on time."

The boys chuckled at the memory of their first meeting on the transport train at Charing Cross station.

"Tardy or not," Thomas said, "I'm glad you both could join us today."

"We all are," Mrs. Sullivan said, patting Frederick's arm.

"I wouldn't have missed it," Frederick said. "We made a promise."

Thomas smiled. "Yes, we did. How have you been?"

"Good. It took some persuasion on my father's part and a sizable donation, but Eton let me return."

His father cleared his throat and raised a warning eyebrow at his son. "Manners, Frederick."

An ashamed blush warmed Frederick's cheeks. "Sorry, sir." He motioned to his Eton uniform. "I'll graduate a year late, but at least I'll graduate and be reinstated into the army."

"The army would be lucky to have you again," Thomas said.

"Thank you." Frederick looked past Thomas to Charlie, who'd joined them along with Mr. Sullivan, Henry, and the twins. "How are you, Mouse?"

"I'm well. It's good to see you, Frederick."

Frederick shook his hand. "You too."

"Come on," Thomas said, leading him down the dock. "Let me show you the first vessel of Sullivan Brothers Shipping's fleet." While General Chamberlain and Mr. and Mrs. Sullivan became acquainted, Thomas and Charlie led Frederick over to the boat.

"*King George*!" Frederick exclaimed with a chuckle as he read the name painted on the stern. "You're a man of your word, Thomas."

"That he is!" a voice called out from behind them.

They turned to see George striding down the dock.

Frederick smiled. "If it isn't the King of the Secret Soldiers himself."

"Former king," George corrected. "I abdicated my throne to become part owner of the newest shipping company in Dover. It promises to be the finest to sail the Channel."

"I had heard rumors of your new venture," Frederick said, extending his hand. "Congratulations, Shillings."

George pulled him into a hug. "Thanks. How are you, Eton?"

"I can't complain."

"Of course you can," George said with a teasing smile. "It's your special skill."

. . .

After Thomas and George christened their new boat, George announced he had something to show everyone.

"What is it?" asked Letitia, bouncing on her toes.

"It's a surprise. You'll have to come with me to find out."

They followed George up a worn path leading to the cliffs of Dover. Max trotted along at Thomas's heels. When Thomas reached the top, he stopped short.

Before him, in the spot where he and James had sat and dreamed about their futures, stood a white cross. A short inscription was carved into the stone.

JAMES M. SULLIVAN
LOVING SON AND BROTHER
1898–1917

Mrs. Sullivan let out a gasp and covered her mouth. Mr. Sullivan pulled her into an embrace, and Letitia and Charlotte fought back tears as they drew close to their parents.

Thomas didn't speak. He stared at the memorial, his face void of expression.

After several seconds of silence, George shifted nervously in his place beside him.

"You did this?" Thomas asked.

"Well, yeah," George said, wary of his friend's reaction to his surprise. "I've been working on it for a while."

When Thomas remained silent, staring at the memorial, George glanced over at Charlie, who shrugged.

"I won some money playing cards with a group of miners in

town," George continued. "Made enough to buy the marble. The chap who carves the gravestones for St. Paul's cemetery agreed to carve and inscribe the memorial if I helped around his shop for a few months. I wanted it done before we launched *King George*. It's quite heavy. Thankfully, Mr. Bartlett let me borrow a cart and pony from the mine to haul it up here. I got it in place just as Eton arrived."

Without taking his eyes off the memorial, Thomas nodded.

"I just thought maybe you needed a place to visit your brother. You know, a place where James can watch over you as Sullivan Brothers Shipping sails the Channel." He glanced over at Mr. and Mrs. Sullivan and the twins. "Where he can watch over all of you."

His eyes glistening with grief and gratitude, Mr. Sullivan nodded, but when Thomas still didn't respond, George stepped closer to his friend and whispered. "I can take it down if you don't like it."

Thomas's eyes welled with tears. "It's perfect. Thank you."

A relieved smile spread across George's face. "You're welcome." He then turned to Frederick. "Eton, didn't you bring a surprise for the Sullivans too?"

"Yes." Frederick stepped before Mr. and Mrs. Sullivan. "My mother had hoped to join my father and me here today, but unfortunately she was called away to London. She did, however, ask me to extend her condolences for your loss and her appreciation for your family's sacrifice."

"Thank you, Frederick," Mr. Sullivan said. "We are grateful

for everything you and your family have done to try to find our James."

Frederick pulled a thick envelope from his coat pocket. "Although the army was unable to recover your son, Mr. and Mrs. Sullivan, my father was able to learn what happened to him."

Frederick's words tore Thomas's attention away from his brother's memorial. "You know what happened to James?"

Frederick nodded and handed Mrs. Sullivan the envelope. "This contains the sworn testimonies of twelve Allied soldiers: six Brits, two Canadians, two Aussies, one Belgian, and one French, all of whom were held as prisoners of war with your son on the German front line."

The envelope trembled in Mrs. Sullivan's hand as silent sobs shook through her. Thomas reached out and took her other hand as Frederick continued.

"Each testimony states that your son's actions early in the morning of June 7, 1917, saved the lives of all twelve prisoners of war."

General Chamberlain stepped beside his son and addressed Mr. and Mrs. Sullivan. "When Frederick told me of George's plans to present you with this memorial, I asked if I might join him today to meet your family." He took a small box from his coat pocket. "Over the last two years, I have had the privilege to meet the families of many of Britain's most courageous soldiers. Men who, like your son James, gave everything on the fields of battle to protect crown and country." He opened the box and took out a medal. A square bronze cross hung suspended from a wine-red ribbon and bronze bar. The cross bore the image of a crown and a lion, along with the words *For Valor.*

"On behalf of King George the Fifth and the British Army, I am honored to present to you the Victoria Cross, for acts of gallantry and extreme bravery performed under enemy fire by your son, James M. Sullivan."

Mr. Sullivan took the medal. "Thank you, General Chamberlain." He then handed the medal to his wife, who showed it to the twins.

After everyone had seen the medal, Charlie placed a small hand-carved wooden frame holding a painting he'd made of James against the base of the marble cross and recited two verses from the poem "For the Fallen" that Father Clark had helped him memorize for the occasion.

They went with songs to the battle, they were young,
Straight of limb, true of eye, steady and aglow.
They were staunch to the end against odds uncounted,
They fell with their faces to the foe.

They shall grow not old, as we that are left grow old:
Age shall not weary them, nor the years condemn.
At the going down of the sun and in the morning
We will remember them.

Following the recitation of the poem, Mr. Sullivan took out his tin whistle to play his eldest son's favorite song. His breath, weakened by decades in the mines and tight with emotion, drew out shaky notes. When he could no longer play, George put a hand on his shoulder and sang. His voice wasn't as deep or rich as James's had been, and he missed the key on many notes, but the lyrics had never meant more to Thomas.

Oh, Danny Boy, the pipes, the pipes are calling.
From glen to glen and down the mountain side.
The summer's gone and all the roses falling.
'Tis you, 'tis you must go, and I must bide.

Thomas and the others joined George for the remaining verses, and as the last mournful note echoed over the cliff, the four secret soldiers stepped up to the memorial and saluted their fallen brother before joining the Sullivans, Henry, and General Chamberlain as they made their way back down the path.

"Are you coming?" George asked when he noticed Thomas lingering by the cross.

"In a minute. There's something I have to do."

George nodded. "Take your time. We'll wait for you at home." He patted his leg for Max to follow. The terrier trotted after George, stopping several times to glance back at Thomas before disappearing below the hill's slope.

After several minutes of standing before his brother's memorial, uncertain what to say, Thomas removed his necklace and looped it over the top of the cross. The saints medals hung below the carved letters of James's name. Tears blurred Thomas's vision as he placed his hand on the marble. "I miss you, James. So much." He ran his fingers over the inscription, pausing over the word *brother.* "I promise I'll always remember you, and I know you'll always watch over me."

Giving the memorial a final salute, he had just turned to join his family and friends when a brisk wind swirled across the cliff top, nipping at his clothes and tousling his hair. With a smile, Thomas patted down his cowlicks and wiped away his tears.

"It's what brothers do."

AUTHOR'S NOTE

THE TUNNELLERS' MEMORIAL website was an invaluable resource in my research for this book. In July 2017, I emailed military historian Jeremy Banning, who was part of the Tunnellers' Memorial team, and he was kind enough to put me in contact with his colleague, historian Simon Jones. Jeremy also recommended Simon's book *Underground Warfare 1914–1918*, which became a main source of information for my research. I emailed Simon after I finished it, and he generously answered my questions. Simon's book also led me to two other extraordinary works, *Beneath Flanders Field* and *Pillars of Fire*. I spent months poring over their pages. Further research uncovered articles, documentaries, and firsthand accounts, including letters home from soldiers on the front lines, which gave me a better understanding of the trials and tribulations faced by the brave men and boys who served on and under the battlefields of the Western Front.

I was shocked to discover that more than a quarter of a million underage British boys served in the four-year conflict. Unlike the child soldiers of the Ugandan Civil War, whom I wrote about in my first novel, *Soldier Boy*, the young soldiers of the Great War were not stolen from their families and forced into combat. The boys who served lied about their ages and volunteered to fight. In my research, I learned about the various reasons that drove a literal army of boys, some as young as thirteen, to the recruiter's table. Some joined out of a sense of duty. Others sought glory. Many joined out of necessity, willing to risk their lives in the trenches for the promise of fare wages and three meals a day. The hundreds of thousands of underage British soldiers with their diverse reasons for joining the war inspired the main characters in *Secret Soldiers* and provided endless sources of tension and conflict for Thomas and his clay kicking crew, who struggled to work as a team and complete their secret mission beneath no-man's-land.

While researching, I discovered that British Prime Minister Harold Macmillan, whose grandfather founded Macmillan Publishing, graduated from Eton, served in World War I, and read Aeschylus' *Prometheus* while in the trenches. I gave these details to my character Frederick as a nod to Farrar Straus Giroux Books for Young Readers, an imprint of Macmillan and the publisher of *Secret Soldiers*.

If reading this book has sparked your curiosity about the tunnellers of World War I and the Battle of Messines, I recommend the Tunnellers' Memorial website and the following wonderful resources that proved so invaluable to me.

"A Memorial to William Hackett VC and the Tunnelling Companies of the First World War." http://www.tunnellers memorial.com/.

Barton, Peter, Peter Doyle, and Johan Vandewalle. *Beneath Flanders Fields: The Tunnellers' War 1914–1918*. Montreal: McGill–Queen's University Press, 2014.

Jones, Simon. *Underground Warfare 1914–1918*. Barnsley: Pen & Sword Military, 2010.

Passingham, Ian. *Pillars of Fire: The Battle of Messines Ridge, June 1917*. Stroud, Gloucestershire: Spellmount, 2012.

Secret Tunnel Warfare. Directed and produced by John Hayes Fisher. Produced by John Farren. Performed by Jay O. Sanders. Public Broadcasting Service. https://www.pbs.org/wgbh/nova /video/secret-tunnel-warfare/